THIS IS
OUR PLACE

Also by Vitor Martins

Here the Whole Time

THIS IS OUR PLACE

VITOR MARTINS

TRANSLATED BY LARISSA HELENA

PUSH

Originally published in Brazilian Portuguese in 2021 as *Se A Casa 8 Falasse* by Alt.

Copyright © 2021 by Vitor Martins

English translation © 2022 by Larissa Helena

Library of Congress Cataloging-in-Publication Data available

ISBN 978-1-338-81864-2

10 9 8 7 6 5 4 3 2 1   22 23 24 25 26

Printed in the U.S.A.   37

First edition, November 2022

Book design by Stephanie Yang

FOR RAFAEL.
WHEN I'M WITH YOU, I'M HOME.

I AM A HOUSE.

Not in the metaphorical sense, like my eyes are windows into my soul or something. I am *literally* a house. Brick, concrete, two bedrooms, living room, kitchen, bathroom, and garage. Wooden doors, built-in closets, rusty pipes that make the shower water smell funny, and an electrical system that hasn't been updated since the 1980s and always melts the fridge's plug and shocks people whenever they turn on the light switch in the small bedroom.

That part's fun. The shock thing.

I could have saved this reveal for the end. Left you with your mouth wide open upon realizing that, this whole time, I was the one telling these stories. Number 8 Sunflower Street. But I'm not great at keeping secrets, and I like wondering how you're imagining me right now. Like those psychological tests where you draw a house to determine your personality type. If you draw a house with no ground around it, just floating on white paper, it's because you think your dad doesn't love you. If your house is yellow with a red roof, that means you have an irrational fear of clowns or spiders. Something like that. I'm not sure how those tests work because I'm not a psychiatrist. Like I said, I am a house.

My story is nothing special. I was built in 1963 in a vacant lot on Sunflower Street in downtown Lagoa Pequena, a rural city in the state of São Paulo that rose to fame in the mid-1990s when it became the setting of a primetime soap opera, but no one gave much thought to this tiny place or its twenty-eight thousand residents after that. But I like it here so much that I never dreamed of moving.

That was a joke.

I can't move.

I thought it best to explain since I don't know if everyone gets house humor.

But I really do like it here. As far as I can tell, Sunflower Street is a great place. Lots of trees, dogs taking their owners for walks, and a sweet flower name that's infinitely better than other streets named after racist members of a monarchy that doesn't even exist anymore, or corrupt politicians who were so honored after they built a school and a clinic. Sunflower Street is an oasis in the middle of all that chaos. As far as I know, anyway. I barely have any time to visit other places.

(That was another house joke.)

The stories that happen inside me are way better than my own. And there are many of them, by the way. Being a house, I've had a lot of different people living under my roof. I'm sure that owned houses are jealous of rented houses; imagine having to live forever with the same family, listening to the same stories, the same gossip about Aunt Silmara who went through a midlife crisis and got herself a boyfriend fifteen years her junior, or Cousin Tadeu who either is gay or finds a new best friend every six-and-a-half months. My stories go way beyond Silmara and Tadeu (both

2

of whom have made perfectly acceptable life choices and do not deserve their cruel, gossipy family).

I call them "my stories" because I'm possessive. And because it works both ways. The residents call me "my house," so I don't see any problem with calling their stories mine. They'll never know, anyway, because I'm very quiet. At least, I always have been. But now I've decided to break my silence.

You know when people say, "Oh, if these walls could talk?" They do. Or, "Careful what you say, the walls are listening"? They are. Or even, "Whoa, it's as if this house can read my thoughts!" Fine, no one ever says that one. But I can. Not every thought, of course. Just the loud ones. The ones that scream in your head, desperate to pop out at any moment. It's impossible not to hear them. It's hard not to notice the details when they're happening *inside* me.

So, the next time a visitor comes over to your house and you say, "Come in! Don't mind the mess," remember: I mind.

I mind the dishes you haven't washed in six days just because the weather turned, and now the dirty coffee mug buried under plates is starting to grow mold. I mind the pile of laundry behind the door and the dust that is accumulating on the top shelf because you think no one will ever see it, anyway. I mind the wine stain on the couch that you tried to hide under a quilt, and the nail holes on the wall that you covered with toothpaste because you read online that it's cheaper than buying Spackle.

But I'm not as focused on the mess in me as I am on the mess in *them*. That's the mess I like to pay attention to. The confusing thoughts that keep them up at night; the tears that fall out of nowhere when an unexpected song starts playing; when they sing in the shower to forget all their troubles; the hours lost in front of a mirror making faces and asking, "What if this were really my face?"; the catastrophic fights followed by apologetic kisses that, deep down, still taste of anger.

I can feel all of it. I pay attention to all of it.

And now it's my turn to speak. Metaphorically, of course. I can't speak.

I am a house.

ANA

Ana knew the Y2K bug wasn't going to happen. In part because her father, Celso Carvalho, the computer genius of Lagoa Pequena and the surrounding areas, had spent the last six months watching every sensationalized newscast on TV, yelling, "Y2K IS NOT GONNA HAPPEN!" while pacing from one room to the other with a cup of coffee in his hand and an old T-shirt that read SUPER DAD.

Celso makes a living taking apart and fixing computers, installing software from a mountain of CDs, and speaking in a technical jargon no one else understands. If your computer has an issue, Celso can take care of it. If humankind is threatened by a mysterious Y2K bug that will cause the loss of data, power, money, and sanity, Celso will reassure you. Because he knows everything, and Ana trusts him.

Still, the two decided to spend New Year's Eve at home, just in case. In the final moments of 1999, Celso doesn't seem too sure that the world isn't about to collapse.

Five . . . four . . . three . . . two . . . one—

The TV is still on, fireworks go off outside, the electricity remains

5

intact, and the computer is working normally. No alien invasion or sign of the apocalypse at the turn of the millennium.

Ana and Celso let out sighs of relief as Celso opens a bottle of hard apple cider.

JANUARY 1, 2000

"You can have a sip, honey. You're already seventeen," he says, serving the drink in two different wineglasses. The family's dinnerware collection is all mismatched because Celso breaks something every time he decides to clean the kitchen.

"I think I'll pass, Dad. I don't really like cider that much," Ana answers, letting it slip that she has tried hard cider before, contrary to what her innocent Super Dad might think. "I mean—*apple*! This is *apple* cider, and I'm not a fan of the fruit—apple—which I have definitely eaten many times because I love to eat fruit."

"Except for apples. Which you seem to hate all of a sudden," Celso points out, not putting any stock in her blabbering.

"Precisely," Ana responds with a silly laugh that only her dad can bring out of her.

"Stop being silly, go on," Celso insists, handing her the prettier of the two glasses. "It's the start of a new millennium! We need to celebrate. What will the next thousand years have in store for us? Where will we be on the eve of the year 3000?"

"Hopefully dead." She accepts her dad's invitation and takes a sip of the acidic drink just to confirm that she does, in fact, hate hard cider.

"You never know," Celso retorts. "Technology might advance in unexpected ways. Maybe they'll put my consciousness in a machine. I could live forever."

Ana laughs at the image of a robot with her dad's face, flannel pants, wobbly aviator glasses, his full head of gray hair hidden under a '98 World Cup hat. That is, if in the future robots have hair. And clothing.

"Dad, imagine what a nightmare it would be to live over a thousand years!" Ana says. "Imagine the amount of stress you'd have! I'm sure they'll come up with a new millennium bug every ten years."

"So a *decade* bug, then?"

"You know what I mean. Living over a thousand years would be the worst thing ever."

"It's only a good thing when it's the vampires of those books you love, huh? Your old man's pushing forty-five, and he's as good as dead," Celso says, lowering his hat to hide a goofy expression.

"Lestat is only two hundred fifty-nine years old," Ana informs, a little embarrassed to have this information on the tip of her tongue, having just reread *The Vampire Lestat*. For the fourth time. "Fine. I'll let you live a little longer than him, okay? Is three hundred years enough for you?"

"I think so," Celso answers after a few moments of reflection. "I could annoy you plenty for three hundred years. Pick on every single boyfriend you bring home."

"Don't count on it," Ana says with a tight smile that wants to shout, "BECAUSE I LIKE GIRLS!"

But despite understanding lines of code, every odd noise that comes from any machine, and blinking lights on a monitor, Celso is terrible at reading between the lines. Ana's heart grows heavy in her chest as she sinks farther into the couch, the cider warming in her glass.

Whenever the conversation turns to boyfriends, she never knows what to do. Ana pulls at the cords of her old purple sweatshirt, asking herself what kind of luck the color purple will bring for the new year.

The TV continues to show fireworks from all over Brazil, and Ana watches the images in silence. People celebrate on beaches, wearing colorful glasses in the shape of the number 2000, their eyes peeking through the two middle zeros. Many make offerings to the sea, hoping that the new millennium will bring brighter days. Footage of the stock exchange shows old men in ties celebrating the fact that the new year didn't cause any damage that would have left them less rich.

Father and daughter watch TV together until the silence grows uncomfortable enough.

"I think I'm going to bed," Ana lies. She won't be able to fall asleep.

"I'll stay here a little longer," Celso answers, pointing at the computer in the corner of the room that just went into sleep mode, displaying a screensaver of a never-ending labyrinth.

Celso is a night owl. He prefers to work when the house is silent, and it's always in the wee hours of the night that he scatters on the table his memory cartridges, hard disks, and spare parts from the computers he's putting together for his clients. During the day, he sleeps like a bat. Or a vampire.

Ana is just like her father, except for the sleeping-during-the-day part. She never sleeps. Not literally, of course. Ana is a human being; she needs to sleep. But sleep is never a choice, she always puts up a fight before it wears her down in the end. Tonight will be one of those nights when her thoughts are so loud that all the fireworks in the world won't be capable of stifling them.

"Don't stay up too late, okay?" Ana says as she gets up from the couch and leaves the half-empty glass of horrible cider in the kitchen sink.

"Sweetie," Celso calls out before she can burrow into her room. "This is going to be a good millennium."

"Kind of risky to assume that of the next thousand years, don't you think, Dad?" she teases.

"It'll be good. Things will change. I can't explain it yet, but I just know it. And I always know these things."

They say good night with a smile and Ana closes her bedroom door, ready to begin her ritual of thinking too much and sleeping too little.

I have two bedrooms: a big one and a small one. Ana took the big one because Celso does all he can to leave the best of everything to his daughter. He sleeps in the small bedroom, containing his twin bed and an old wardrobe he bought secondhand, covered in stickers on the inside of the doors. But it's not as if he didn't take up half the living room with all the paraphernalia required in his line of work.

In the big bedroom, Ana created her own universe. The bed sits in a corner, right next to the window, and is surrounded by posters of *Buffy the Vampire Slayer*, clothes strewn all over the floor, piles of books that she intends to read someday, and a little shelf where she keeps the CD collection she just started.

That's another perk of being Celso's daughter: She can score the newest technology before anyone else in school. Ana was first in her class to get a Discman and, despite the annoying speed at which the device consumes batteries, she cannot live without her portable CD player. Being able to lie in bed, cozy up with a blanket, and put her headphones on maximum volume so the music plays louder than the thoughts in her head is one of Ana's favorite parts of a normal day.

Here is a list of the thoughts inhabiting Ana's mind these evenings:

I wonder if deep down my dad still blames me for the loss of my mom.

I wonder if my principal in fifth grade was right—that I am the way I am because I didn't grow up with a mother figure?

I wonder if one day I'll wake up and know exactly what I want to be when I'm older.

I wonder if the way I think compulsively about Leonardo DiCaprio in Romeo + Juliet *actually means I don't like girls exclusively, or just that he looks like a cool, determined lesbian in that movie?*

I wonder if one day I will be a cool, determined lesbian.

I wonder if the future will be a little less complicated than the present.

I wonder if Letícia is thinking about me right now.

I wonder if I'd look good if I dyed my hair and cut it short just like Leonardo DiCaprio in Romeo + Juliet, *or if I'd run the risk of looking like Macaulay Culkin in* Home Alone.

Letícia, Letícia, Letícia.

Sometimes the order of these thoughts varies. They also don't all come at the same time every day. The haircut thing, for instance, comes about only once every fifteen days. The stuff with her mom is a weekly occurrence. But for the last six months, *Letícia, Letícia, Letícia* is a recurring theme.

And it's Letícia Ana thinks about as she slowly riffles through the CD rack, trying to decide which one will be tonight's soundtrack. The first night of the year 2000 has to be special. Ana puts a lot of stock in first times within new cycles. The first song played in a year, the first socks worn on the first day of school, the first movie watched after the nearby theater was renovated. Silly things she won't even remember two months later, but that, in the moment, feel important.

Unlike the rest of the bedroom, the CD rack is well organized. Each CD is arranged alphabetically by artist, and sub-arranged by year of release for artists that have more than one. But today her three latest additions to the collection sit messily on top of the rack.

Madonna's *Ray of Light*, which she bought on a complete whim on one of her visits to the record store down the street. Ana didn't have it in her to buy *Com Você . . . Meu Mundo Ficaria Completo* by Cássia Eller out of fear of what the middle-aged clerk would have thought of her, as everyone knows Cássia Eller likes girls. But she refused to leave the store without a new album with a beautiful woman on the cover.

Ana eyes the album next to Madonna's, from which five men wearing all white gaze back at her with mysterious eyes on the cover of *Millennium* by the Backstreet Boys. That one was a Christmas present from her dad, who probably went to the same record store where she'd spent twenty-seven minutes staring at the album cover photo of Cássia Eller wearing nothing but an oversized T-shirt and panties before Ana gave up on buying it. Celso would have walked up to the clerk and asked what the best present for a seventeen-year-old might be. Ana had only listened to the album a couple times, because she thinks she's too old for Backstreet Boys, but she sings "I Want It That Way" in the shower when she's alone and has included Nick Carter in her list of blond men with hair parted in the middle that she's still not sure whether she finds attractive or if she just wants their haircut.

Last, Ana holds firmly in her hands the most important CD of them all. Partially for its sentimental value, but also because the plastic case is broken and at risk of falling apart at any moment. *Enema of the State* is the most battered album in Ana's impeccable collection. Theoretically it's not Ana's, but she doesn't plan on returning it to Letícia because Letícia doesn't care at all about objects with special meanings, and to Ana, this Blink-182 album marks the beginning of it all. The beginning of the two of them.

Ana believes that this could be a good way to start the year and, with all the care in the world, she removes the disc from the dilapidated case and puts it in her Discman. She skips the first song because the CD is scratched and that track stops playing after one minute and thirty-eight seconds. Ana once again wonders if she will ever know how "Dumpweed" ends.

She adjusts her headphones on her head and lies down in a comfortable position to let the volume of the drums and the electric guitar take over her body as she attempts to fall asleep. How she's able to fall asleep with this loud music in her ears is a mystery, but that's how it goes with Ana. She doesn't fully understand the lyrics in English and, for the parts that her brain cannot translate, she just makes up something that works in Portuguese with words that rhyme. Maybe this exercise is exhausting enough to force her to get some rest, even if just for a couple of hours.

Today there's no room for haircuts, conjectures, memories of the mom she hasn't met, or attempts to figure out her own dad. Today in Ana's mind there's only Letícia. What wouldn't Ana give to be a billionaire, own a cell phone, and use it to call Letícia. Create an environment with just the two of them, no interference. No "Hi, Dona Celeste, this is Ana. Is Letícia around?" But if Ana were indeed a billionaire, the last thing she'd worry about would be a phone to speak to Letícia. She would buy a car and run away with her to a different place, leaving no trace behind. Assuming Letícia knows how to drive, of course. Because Ana doesn't and is generally terrified of cars. A plane trip could be a good plan B. Leave to a different country. Somewhere where she and Letícia can go for a walk holding hands and not be afraid.

Ana thinks of Letícia's hands. She has big hands with long fingers, which is crucial for volleyball. Letícia is that kind of girl, the kind who plays volleyball for fun. That's what makes Ana believe that Letícia knows how to drive. Sports and cars are interests that go hand in hand.

Hands . . .

Letícia's hands.

The two met unexpectedly. They go to the same school, same class, but it always seemed as if they belonged to different worlds. It's kind of weird to think that a classroom is much smaller than a house and that, even so, it is possible to share that space daily with someone and live a full year completely unaware of their existence. Ana has always been the kind of girl who sits in the front row, pays attention, and stares at the teacher even when she's not interested so they don't have to feel that they're talking to the walls. Or at least that's how she sees herself. Every time she thinks of Letícia, she imagines her sitting toward the back, but not all the way to the back, and chatting with everybody.

It happened on a field trip when the seniors were loaded onto a school bus and taken to the Federal University of Lagoa Pequena for a career aptitude test with undergrad psychology students.

The first step was to answer a ten-page notepad of multiple-choice questions "where there were no wrong or right answers." (Imagine I said that last part making air quotes with my fingers.) (Just kidding, I don't have fingers.) Ana keeps the notepad in the third drawer of her dresser to this day and, in evenings when the uncertainty of the future is the main topic of her loud thoughts, she rereads the questions, trying to understand what she got wrong. Because it's not possible that she didn't get it wrong. Even though she knows there are no wrong answers on this test.

The second stage divided the students in groups, and maybe that's where the mistake was. Ana was in the same group as Letícia and two boys in their class whose names were Maicon and Brickwall. Ana never knew what Brickwall's real name was; everyone calls him this because he is tall, large, and very white. The class that fit that group best was physical education, and Ana spent the next forty minutes listening to an overexcited undergrad student talking about the things she liked best in her classes and how happy she was to meet future physical educators that morning.

Future physical educators, what a joke!

Ana laughs about that to this day because, really, she must have picked all the wrong answers.

The speech made all the sense in the world to Maicon, Brickwall, and Letícia. But to Ana? Completely addicted to staying in bed and unable to educate anyone about anything because every time she needs to answer the same question more than once, she feels ready to completely give up? No way.

If Ana believed in God, she'd say he writes straight with crooked lines, because it was the result of that nonsensical test that had her next to Letícia, and all a girl like Letícia needs is a first hello to fill the following days with hellos.

It's not as if Ana doesn't have any friends. She kind of does. But on the days following the test, hearing a good morning from Letícia made her feel seen. It's as if she had existed only inside her own head and, all of a sudden, she started living in the real world.

Six months ago, Ana was at the bus stop, still trying to get used to her own existence in reality, when Letícia appeared by her side after class.

"Did I just miss the 74C-10?" Letícia asked, probably just trying to make conversation, because anyone in town would have known that the 74C-10 bus was still ten minutes away.

"Sorry?" Ana didn't get the question, because of the music pumping through her headphones.

"What are you listening to?" Letícia asked, changing the approach completely now that she had Ana's attention.

"Rock," said Ana, because it was a new album, and she couldn't remember if the band's name was Red Hot Chili Peppers or Hot Chili Red Peppers.

"Are you into rock? I think you'll like this one," said Letícia, getting the beat-up CD from her backpack. "I share our stereo with my brother, and he has it this week, so you can listen to it and bring it back to me next week." It was the Blink-182 album. Ana never returned it. Letícia never asked for it back.

"You look like the nurse on the cover," Letícia went on, trying to get a conversation going with Ana, who still seemed stunned and lost with the sudden interaction.

Ana laughed, of course. Because she didn't look *in the slightest* like the nurse on the cover. Her hair was darker, and her boobs were way smaller. But she didn't refute Letícia's comment because she thought it would be rude.

That was when the whole *Letícia, Letícia, Letícia* thing started. I've memorized every single detail because Ana replays their first interaction in her mind over and over before going to sleep, and today it's no different.

She considers everything the new millennium has in store for the two of them. And, if her dad is right and she really can live for three hundred years with her consciousness transferred to a robot body, Ana wonders if Letícia would like to be a happy robot by her side.

Fembots?

Ana wonders if there is a feminine word for robot. Probably not. Or maybe there is one, but it's like *she-bear*, which actually exists but sounds made up. Just like Ana and Letícia's romance, which is real but that, even after all these months, still feels like a dream.

I guess I fast-forwarded the story a bit just now. I get excited with any spark of romance, I have to admit it. But here's what happened: Right after the bus stop loan, Ana and Letícia started speaking every day. They exchanged more CDs, worked on a project together, and had their first kiss in the Municipal Library of Lagoa Pequena, right under the M–O section of the self-help shelves. It was risky, and the two of them were afraid. They've never done a crazy thing like that in public again. But they continued to see each other, kiss, and exchange promises as well as CDs. Promises that they'd do whatever they could to keep that love alive. They exchanged their very first "I love you" right here in this bedroom, after they watched the *Clueless* VHS that Celso had grabbed at the video rental store on their street, swearing it was the type of movie Ana would have loved. She hated it. Letícia loved it.

Too bad this is not a love story.

On the first evening of the year 2000, Ana reimagines every important moment of her story with Letícia like a black-and-white movie, and when the album in her Discman is over, she's already asleep. Ana's mind finally rests—just like the CD, tired of all the spinning.

———

Ana wakes up on autopilot.

She ties up her hair in an attempt to get the volume under control, cleans her eye boogers, brushes her teeth, and brews coffee for her dad. Ana doesn't drink coffee. Except for once in a while, and with lots of milk, which she adds to the glass little by little until the beverage is more or less the color of the sand at a reasonably clean beach. But preparing a drink is one of the many ways Ana has found to display her love for her dad without having to say, "Love you, Dad." Besides, the process of putting the grounds and water in the coffeemaker, hearing the noise of the machine boil water, and watching the dark liquid drip into the glass pot little by little calms her down. And even though she uses the same measurements every day, Celso always says that today's coffee is better than yesterday's. Of course, it's not true; there are days when the coffee tastes awful. But her dad compliments it anyway, because this is one of the ways he found to display his love for his daughter without having to say, "Love you, daughter."

But when Ana gets to the kitchen, there's already coffee. And, by the amount left, it was prepared a few hours ago. Time enough for Celso to have a couple of mugs and leave just a little at the bottom of the container that will caramelize in the heat of the coffeemaker until it turns into a black sticky goo. Pulling the cord out of the outlet, Ana turns off the coffeemaker so she won't have to deal with the black goo later since it's Monday, and on Mondays, it's her turn to take care of the dishes.

"Dad?" Ana calls.

From the living room, he grunts in response, but not in a bad mood. Celso is almost never in a bad mood. His grunt sounds more like that of someone who hasn't slept at all at night because he's been trying to find the best words to share important news with his daughter. Not that she can notice anything beyond the lack of sleep, but I'm a house, and being a house has some advantages according to the laws of the universe.

"Honey, come here," he whispers, and Ana can hear him because I'm a small house.

"Good morning. You already made your coffee? Got sick of mine?" Ana jokes, because she still has no idea what Celso is about to say.

"We need to talk," he says in a serious voice, rotating his body on the old office chair with the jammed wheels to face Ana.

She freezes for a moment and hides her fists in her pajama pants. He figured it out. That must be it. He knows about Letícia. Some neighbor must have told him about the girl who is always over when he's away. Someone must have seen them kiss in the library and the information passed from person to person until it reached her father. Or it was the damn record store clerk. He must have said something about the album covers Ana looks at. Or maybe her dad is not sure about anything. He just thinks Ana is a lesbian and believes the best thing to do is to have this conversation now before the worst comes to pass. It must have been her posture, her attitude, her inability to paint her own nails, or the way she said, "Don't count on it" on New Year's Eve. That sentence was too bold. Ana needs to be smarter and stop dropping clues all the time. She is going to lie. Say she doesn't know what he's talking about. She'll learn to paint her own nails and try never to be seen with Letícia in public again.

Letícia.

How is she going to talk to Letícia? She can go out and walk in circles in front of her girlfriend's house until she decides to look out the window.

Or would that be even riskier? She couldn't possibly wait until classes are back to tell her everything. That would be impossible. Or maybe Celso would want to tell Letícia's parents about it?

Ana knew she should have gone ahead with the idea of the secret code for bad things. When they speak on the phone, Ana always ends the call saying, "I still have that CD of yours," which means "I love you." Letícia answers, "You can keep it for as long as you need," which means "I love you, too." But when Ana suggested they create a secret code to ask for help, Letícia thought that was silly. Said she'd always protect Ana above anything else. Well, where is Letícia right now?

"Honey?" Celso gets her attention again, since Ana has spent the last thirty seconds frozen, watching the emptiness with her mouth agape, not saying anything.

"Hey, Dad," she replies, snapping out of it, but still choking on stress.

"I've known about this for some time now, but I've been waiting for the best moment to talk to you about it because, well, this is going to affect both of us. I wanted to get all the information before talking to you, but I've been afraid to have this conversation, and . . ."

I'm scared of this conversation, too, Ana thinks.

"But time passed and passed, and you know what I'm like, honey. I hate conflict."

I hate conflict, too.

"But now I can't delay it anymore because we got to a point where I don't know what else to do. I need you to understand you're the only family I have, and that everything I do is always thinking of what's best for you, so . . ."

20

Dad, just spit it out. Say what you know, or what you think you know, whatever. Just get this over with once and for all.

"We're moving," Celso concludes.

Ana's breath gets caught when she tries to do a deep inhale and let out a relieved sigh at the same time, resulting in a coughing fit that lasts a few seconds.

"You went around in circles for all this time just to tell me we're going to live in another house?" she asks, her face red from all the coughing and her forehead sweaty from all the worrying.

"In another city. Technically another state. We're going to Rio de Janeiro," he replies, shrinking as he speaks.

All the relief she felt for not having to deal with the "So, honey, are you a lesbian?" question flies out the window. She's no longer relieved. She's worried. Upset. Sad. Pissed out of her mind. She's never felt all these feelings at the same time. Ana is still standing, just as she had been when the conversation started, but now her legs are shaking and she needs to sit down before she collapses on the floor. Her legs carry her slowly to the couch where Ana plops down, processing the information like a slow, broken computer for her dad to fix. However, in her case, Celso is not here to fix anything. He's here to break it further.

"Say something," Celso asks, his voice filled with remorse.

"When?" asks Ana. "When are we moving?"

"In two wee—"

"TWO WEEKS?" Ana yells before he can finish his sentence.

"I know, honey, I know. It's not long, it's just that everything happened so quickly and—"

"What happened so quickly? Go ahead, explain," she demands, frenetically twirling the ends of her hair around her pointer finger. She always does this when she's nervous.

"In October, I got this phone call—"

"OCTOBER? You've known this for . . ." Ana pauses to count the months on her fingers because math is not her forte, especially when she's nervous. "Three months! You've known for *three months* and decided to tell me only now?"

"It's a job opportunity. An offer I can't refuse," Celso retorts firmly, trying to show her who's boss. "To be an IT technician at a very big company. We'll lead a very comfortable life. Things were uncertain with all this Y2K craziness, but now it's official. Honey, I just want what's best for us."

"You want what's best for *yourself*, you mean. You don't know what's best for me. You have no idea who I am. I don't even like the Backstreet Boys!"

Celso looks confused, unsure what the Backstreet Boys have to do with this.

"If you want some time to think, we can talk later, when we're calmer," he says.

"Ah, thank you so much for giving me *time to think*, Dad. Whoa. I really appreciate it," Ana says, lifting off the couch like a rocket and dashing to her room.

Her mind repeats *Letícia, Letícia, Letícia* as she takes off her pajamas and puts on the first thing she sees in front of her: an old pair of jeans, a loose T-shirt, and a pair of sunglasses because the sun is shining and she doesn't want anyone to notice she's about to cry.

After tying her white Keds in a rush, she opens the door to leave.

"Honey, I . . ." Celso tries to start the conversation over again.

"Give me some time, Dad. I just need some time," she says without looking back, then slams the door behind her.

"I love you," Celso whispers to the walls, but no one is around to hear him.

I told you this isn't a love story.

It's a goodbye story.

GREG

Gregório Brito barely had a chance to say goodbye.

He'd been living a normal Sunday like any other when his mother entered the room hysterically demanding he pack his bags to go spend a few days at his aunt's house. An aunt he barely knew. His parents were having "a few grown-up issues they needed to work through." That's how they talked about their divorce, always sugarcoating things for their son, as if he were still a little boy. Greg knew his parents were about to get a divorce. The constant fighting over the last couple of years made that very clear. He'd totally be able to deal with lawyers coming and going and his father's yelling, drowning out his mother's voice. But Greg's mom wanted to spare him, and that meant boarding him on a bus to a little rural town, where he'd stay until further notice, while they figured out their "grown-up issues" in the family's giant apartment in São Paulo.

Now, as he spends his very first night in Lagoa Pequena, Greg lies facing the ceiling, wondering what good can come from him being in this town while he tries to calmly fall asleep.

And obviously fails.

Coming here was poorly planned, it all happened so quickly. According to his mom, Aunt Catarina would be very pleased to welcome him since she felt so lonely and loved having people over.

Catarina was not lonely and, for lack of a better word, *hated* company. Human company, at least. Her dog, Keanu, doesn't count because Keanu is the perfect company.

But Catarina liked her calm life and didn't expect to suddenly have a teenager under her roof for who knows how long. She didn't know how to say no to her sister, Carmem. Not after all the times Carmem had lent her money to fund her fraught business initiatives.

Catarina still owns a home video rental store. In 2010. I rest my case.

———

I feel dishonest now because I started this story by telling you that I am a house. And yeah, I'm still a house. But now I'm also a home video rental store, where my garage used to be.

It's a long, boring tale, but suffice it to say: After Ana and Celso (spoiler alert!) left, Catarina was interested in renting me. But she didn't know where to keep her car, and the landlord said he'd been thinking of building a garage where the front porch used to be, because he thought it would increase the property value.

It turned out awful, if you want my opinion.

The porch had been wide, inviting, and the floor made of little red-and-yellow tiles. The garage made it all dark, metallic, and pointy. But it had been the start of the new millennium, and people were obsessed with the idea of having a car *and* the idea of increasing property value. As soon as the renovation was done, Catarina moved in. Her video rental store, Catavento Video, had already been operating farther down at Number 23 Sunflower Street. She had the best days of her life there. Movies with friends, wine every Wednesday, a romance here and there, the day she adopted Keanu Reeves—who filled all the rooms with life and covered the walls with paw-shaped stains—and a car in that horrendous metallic box.

The car was the first to go. When business started to slow down, Catarina sold her car, telling herself nobody needs a car in a city so small (or pequena), it's even in the name.

But that was just the start. Business went from bad to worse, and the money her older sister lent her helped her keep things together, until she had to give up the store entirely. But that wasn't the end of Catavento Video, because Catarina had a strong will, a big garage, and no car.

And this is the story of how, for a short period of time, I was also a video rental store.

———————

"He can help you take care of the store" was Carmem's line to Catarina during the call where she asked her sister to take care of her sixteen-year-old for a few days. She could have just said "watch your nephew for a few days because you owe me money," which would have been enough. But it didn't seem like a bad idea to have a new employee working for free to help the rare customer who still stopped by looking for a movie to watch over the weekend.

Those are Catarina's thoughts as she stares at the ceiling on that first night Greg spends in Lagoa Pequena. She would treat her nephew as an employee, not as a relative. It was bad enough that she had to work on her failed business and try to find moonlighting gigs to keep her home in order and feed a sloppy three-legged mutt. Impossible to add a teenager to this equation.

Separated by a wall, the three residents submerge in their own thoughts. Greg wonders how long this visit will last. Catarina wonders how she will manage to keep the store open, have enough money to pay the bills, and stop feeling frustrated that, at thirty-six, she hasn't accomplished anything worthwhile in her life. Keanu wonders when he will get treats, because Keanu is a dog.

JANUARY 18, 2010

When the sun rises, Catarina gets up to make some coffee and a grilled ham-and-cheese sandwich. Not because she wants her nephew to feel at home, but because she wants to show she's got everything under control.

"Morning, Aunt Catarina," says Greg, coming into the kitchen to an enthusiastic welcome from Keanu, who scratches his legs and barks with his tongue lolling out like a good boy.

"Morning, Gregório," Catarina replies, hiding her face behind an enormous coffee mug.

"You can call me Greg. Everyone does," he says timidly, grabbing a glass of water.

"Did you have trouble organizing your things in the bedroom?" Catarina asks.

"None at all, it was easy. It's not as if I had that much . . ."

Greg had arrived the previous day carrying a small suitcase. Some changes of clothes, his laptop, and a Nintendo DS. He didn't know how long he'd stay in Lagoa Pequena, so he thought that would cover his needs (getting dressed, going online, and catching new Pokémon).

The two of them had breakfast in awkward silence. Despite being relatives, they've never had much contact beyond the occasional Christmas get-togethers. Greg knows almost nothing about his aunt, and she knows even less about him.

"Thank you for having me over," he says, trying to be polite without sounding sorry for himself.

His technique fails, because Catarina looks at him the way one looks at a child who was left wailing at one's front door in a box.

She'd like to know more. She'd like to know how her nephew is dealing with the whole divorce thing. She'd like to know if he *knows* about the whole divorce thing, because his serene, unworried expression makes her think Greg has no idea what's going on. Or maybe he knows and doesn't care. Teenagers these days are basically born with a computer in their hands and divorced parents. *It's standard*, she tries to remind herself.

Catarina remembers every single time her sister called just to chat, talking about how worried she was that Greg was becoming a man and that, despite being a very smart kid, she was afraid of the "choices" he'd been making and how he could at any moment "go down a dangerous path." But looking at him now, sitting on the other side of the table, he seems almost . . . harmless?

Greg's frame is slender, with thin wrists covered in colorful silicone bands. His light brown skin, a few shades lighter than his aunt's, is full of freckles around the cheeks. His short hair is curly and his giant pair of glasses covers practically his entire face. Just like Catarina, Greg has a dimple on his chin—a subtle reminder that, despite being a total stranger wrecking her quiet routine, he's still a family member.

"No need to thank me. That's what family is for," she says, subconsciously bringing her hand to her chin. "Besides, you're going to work for me, isn't that right?"

"My mom told me about the store. I have no work experience, but I'm a quick learner."

Catarina tries not to huff impatiently at him. Having someone to watch her store while she does odd jobs around town seemed like a good idea at first, but she'd completely forgotten that the kid had never had a job in his life. Training employees was always a pain, and Catarina hadn't done it since Catavento moved into her garage and she became the only one in charge of its operations.

"Here's how it's gonna work," Catarina says, slamming her mug on the table and making more noise than she intended to. She clears her throat and lowers her voice because she also doesn't want the kid to think she's a tyrant. "The store opens at nine and closes at seven. Today is Monday, which means it'll be busy. Lots of people will come in to return the movies they rented for the weekend. The secret is to recommend a similar one and not let the client leave the store without first renting another. Do you know anything about movies, kid?"

Greg blinks slowly, as if he were still taking in the opening hours. At this specific moment, he doesn't look like the smart kid his mom's been gushing about.

"Never mind. Come with me, it's easier if I show it to you," she says, dropping her mug into the sink and pushing him by the shoulders.

Greg isn't sure what's going on, so he shoves the last bite of sandwich in his mouth and follows her.

The two are in the garage. The place is dark, and the walls are covered with movie posters. At first glance, Greg can't find a single poster of anything that came out in the last five years. This is going to be a challenge.

Aluminum shelves with several piles of DVDs are spread throughout the garage. No Blu-rays. The place looks like an antiques store. Identification tags printed at home organize the titles in different categories: new releases, drama, thriller, comedy, kids, Keanu Reeves . . . Yes, there is a shelf dedicated to Keanu Reeves films. That might explain the dog's name, who followed them into the garage and is lying down in a little bed hidden behind the counter.

"Well, then," Catarina says, ambling around the narrow corridors with her hands on her waist. "If a client comes in to return . . . this one."

She takes a random DVD from the fantasy section and puts it on the counter.

Greg scans the cover. *Stardust*. Luckily it's a recent movie, one he knows.

"Hello, good afternoon, I'm here to return this movie. It's really good, you know!" Catarina says in a different voice, as if she were a customer. "Catarina's recommendations always amaze me."

"Hello! Good afternoon," Greg says, positioning himself behind the counter and puffing up his chest to play along.

But he has no idea what to say next.

Catarina lets out a frustrated sigh.

"So then you type the movie's title here." She points at the search field on the screen of her prehistoric computer. "And while you're processing the return, you should already be suggesting something else. Go, quickly. Make a recommendation."

Greg's heart hammers in his chest. This is essentially his first job interview, and even though he knows he already got the gig, he's afraid of making a mistake. Greg hates making mistakes.

"Hmm, have you seen *The Brothers Grimm*? If you like fantasy films based on fairy tales, I think you'll enjoy that one, too," he says, forcing a smile and, for some reason, changing his tone of voice a little.

"Good thinking," Catarina says with a thumbs-up. "But I don't buy Matt Damon movies. This is a one hundred percent Matt Damon–free movie rental space. I should put that on the sign."

"Wh-why?" Greg asks, afraid of the answer.

"Long story. I had an ex who looked like Matt Damon. Trauma. Suggest something else, go, quick," she says, as if they were on a game show and there was an alarm about to go off somewhere.

"You might enjoy . . . *Coraline!*" he yells. Keanu barks. "Which is another movie also based on a novel by Neil Gaiman."

He smiles, proud that his quick thinking didn't fail him twice in a row.

"Hmm, you know books. That's a good balance for me. I don't read books. You can watch, like, fifty movies with the time it would take you to read a book. That's why I own a video rental store and not a library. But very good. And what would you recommend to someone who came to return . . . this one?" She places another movie on the counter.

While he examines the cover of *The Mummy*, Greg tries not to feel offended by the whole spiel about not reading books.

"I've never seen it," he answers, reading the credits on the back cover. "I was six when it came out."

"When I was six, I already had solid opinions on Oscar winners," Catarina retorts.

"What you just said doesn't make any sense," Greg points out, somewhat questioning his aunt's intelligence.

"Clock's ticking. The client is leaving," she whispers, walking back toward the door and tapping her pointer finger on her wrist.

"Hmm . . . Uh . . . *The Mummy 2*! Probably."

"*The Mummy Returns*," Catarina corrects him. "You should watch it. It's the kind of movie that makes you feel like a different person after watching."

Greg laughs, surprised because, after all this time, he never thought he had an aunt with a sense of humor. Catarina stares at him in confusion, which makes him realize she was serious about *The Mummy Returns*.

They continue to "play" for a while longer and, as Greg observes the DVDs on the shelves, he begins to notice that it's possible to recommend movies he's never watched based solely on the covers. If you liked a romantic comedy in which a straight couple hugs against a white backdrop, there are ten more of those. If you enjoyed an action film with a middle-aged hero running with a gun as bombs explode in the background, you might enjoy all of these that look just the same. And if all you want is an excellent film, you can choose one from the Keanu Reeves section (according to Catarina).

In only a few minutes, Greg learns how to work the computer system and register rentals and returns. By the time the store opens, he feels readier than ever.

Greg knows this will be an easy job. Maybe he shouldn't even call it a job. But, more than anything, he's excited by the possibility of no longer being treated like a child by everyone around him.

Catarina opens the garage door. It's a normal summer day, and Sunflower Street is peaceful and sunny. She explains that she'll leave Greg alone for a few hours in the morning, and he's surprised by the confidence she already has in him. They had never exchanged more than two full sentences until this very morning! Greg's shock is so evident that she feels like she needs to say something.

"You're family, Gregório. I trust you. Besides, what would you possibly do? Put Keanu in your backpack and run away?" She stops and thinks for a moment. "Please don't put Keanu in your backpack and run away."

He smiles. So does Keanu (in that way dogs smile).

"And where are you going?" he asks, unafraid of overstepping.

"To work, where else?" Catarina answers casually, while cleaning Keanu's shelf with a damp cloth.

"I thought the store was your work," Greg admits, a little confused.

Catarina lets out a sort of villainous laughter, as if she were the evil stepmother in a teen movie about twins who were separated at birth and found each other years later, then hatched a plan to bring their biological parents back together. Yes, this example is, specifically, *The Parent Trap*. Greg and Catarina's story always puts me in that kind of mood.

"Will you be back for lunch?" Greg asks, finding a smart way to talk about food without directly asking what's for lunch.

"No. Not until later. But Tiago will stop by at noon to bring food."

"Who's Tiago?"

"The guy who will stop by at noon to bring food," Catarina repeats slowly, as if she were talking to a child.

Greg decides not to press the subject and to trust Tiago, the guy who will stop by at noon to bring food. He regrets not having taken the opportunity to eat more at breakfast.

When Catarina leaves, Greg feels a sense of freedom. At home, there were rare moments when he could be alone and, in recent months, with his mom trying so hard to maintain the appearance of a happy family to their holiday guests, the situation only worsened.

The store's computer is old, but functional enough for him to open his email server and send Sofia Karen some updates. Greg is not much of an email guy, of course. He's a teenager who spends most of his online time on Pokémon forums. But email turns out to be the most efficient way to keep in touch with his best friend. Who's also his dad's personal assistant.

Greg's father is a plastic surgeon. The reasonably well-known Alexandre Brito, who owns the aesthetic clinic Britto Beauty, spelled with two *t*'s either because of numerology or because his dad thought it would look fancier that way. Greg hates the company name and would never take a clinic called Britto Beauty seriously if one day he were to consider any cosmetic procedure, which he wouldn't because, unlike other gay boys his age, Greg likes the way he looks. It's astounding.

Things started to change in 2007, when his dad did a procedure on someone who had participated on that reality show *Big Brother Brasil*. At the time, Greg had no idea who it was because in the Brito household nobody watches reality TV. All it took was one interview on a gossip website for Alexandre to become a household name in plastic surgery for B-list celebrities. Money, recognition, one appearance on a TV show that offered middle-aged women plastic surgeries and gift cards for department stores, and Alexandre's life was set. Greg never complained, because his dad's sudden success greatly improved the family's quality of life and brought with it Sofia Karen.

Sofia is a young woman whose dream is to be a reporter, and who makes a living by booking interviews and buying suits for Greg's father. The two of them used to spend a lot of time at the Brito home, where Sofia worked, and Greg got attached. He'll never say this out loud, but when his sudden trip to Lagoa Pequena was announced, the first thought he had was of how he'd miss spending afternoons with Sofia. Then he thought he'd really miss his room, the fast-paced São Paulo lifestyle, his mother, and many other things before he got to his father.

Patiently, because it's a slow computer and it takes a few seconds for the screen to register what's being typed on the keyboard, Greg writes Sofia an email:

Monday, January 18, 2010. 9:37 a.m.
From: geodude1993@email.com
To: skaren@brittobeauty.com.br
Subject: I'm alive!

Hi, Sofia, I'm here at my aunt's. Sending a note just so you know I'm okay,

because we barely had a chance to say goodbye. But I think you know where I am because you were probably the one who bought my ticket.

My aunt is weird. She acts funny for someone who's over thirty. But I'm not complaining. Maybe I'm used to adults being horrible and she made me think there's a chance I could be a cool adult one day.

I'm in charge of her video store and her dog, can you believe it? Who even OWNS a video store these days? The dog is great. A gray mutt with dark spots all over his body. And he has three legs. Not that it makes any difference, but I want you to imagine Keanu exactly the way he is. His name is Keanu Reeves because, it seems, Aunt Catarina is obsessed with the actor. I was afraid if I told her I've never watched one of his movies, she would kick me out.

Did you get me a return ticket? I'd like to know when I'm coming back. I wish my mom would tell me things. Classes won't start again until after Carnival. I don't want to be here on Carnival. I was almost sure that this year I'd finally have my first kiss. I even got a fake ID to go out! Everyone kisses on Carnival. Lagoa Pequena feels like the kind of place that doesn't have any boys my age around to kiss.

Other than that, I will survive.

How's my parents' divorce going?

Keep me posted!

Your best friend,
G

Greg carefully watches the green browser bar load, and when his email finally gets sent, he notices a middle-aged woman standing by the counter. Greg has no idea how long the short woman with gray hair and plump, white arms has been standing there, but she doesn't look upset. Just frozen in the same position for decades.

"I didn't want to bother you, you seemed focused on the computer," she comments, slowly blinking her huge and slightly scary eyes.

"How may I help you today?" Greg asks, frowning internally at his voice automatically going into polite mode.

The customer returns *Die Hard* and *Die Hard with a Vengeance*, and when Greg asks if she would like to rent the second installment, thinking she might have made a mistake with the order of the movies because all the covers are identical, she politely declines, saying with conviction that she hates *Die Hard 2* because she's afraid of planes.

Greg missed the opportunity and the lady (whose name is Leda, according to her registration in the system) leaves without renting anything else, but she promises to come back on Friday.

The morning drags by, and the store remains nearly empty. A mom and daughter stop by to return *Chicken Little* (according to the system, this is the eighteenth time they've rented the same movie). The mom's tired look makes it clear she can't stand her daughter's obsession with the bird. Greg reserves judgment because deep down, and secretly, he thinks it's an excellent movie. Someone else comes into the garage, but not a customer. Just your average Joe asking about the nearest gas station. Greg doesn't know the answer.

It's past noon and Greg is starving and impatient with the slow internet, which takes an eternity to load photos of his Facebook friends. He knows Facebook is a portal to everything he wished he were experiencing during his school break (in São Paulo, far away from Lagoa Pequena), so the slow internet might be more of a blessing than a curse. A long shadow appears on the floor of the store, and Greg raises his eyes dramatically to see the tallest guy he's ever encountered in his entire life standing at the store's door.

Greg likes to exaggerate. The guy isn't even that tall. Just a little taller than average for boys their age. But the dark, tight jeans and the black hoodie with sleeves longer than his arms build up the illusion. The hoodie has P!ATD printed on it, and Greg knows it means Panic! At the Disco because he used to watch the band's music videos on MTV. It's hot out, but the guy doesn't seem to mind it, in all his layers of black clothing. His dark, straight hair falls over his eyes, hiding half of his pale and sweaty face. It's intriguing to Greg how this guy can completely don the look of a 2010 emo. He either takes his musical taste very seriously, or Lagoa Pequena is the kind of place where trends arrive late, and the emo style just got here.

This is Tiago, the guy who stops by at noon to bring food.

He's emo. And he's late.

"Hi," he says. "Catarina asked me to drop this off. Sorry I'm late. Lots of deliveries today."

"Hi," Greg replies, still staring at Tiago with a mix of curiosity, interest, and, maybe, desire.

Tiago is carrying a take-out container in his right hand and, in his left, an MP3 player with earbuds that go into the hoodie and are dangling out of his collar. The music is loud enough that Greg can hear it from behind the counter. It sounds like rock, or maybe a man letting out a terrified scream because someone is pouring acid on his face.

"Are you coming to get the food, or should I bring it to you?" Tiago asks, in the same tone of voice as before. As if he were about to die of boredom.

The two remain ten feet apart. It's the clunkiest social interaction I've ever witnessed.

"You can leave it here on the counter," Greg says without moving. "Maybe you could . . . watch the store. And the dog. Just for a couple minutes? I need to go to the bathroom, and I've been alone all morning."

Tiago nods. Greg runs inside.

He feels ridiculous that he was all awkward in front of a guy who seems like the leader of a ghost-type Pokémon gym. Or like a vampire.

When Greg comes back to the store, the food container is on the counter, giving off an aroma that he identifies as mashed potatoes and steak. Tiago is sitting on the floor, Keanu licking his face. He smiles as if he'd completely forgotten the emo role he'd been playing but assumes a serious expression as soon as he notices Greg's presence.

"I'm off," Tiago says, more to Keanu than to Greg.

"You don't want to rent a movie?" Greg asks, because he wants to surprise his aunt with more rentals than expected (she expects zero) and because he wants a few more minutes in the company of this mystery boy.

"I don't have time to watch a movie today," Tiago says, getting up from the floor and running his hands over his clothes in a failed attempt to get rid of Keanu's fur.

"You can return it whenever you'd like," Greg tries, making up new rules, which probably won't make his aunt very happy.

Tiago half smiles.

"Do you have *Scooby-Doo Two*?" he asks, as if he's known for some time which movie he'd like to watch.

"The second one?" Greg is confused because he knows nothing about Scooby-Doo.

"Yeah. One of those movies with real people—flesh-and-bone humans— and a computer-animated dog," Tiago explains. "I watched it a million times when I was younger, but I think my mom lost the tape and I never found it anywhere else. Do you have it here?"

Greg looks up the movie in the system but can't find anything.

"I'm sorry, guess this isn't your lucky day. I think my aunt never saw any potential in *Scooby-Doo*. Or maybe it has Matt Damon, and she refused to order it."

"Catarina is your aunt?" Tiago asks.

"Yeah, why?" Greg snaps back defensively, pressing his thumbs hard against the counter.

"Nothing. She almost never talks about her family. I thought you were just a cute guy she hired."

!!!!!

Greg swallows hard. Keanu barks. Tiago turns his back on him.

"Eat it before it goes cold. I'll be back tomorrow."

And, in the blink of an eye, the seven-foot-tall emo boy disappears.

Greg, still stunned, opens the food container and finds mashed potatoes and steak, just as he'd hoped. He smiles at the steak, suddenly remembering how hungry he is.

On the computer screen, his inbox beeps with an incoming message. Sofia Karen just replied. Greg reads the email while chewing on a piece of steak.

Monday, January 18, 2010. 12:58 p.m.
From: skaren@brittobeauty.com.br
To: geodude1993@email.com
Subject: Re: I'm alive!

Hi, Gregório. I'm offended to learn that you're used to horrible adults when I literally am an adult AND we spend a lot of time together.

You've never seen anything with Keanu Reeves? Not even the one where he's a go-go boy? Not even *The Matrix*??? I thought teachers made kids watch it in school or something. I don't know, I would. If I were a teacher.

Your parents still haven't asked me to buy your return ticket. I'll let you know as soon as I have any news. Unlike any other news about their divorce, which I do not intend to share with you because that is none of my business, so stop asking me about it. I'm sure your parents will have a talk with you when everything is official.

I also shouldn't know anything about your fake ID. Or your potential first kiss. Don't put me in a difficult position, Greg. I'm just an employee of this family. Of your dad, in fact. If you commit any crimes with this fake ID, these emails might make me an accomplice or something. Maybe I'd get arrested. I'm not sure how the law works. Despite being an adult who knows many things about everything.

Anyway, do not commit any crimes! I beg of you!

And stop worrying so much about this first kiss of yours. When the right time comes, you will know.

From your dad's employee who's not even close to being your best friend,
Sofia Karen

Greg reads the message twice because Sofia's words make him feel at home. He replies right away, since he's got nothing better to do.

Monday, January 18, 2010. 1:07 p.m.
From: geodude1993@email.com
To: skaren@brittobeauty.com.br
Subject: Re: Re: I'm alive!

The right time has come.

There's a guy here. He brought me food.

And I might be way off, but I'm pretty sure we're gonna kiss.

From your eternal friend and confidant,
G

Sofia doesn't seem to be very busy, because her answer arrives right away.

Monday, January 18, 2010. 1.09 p.m.
From: skaren@brittobeauty.com.br
To: geodude1993@email.com
Subject: Re: Re: Re: I'm alive!

You've said that every other time.

But I shouldn't even know that, since I'm JUST YOUR DAD'S EMPLOYEE AND NOT YOUR FRIEND.

(But anyway, good luck. Tell me all about it later. In the totally impersonal way you'd tell it to an employee, etc.)

Sofia Karen

As soon as he's done reading the reply from his friend/employee (I still haven't completely understood the relationship between these two), the afternoon sun blasts on the roof of the garage, heating it up, and Greg would give everything for a nap. He would have fallen asleep on the keyboard if it weren't for the arrival of another customer, which made Keanu get up from his little bed and bark while trying to bite his own tail.

"Hi," says the man, his deep voice a little raspy.

Greg lets out a long sigh because, well, it can't be possible that all the people in this city are extremely attractive in a mysterious and slightly dark-and-handsome way. The man standing by the front door doesn't resemble Tiago, not even remotely. He's not an emo adult. Just a . . . handsome adult. The red undertone of his skin shows that he spends a good amount of time in the sun, and his gray hair, that he must be at least fifty. He's

43

unnecessarily muscular. He's not young enough to look like a superhero, but he is charming enough to look like the father of a teenage superhero in a poorly produced TV show that got canceled in the second season.

"Hi," Greg says, gingerly touching his face to check if he has any mashed potato on his chin.

And he does.

"Is Catarina around?" the man asks.

"No, she went out. I'm her nephew. Gregório," he introduces himself.

"Right," the man says without looking Greg in the eye. "Thanks."

Then he leaves. Without introducing himself. Without even giving Keanu a quick pat, even though the dog seemed very excited by his presence.

Greg decides to make it up to the needy dog and, just like Tiago had done a few moments earlier, he sits on the floor, pets the mutt, and receives a series of face licks in return.

For a brief second, Greg feels at peace. He feels that maybe, *just maybe*, Lagoa Pequena might not be so bad after all.

BETO

Beto hates Lagoa Pequena.

He hates its silly streets named after flowers, the tiny square with live music every Sunday, and the way every single resident seems to know someone who knows you. He hates how people in this town start playing Christmas music at the end of October, and the fact that young people's greatest accomplishments here amount to a big party when they turn fifteen (for girls) and buying the latest video game (for boys). He also hates how everything is meticulously divided by gender, and how your destiny seems to be stamped onto you the moment you're born. But, above all else, he hates how Lagoa Pequena always finds a way to crush his dreams, little by little.

Beto takes photos.

He still doesn't consider himself enough of a professional to call it being a *photographer*. But over the past three years, at every birthday party, wedding, engagement party, and even some wakes, graduations, and gender reveals, you could always find Beto wearing his black vest, his semiprofessional camera, and a forced smile.

Beto also hates gender reveal parties. For the money, he had to endure three years of taking photos of couples cutting cakes with either pink or blue filling. Always for the money.

He had a simple plan: Save as much as possible, move to São Paulo, enroll in a photography course, and work with things that were actually important. To see his photos in magazines, big campaigns, and Instagram ads that most people ignore. It wasn't that absurd of a plan. Lara, his older sister, went to São Paulo with much less of a plan, and it had all worked out.

The only thing is, when Lara moved to the city, there was no mysterious virus spreading throughout the world and forcing society to adapt to a new and scary reality. Beto isn't stupid; he knows there are people going through much worse because of this virus. He reads the newspaper, follows the climbing death rates, and knows that his move can wait. Spending a little more time in Lagoa Pequena is no huge sacrifice.

But when no one is looking, when he's alone in his bedroom staring at the ceiling, Beto can't help but feel frustrated that, seriously, when it was *finally* his turn, a damn virus *had* to come into the picture?

The mayor of Lagoa Pequena issued an order for social isolation right when things started. The whole city is shut down, the streets are empty, and the houses are full.

Without any prospects for when all this will get better (a few months? Maybe years?), Beto spends his days trying to make himself numb to the worries. He walks from one room to the other, trying not to seem too sad because he doesn't want to have an honest conversation with his mother.

Being the son of a psychologist is not without its advantages. Helena, Beto's mother, has never questioned her children about their professional choices. She's always offered all the support that Beto needed to follow his passion for photography and defended her son from nosy relatives who would seize any opportunity to say that taking photos doesn't pay the bills. Helena likes to have conversations, to understand his problems, and to be a part of the solution. That's a good thing, right? There are parents who, for a lot less, would already be shoving a little public service prep course down their kids' throats.

But not Helena. She's a cool mom.

Or at least she used to be. Before it all began.

With her downtown practice shut down, Helena has been seeing her patients over videoconference. She transformed her bedroom into her office and spends most of her time locked in there. Beto tries not to make noise because he knows how important work is for his mother.

But every day, around seven o'clock in the evening, when she leaves that room, she seems starved for human interaction. Thirsty for a conversation while staring into someone's actual eyes, some dialogue without the constant "Oops, I think you're frozen," or "Can you still hear me?" or "You're on mute." And the victim of this desire is always Beto because there's no one else around to listen to what Helena has to say.

Today marks a month that they've been isolated. Enough for Beto to miss every tacky event that he used to photograph around the city. He misses waking up early on Sunday and going outside to take photos of people at the park. He misses finding the beautiful contrast between a bare tree and the cloudless sky, and watching the branches form abstract patterns through his lens. But today, with no school, no work, and not a single good night's sleep in days, Beto doesn't even know whether it's Sunday or not.

It's not Sunday. It's Tuesday.

"Honey, what if I dyed my hair red?" Helena says. "Not like *red* red. But, I don't know, auburn. Do people still say *auburn*? It sounds like an old woman's hair color, doesn't it? That's not what I want. To seem older. I just wanted, I don't know, a new look. I could order the dye from the pharmacy and do it at home. Can't be too hard, can it? I'm sure there's a video online that shows you how to do it. Look it up— DIY hair dye."

It's nearly nine at night and the two are seated on the couch. The TV is on mute because the news is too terrible to watch after dinner, but, in a way, seeing the soundless image of the local news host makes them both feel less alone.

"I think so," Beto answers without paying his mom much attention.

"Yes, I'll look good with red hair, or yes, we can do it at home?" she asks, her eyes fixed on a historical romance that she started reading the day before and is now past the hundredth page.

Beto never understands how she can read, talk, and plan a new look at the same time. He didn't inherit this multitasking gene.

Right now, for instance, he can barely pay attention to his mom and scroll his infinite Instagram feed without totally losing focus on both. Beto puts his phone aside and looks at his mom because he's polite. And because he doesn't feel emotionally ready to see photos of beautiful people on his phone on a Tuesday night when there's no guessing when he'll be able to leave the house again.

"You'll look beautiful no matter what," Beto tells his mother. "And maybe you don't even have to look up how to dye your hair online. Don't these things come with instructions on the box?"

Helena abandons her book and uses the front camera of her phone as a mirror, rearranging her hair and trying to imagine its strands in a different color. She smiles, then looks serious, then makes a face, watches her face attentively, and runs her fingers over her cheeks, which, just like Beto's, are plump and rosy.

"I'm a visual person, Roberto. I need to *see* it," she says.

"You can see the words and interpret the sentences and understand how to dye your hair at home. You literally have a PhD, Mom. I trust your ability to read a manual and know what to do," Beto replies with a cheeky smile.

He's not worried because he knows that even if his mom's hair dyeing goes wrong and she somehow ends up with blue hair, she'll be able to see the bright side of it all. That's just what she's like. At least she's not annoying and unrealistic, like those people who believe that every bad thing happens for a greater good, and that a virus spreading around the world might have a positive side because now they get to spend more time with their son. Helena knows that some things have no positive side, but she can still rationalize things enough to understand that not everything is the end of the world.

(Unless this virus actually *is* the end of the world, too soon to tell.)

Helena opens her mouth to answer, but she's cut off by her phone ringing. Beto makes a mental note to change his mom's ringtone as soon as possible because, now that the two of them spend all day together, that annoying sound like something from a rave for robots is starting to get to him.

"It's your sister," Helena mentions as she sees Lara's photo flash on her phone screen, then picks up the call on speaker because this is a family without secrets.

"Hi, Mom," Lara says on the other end of the line.

"Hi, honey. I'm here with your brother. On speaker," Helena warns, just to be safe, because who knows if this is the one time Lara was planning on telling her a secret.

"Hi, Beto," Lara says.

"Hi, Lara," he replies.

Oh my god, this conversation is going nowhere.

"So, I was thinking of spending a couple days with you. Just until this whole thing is over, I don't know. Our entire office is working remotely, and my classes are online now, so I wouldn't really be missing anything. And I'd get to spend some time with the two of you. I don't know, I just miss you," Lara says all at once so her mom won't have much time to think about it.

"We miss you, too, sweetie, but I'm not sure it's safe for you to come over now. Besides, the buses to Lagoa were shut down. God knows when they're going to start running. And, even if they were running, can you imagine being trapped in a bus with two hundred people?" Helena counters, pondering. "I'm not sure that's such a good idea, honey."

"You can't fit two hundred people on a bus, Mom," Beto points out.

"There's a ride app that a lot of my friends use. You can do ride-sharing with someone who's headed to the same city as you, and it's a lot cheaper than taking the bus. And there aren't two hundred people in the car," Lara explains.

"That's even worse, Lara. To hit the road with a *stranger*?" Helena protests immediately.

"Well, it's just that I found this woman on the app who's offering a ride to Lagoa Pequena."

"Don't even think about it, Lara. *Don't you even think about it.*"

"And she's great, she's already offered more than a hundred rides through this app, and she has a five-star rating," Lara justifies.

"Honey, that's just a number on your phone screen. Who can speak to her *character's* five-star rating? She might be a kidnapper. Or worse. She might be infected!" Helena says with terror in her voice.

"I'm pretty sure a kidnapper would be worse," Beto points out.

"Well, the good news is that she did not kidnap me," Lara says in a voice so low they can barely hear it.

"LARA, WHAT ARE YOU SAYING?" Helena's scream is so loud that all of Sunflower Street might be able to hear it.

"I'm almost on our street, come open the gate to let me in, bye," Lara blurts out, and hangs up.

Helena is astonished and annoyed but can't hide her smile, knowing she will see her daughter long before expected (there was no date when she expected to see Lara). Beto is happy, too, but, practical as ever, he's thinking about how he'll have to clean up the mess in his room to welcome his sister, who hasn't slept there for over three years now.

In less than two minutes the doorbell rings, and Lara comes in dragging a small suitcase behind her. Her face is covered with a mask and, before coming in through the front door, she takes off her shoes, her jacket, and her pants. She wants to be as careful as possible before she finally hugs her mom, who in turn tosses a tube of hand sanitizer her way, along with a plastic bag for the clothes. This whole cleaning ritual happens while Lara apologizes for showing up unannounced, Helena tells her daughter to stop apologizing because this will always be her home, and Beto cracks a goofy smile because he just realized his sister will be able to help his mom with the whole hair-dyeing thing and he won't need to take part in any of it.

It's not that Lara necessarily knows about hair just because she's a girl. Beto isn't sexist like that. I'm not sure if it's the vibes I give off, but I've never had that kind of prejudiced person living under my roof. He knows his sister will be able to help because she's been dyeing her own hair since she was fourteen. Today it looks shorter than ever, dyed a fading green, the black roots long and the dry ends pulled up in a loose ponytail.

Lara's whole cleaning process takes some time, and Helena doesn't allow family hugs until after her daughter showers. Then, fully showered and wearing her pajamas, Lara is squeezed by Beto and Helena, one on each side. Beto is the largest in the family. His body is the fattest, and his arms are the longest. He can envelop his mom and his sister at the same time, and despite not being the kind of person who offers constant displays of affection, he feels good during the hug. Even with Lara's periodic visits before the pandemic (she used to come to town every three months), Beto can't recall the last time he's felt so at home. It dawns on him how this is good and bad at the same time.

Helena prepares a pasta dish for her daughter with yesterday's leftovers, despite Lara's insistence that she's not hungry because she ate before leaving home. Helena doesn't believe her because she thinks her daughter doesn't eat well in São Paulo. It's obvious how much weight she's lost since she moved to the capital.

Lara is seated on the couch with the plate of food propped on a pillow, Helena next to her and Beto on the floor because the couch cannot comfortably accommodate the family's butts.

"Where did you get this idea of coming home out of nowhere, honey?" Helena asks while Lara calmly twirls pasta on her fork.

"Lu went back to her grandmother's in Fortaleza, Gi was annoying me, bringing her boyfriend home every day, and Ma spent all day locked in her room," Lara answers with her mouth full.

Lu, Gi, and Ma are Lara's roommates in São Paulo. Probably Luciana, Giovana, and Mariana. Or Luana, Gisele, and Marcela. Whatever. Beto never asked. It's a São Paulo thing, referring to people by the first syllable of their name. He thinks it's ridiculous but, deep down, all he wants is to be there, too, and to no longer be Beto, just Be.

"And you've been watching the news, right?" Lara keeps going. "At first I thought it was going to be quick. A month or two, tops. But around the world the virus has been out of control for way longer. God knows how long it will take to get under control here in Brazil . . ."

"If it's up to our government . . ." Helena doesn't finish the sentence.

It will probably last forever, Beto completes it in his head, watching his life unravel in front of his eyes.

"So then I talked to Cleo, my boss, and she said it was fine if I wanted to come over. I might have made up a sickness for you, Mom," Lara admits, and Helena immediately shoots her a disapproving look.

"*Lara!*" Helena reprimands her.

Beto laughs.

"I just didn't want her to think that I was, I don't know, trying to go on vacation, know what I mean? I wanted her to see that I had to come back."

"To care for your sick mother, of course," Helena says, still hurt.

"Anyway, she let me, so I came. I hope it's not a problem," she finishes, taking one last forkful of pasta.

"As I said, this will always be your home, honey," Helena tenderly reaffirms. "Now go wash this plate because—*cough, cough*—your mom is sick."

Beto laughs again.

But deep down he feels like crying.

He just can't quite understand why.

———

Beto's bedroom is the smallest one. It's the bedroom he shared with his sister until she moved out to study journalism in São Paulo three years ago. Of course, a lot has changed in three years. The room is messier because Beto produces by himself the equivalent mess of three people. The walls no longer display all the framed dried flower collages and gold medals Lara won at a poetry contest and a swimming competition, because she is *that* talented. Lara took most of these awards to her new apartment, and the currently empty walls remind Beto that he's never won any gold medals.

The bunk bed hasn't changed. Helena never bought Beto a different bed, and he never minded having a bedroom meant for two. He always slept on the bottom due to his irrational fear of falling from the top bunk, but Lara is no longer used to the top bed. She must have developed the same fear her brother has because instead of climbing up, she takes the mattress and places it on the floor next to Beto.

"I always thought it was weird to sleep that close to the ceiling. It seems like the whole house is going to come crashing down on you," she justifies while grabbing a blanket from the built-in closet, then plops down.

I don't understand this fear people have of being smashed by their own house. I would never collapse on any of them. Not on purpose.

It's past midnight, and the last few hours were filled by family conversation about every topic imaginable. Most of the time, Beto only watches and laughs, relieved that now his mom has a new pair of ears to listen to her.

But now it's just the two of them, and it's weird to have his sister back for an indefinite amount of time.

"Why did you decide to come here?" Beto asks, lying on his side to observe her.

"I already told you, Lu went to Fortaleza and—"

"No, Lara," he interrupts. "Tell me the truth. Not the story you told Mom. The story you would tell me."

"I was so alone," she answers, without stopping to think for even one second.

Beto laughs because, to him, being alone has always seemed like *the best*.

"But you live in the largest city in the country, Lara. São Paulo has everything. Why come back to Lagoa Pequena?"

"São Paulo doesn't have the two of you," Lara says and, immediately feeling that her answer was ridiculous, continues, "and besides, when we're in a crazy situation like this one, where all we have is our family, it's kind of horrible not to be here."

"But you live in an amazing apartment! The door to your living room is purple," Beto reasons, remembering a detail that was etched in his memory since he last went to visit his sister.

Beto spent one week in São Paulo at the end of 2019. He went there for vacation after he graduated to get to know the city, look for calm neighborhoods, and research rent prices. It wasn't even that long ago, but now, with his moving plans totally on hold, it seems like an eternity ago that he saw his sister's purple door and realized that he could paint his door whatever color he wanted.

"Look, Beto, I know I'm going to sound like an eighty-year-old grandma," Lara says as she spreads moisturizer on her legs and elbows. "But I was exactly like you. I also thought São Paulo was the best thing since sliced bread and that I'd never come back to Lagoa Pequena. There was this one evening—it was my first month living there—when we went out to drink with one of Ma's friends. That was the first time I tried a gin and tonic. People there are *obsessed* with gin and tonic. You can get it in any flavor. But this guy, Ma's friend whose name I can't even remember, has one of those cars with a sunroof, and when we were driving back home, I asked to put my head out and scream, because that's a thing we see in movies and I've always wanted to do it. He didn't let me, because apparently there are traffic laws that forbid it, but I did it anyway because I was totally drunk and happy. So then I literally yelled, 'I WILL NEVER GO BACK TO LAGOA PEQUENA!' and, well, look at me now."

Beto laughs. He had missed these stories full of unnecessary details his sister tells. Moments like these make him certain that she was born to tell stories.

Lara works for a news portal called Telescope, a huge website with different sections from political coverage to quizzes like "Find out which vegetable sculpture you are based on your favorite dress from the Academy Awards." She writes about behavior and fashion, which is kind of weird because she always wears the same dress with pockets in different patterns, and Beto's not too sure what the behavior section is supposed to be, but he's never asked.

"The thing is," Lara continues, "all of it has a negative side I've never talked about. I don't want Mom to worry, you know. Sometimes it's really stupid things like when I almost set the kitchen on fire when I first tried to make a risotto, and sometimes it's serious problems, like when I started crying on the subway home and people gave me weird looks, and I started crying even louder because I didn't understand why I was crying."

Beto takes a deep breath and swallows hard. He knows very well what it's like to cry without knowing the reason. In his case, it's also called *a Thursday like any other.*

"I know what you mean, and I know big-city life sounds a lot more exciting when you're not actually there. But I just wanted the opportunity to learn those things myself, you know?" Beto says, a little frustrated that he's not able to put his feelings into easily understandable words.

"It's okay to feel frustrated by things you can't control, Beto," Lara says, her voice soft and calm.

Beto turns around so his sister won't see his eye roll. It's very annoying how Lara is slowly becoming their mother. Always understanding, using these internet-psychology words, trying to get how he feels, but still maintaining her distance.

All Beto has wanted is to get away from this place, but a freaking virus locked the whole world in their homes. This is not "frustration over things he can't control," Beto wants to scream. Put his head out through a car's sunroof against every single traffic law and howl. He wants his sister to look at him and say, "You're right, this situation SUCKS!" as the two of them let out their hate around the house until their lungs are on fire, then start laughing because people are dying all over the world while they're suffering over something so silly.

He knows it's all silly.

He knows it will go away.

But Beto doesn't just want someone to tell him that it's okay to feel this way. He wants to change the way he feels about things. Maybe it is frustration over what he can't control after all.

"I got you a birthday present!" Lara cries out, sensing that her brother was quiet for way too long and trying to improve the mood.

"My birthday isn't until October, Lara. You're about six months early," he says, caught by surprise.

"But I feel like you need a present now. To put a little smile on that face," Lara says, softly pinching her brother's cheeks.

"Ah, of course. Because buying happiness with presents always works out," Beto counters.

Lara ignores her brother, walks up to her suitcase, and pulls out a box.

"I didn't have time to wrap it because I thought I'd have more time to think about the wrapping paper, but . . ."

Beto's eyes widen when he realizes what his sister is holding.

"Forget what I said. You just bought my happiness. Apparently, it actually works out *really well*. Now I'm really happy!" he says, reaching out like a spoiled child who can't wait to get a new toy.

Beto's hands are trembling as he holds the box. It's a telephoto lens for his camera—one that he's always wanted but has never been able to afford. One that can capture close-up shots of faraway objects and, for people who know how to use it, allows for incredible photos taken from a distance. Beto knows how to use it. He's already watched hundreds of YouTube videos about this lens.

"Lara . . . dear god . . . Lara . . . This is . . . God, Lara!" Beto doesn't have a way with words when it comes to expensive presents.

"Well, from how you keep saying my name, I think you like it," she says with a proud smile.

"I *love* it! I've never loved a present so much in my entire life," Beto says, opening the package carefully and inspecting every single brochure and instruction manual as if they were old parchment that held the history of humankind. "But this is . . . this is very expensive."

"I found a good Black Friday deal!" Lara says, not wanting to go into detail about the price of her brother's present.

"You bought this back in November? Why didn't you give it to me for Christmas?!" Beto asks, not realizing this is a jerk thing to say.

Lara doesn't mind.

"I'd already bought your Christmas present. I got that vest during a Father's Day sale," Lara answers. "See? I'm officially an old lady now. I plan presents ahead, take advantage of deals, and save coupons for cooking pots."

Beto remembers the photographer's vest he got from his sister for Christmas, with six pockets in front and a rainbow flag that she had embroidered on the collar. That was a special present. Lara is good with gifts.

"I don't even know how to thank you," Beto says with a genuine smile.

"I'll want some free photos, obviously. With the new lens. Across from the living room window when it gets the morning sun. Maybe like this"— she turns around and looks at Beto over her shoulder—"to show my latest tattoo."

Lara points at the tattoo on her left shoulder, and Beto smiles at the picture of a dinosaur wearing rain boots. He would ask what it means, except he already knows the answer would be something like, "I woke up and I thought, *Hmm, dinosaur in rain boots!*" Because that's how Lara explains every single tattoo except for the little sunflower on her ankle. "So I'll always remember home" is what one of her Instagram posts says.

Beto is still skipping with excitement when he gets up to get his camera and test it. Of course, locked at home with his sister in the middle of the night, there isn't much use for a long-focus lens. But he tries anyway. With his eyes glued to the viewfinder, he focuses and unfocuses on Lara's face, his crumpled clothes on top of a dresser, a spider web in the ceiling.

"I'll be able to get some incredible photos at the square," Beto says without thinking.

Lara swallows hard.

"After all this is behind us, of course," he adds with a sigh, already tired of saying "after all this is behind us" for everything.

"I know it's hard," Lara says. "Not knowing when it's going to end. But there's less left than what there was when it all started."

"Mom used to say that when we drove to Grandma's and I kept asking if we were almost there," Beto says.

"You see? I now use Mom's phrases! What have I become?" Lara jokes, throwing herself on the mattress. "Besides, until you can go and take photos at the square, take some photos through the window. Use that lens of yours to find a cute neighbor."

"A cute neighbor on our street? I'll most likely find a criminal and put all our family at risk because I have evidence of his crimes."

"Like *Rear Window*," Lara says.

"Or that Shia LaBeouf movie."

"That was a shameless copy of *Rear Window*," she says.

He'd missed this. This thing he has with his sister in which, for a few seconds, the two of them feel fully connected, as if their brains were thinking the same thought at the same time before each one returned to their own private world.

"Can I turn off the light?" Beto asks after putting his early present away with excessive care.

Lara nods.

"I'm glad to be back," she says when they're in the dark. "I swear I won't be a boring guest. If you need privacy in your room to . . . I don't know, you know—"

"Lara!" Beto yells, but he doesn't complete the sentence because the lack of privacy to . . . I don't know, you know . . . was literally the first thing he thought when his sister walked through the door.

"Good night," Lara says.

He waits for her to close her eyes and turn around before finally pulling out his phone to check Twitter for the results of today's post. He spent the day trying not to do that because following the numbers of likes and comments makes him anxious. Beto bites his lips as the app loads. Nine likes. No comments. Whoa.

Earlier in the year, Beto decided to start a personal project of daily photos, kind of inspired by Andy Warhol's Polaroids: a simple and unpretentious photo of a person, an object, a landscape, or himself. The idea was to practice his skills and, at the same time, to make a record of it on Twitter. Almost like a photographic journal for himself, without caring how many people would like it or not. But Beto does, of course, care. He stares at the photo he posted this morning—a ceramic chicken that his mom put on top of the fridge—and lets out a frustrated sigh. He doesn't know what else to photograph inside the house and thinks the easiest thing to do might be to give up on the project entirely. It's not as if anybody would *miss* the photos, after all.

His screen flashes with a notification that gets his attention.

A new text from Nicolas.

Nico

> Loved today's pic ☺

Beto reads it but doesn't reply. Talking to Nicolas will only make things worse.

"Good night, Lara," he whispers, but his sister is already snoring.

ANA

After she discovered her move from Lagoa Pequena to Rio de Janeiro had a set date, Ana made a dramatic exit that, in the end, was for nothing. She had wanted to see Letícia but left in such a hurry that she didn't bring cash for the bus, and walking to her girlfriend's house, besides taking too long, would have been a real torture under the January sun. Ana couldn't just go back home real quick, get the bus ticket in her bedroom, and slam the door again. That would have killed the impact of the fight she'd just had with her dad.

So she walks around the block for thirty minutes and then goes back home, making sure she still looks sulky enough to make Celso uncomfortable.

When she opens the door, her dad is in the exact same position (sitting on the couch, his legs crossed), leafing through a computer magazine. She was only away for thirty minutes, after all. Celso doesn't say anything because he knows Ana, and he knows that in moments like these she needs her own space.

But what Ana really needs is an honest conversation with her dad about everything she has to lose if they leave Lagoa Pequena. So, all things considered, it seems that Celso doesn't know Ana that well after all.

"Can I use the phone?" Ana asks, still annoyed.

"Of course, honey."

She knows her dad would have done anything to please her now, but she decides to ask for permission anyway because she's trying to save his willingness for the following question.

"Can I ask Letícia to stay over?" Ana's voice is nearly a whisper.

Celso hesitates.

One important thing about Celso: He's a cool dad, easygoing even. He's never breathing down Ana's neck and always says yes to nearly anything his daughter asks (except for dyeing her hair because he read somewhere that hair dye can give you cancer). But when it's about having people over, Celso always shows some resistance.

The short of it is that the house is always a mess.

The more complex reason is that the mess might make people think that Celso is incapable of caring for his own daughter by himself and, with his ingrained patriarchal ideas, he still believes that the house would always look neat if a woman lived here. Ana's mom. And Celso doesn't need anyone doubting his ability to give his daughter a happy life because he's already pretty good at doubting that himself.

He obviously doesn't know about all the afternoons Letícia has spent here, locked in the bedroom with Ana, listening to loud music, talking about life, and doing what two teenagers do when they're in love and alone. Letícia never minded the mess, or the mismatched cutlery, the laundry piling up, or the computer parts scattered around the living room that made the place look like an electronics junkyard. She loves being here with Ana. She even jokes about how the mold stain on the bathroom ceiling is shaped like a heart.

But Celso doesn't know that Letícia doesn't mind because the truth is he barely knows Letícia. He has no idea who this girl who changed his daughter's life is. Celso and Ana need to talk.

"Can I?" Ana is still waiting for her dad's answer, holding the receiver to her ear, her finger on the prongs to avoid making the line busy.

"Yes, for sure," Celso gives in. He doesn't want to disappoint Ana one more time.

Ana smiles but doesn't thank him. Her dad doesn't deserve gratitude at the moment. Her fingers shaking with anxiety, she types the number sequence she already knows by heart and listens to the beeps as she imagines the phone ringing at Letícia's house.

"Yes?" Letícia's mom answers. Ana thinks it's funny that she says "Yes?" instead of "Hello?"

"Hi, Dona Celeste, this is Ana. Can I talk to Letícia?" she says, almost in a whisper, because her dad is still around and, for some reason, she believes that saying Letícia's name out loud makes her too vulnerable.

"Good morning, Ana, dear. *Happy New Year!*" Dona Celeste says, not to be polite, but to highlight how rude Ana is being.

"Ah, yes, of course. Happy New Year to you, too. Much peace, health, and prosperity," she says, spitting all the cliché greetings from Happy New Year cards at the woman.

It's funny how Ana has already completely forgotten that this is the start of a new millennium. Nothing about today feels like a beginning. This day started out feeling like an ending.

"I think Le is still sleeping, Ana. But I can knock on her door."

"Yes, please, it's kind of important," Ana begs, feeling her hands sweat while she firmly holds the telephone.

From the phone, Ana can hear Dona Celeste knocking on Letícia's door and yelling "Phoooone for yooooul!" and then more doors slamming and impatient steps before Ana finally hears the voice she's been hoping for on the other end of the line.

"Hello?" Letícia picks up, her voice still sleepy and lazy.

"Hi, Letícia, it's me."

"Happy New Year! No Y2K bug after all! Your dad was right," she says excitedly, leaving any trace of sleepiness behind her, as if her girlfriend's voice were the fuel she needed.

The mention of her own dad makes Ana roll her eyes.

"I know this is going to seem weird but . . . could you come stay over tonight?"

Letícia doesn't reply right away and, from the noise, Ana imagines her girlfriend pulling the phone somewhere quieter, looking for privacy. At this point, they should have come up with more codes for their calls.

"Is your dad going to be out?" Letícia finally asks, probably hiding behind the couch or whatever.

"No, no. He is going to be here. But he knows—"

Letícia lets out a scared sigh.

"He knows you're coming. That's all. It's complicated. I just need you to come. Do you think you can?"

"Today I have a family lunch, one of those that last a whole afternoon. But I can leave in the early evening."

"And your mom?" Ana asks, concerned.

"I'll figure it out. I'll call if anything comes up."

"Okay. Waiting for you."

"Okay."

The two of them go silent for a few seconds, and Ana thinks of everything she'd like to say if things were a little bit simpler.

"That CD of yours. I still have it," she finally says.

"You can keep it for as long as you need."

Ana hangs up with a smile and, when she turns around to her dad, she wipes it off immediately.

"Letícia is coming over later," she tells him.

"The heavy one?" Celso asks, without taking his eyes off the magazine, as if there were another Letícia, and as if that were a totally appropriate way to talk about her. As if Ana had a lot of friends and he needed to make sure which one was going to spend the night.

Ana hates her father so bad right now. But she's too emotionally exhausted to retort, so she just nods and goes back to her room.

Celso waits until Ana leaves the room and cracks a smile, having absolutely no idea how far he is from being a Super Dad today.

———

In the afternoon, Ana gets anxious. It's not the first time Letícia will be over, but she wants to make sure everything will be perfect. With her dad's money, she goes to the market to get some premade dough, cheese, tomatoes, and oregano for mini pizzas, because mini pizzas are a source of comfort to Ana. You can eat them in a few bites and they're fun to prepare. Ana organizes all the ingredients on the kitchen counter, imagining a romantic comedy scene in which she and Letícia prepare mini pizzas and kiss in the process, playing with the ingredients and throwing flour at each other's faces.

This, of course, is never going to happen because Ana can't kiss Letícia in a place as exposed as the kitchen. And because the dough is ready-made and there's no flour in the house. Which is a good thing, in fact, because if the flour war were to happen, Ana would be the one to clean it all, since today is her day to clean the kitchen. And she doesn't want to spend even one extra second doing chores while Letícia is here, because this might be their last night together.

This thought makes her stomach churn as she considers the best way to tell her girlfriend about the move. She needs to tell her today. It has to be today. Postponing the news would just mean Ana is as terrible a person as her dad.

But the idea that moving out of Lagoa Pequena might mean breaking up with Letícia makes her feel like an electric wire is inching its way down her spine and numbing her body. It doesn't have to be that way, does it? It doesn't have to be the end. They can figure it out, can't they?

Questions about the future twirl inside Ana's head, tap-dancing all over every sliver of optimism that she still holds on to and, when she hears the three knocks on her door at about 6:20 p.m., she realizes she didn't even have a chance to try and look good for Letícia. She puts up her brown hair that hasn't been anywhere near a comb the entire day and runs to answer the door. Before she does, she shoots her dad a sharp look. A look that says, "Don't you dare mention the move, let me bring it up. Do not make any comments about Letícia's body. In fact, make no comments at all. Stay very silent. If it's not too much to ask, lock yourself in your bedroom and I will slide mini pizzas under the door, because I might be furious at you, but I don't want you to starve." But Celso is incapable of deciphering seventeen-year-olds and all he understands from Ana's look is "Grrrr, I hate you!"

"Hey! I locked my bike on your porch, is that okay?" Letícia says as soon as Ana opens the door.

Ana just smiles like an idiot and doesn't reply right away. She absorbs everything she sees. Letícia biked here, and the ride from her place must be at least a half hour. Her forehead is a little sweaty, but she doesn't look at all exhausted. Ana thinks if she were the one biking for the past thirty minutes, her legs would be swaying, she'd be drenched in sweat and begging for a glass of water. But that's not what Letícia is like.

Her body is short, with wide hips and big arms that are slightly muscular from volleyball. Her skin, usually a light brown, is more tan and golden because Letícia went to her grandparents' beach house for Christmas. Her black straightened hair is tied in a ponytail, hidden under the helmet she's still wearing.

Letícia finds Ana's awkward silence strange and starts trying to find the reason.

"Ah, the helmet," she remembers.

When she takes the opportunity to let her hair down, too, Ana wonders if it's just her who's seeing everything in slow motion. How can such a beautiful girl be here, standing in front of her? How can this girl have been her girlfriend for the past six months? Ana feels so lucky.

Until she remembers the reason that made her invite Letícia here last minute.

"Hi, Letícia, good evening! Come on in," Celso says, since Ana is still silent and gaping.

"Yeah, yeah, come in, make yourself at home," Ana adds.

Everything is too embarrassing.

Celso and Letícia have seen each other a few times. She's always here, stopping by briefly to get a CD from his daughter or something like that, but he behaves in a weird, stiff manner. As if he's trying too hard to score some points with Ana in a game he doesn't know how to play.

"My mom sent you this," Letícia says, taking off her backpack and pulling out a bottle of white wine.

"Oh, there was no need," Celso says. "But thank you so much!"

"It's no big deal. She got it in a Christmas gift basket from work and no one at home drinks, except for my brother, but my mom doesn't know he drinks. Or maybe she does and pretends she doesn't. Anyway, she was going to throw it out but then she saw that this bottle costs like forty bucks, and she couldn't bring herself to do it. My dad suggested they do a raffle with this as the prize, but my mom thought that was ridiculous because people might think we're on the brink of bankruptcy if they saw us raffling off an expensive bottle of wine, so she just handed it to me and said, 'Get this out of here because your uncle is coming tomorrow.'"

Ana and Celso stare at Letícia with tight smiles.

"My uncle is an alcoholic."

More silence.

"I bought us mini pizzas for dinner," Ana says.

"Great!" Letícia and Celso answer at the same time, relieved that they don't have to keep talking about the alcoholic uncle.

"Le, wanna leave your backpack in my room?" Ana offers without any hint of subtlety, pulling Letícia by the arm.

"I'm gonna go open this," Celso says, waving the bottle in the air, feeling that he, too, should announce what he's about to do.

Would this be kind of like a slumber party? Was he invited to participate as well? So many questions.

As soon as the two are in the bedroom, Ana closes the door and hugs Letícia with all her strength.

"What just happened?" Ana asks, laughing.

"I don't know, I couldn't stop myself from talking. I'm nervous, I think. It's as if I'm being introduced to my girlfriend's father for the first time and really needed to be a pleasant person," Letícia answers embarrassedly, then laughs.

"By bringing up your alcoholic uncle," Ana points out.

They laugh again.

"Why did you invite me over? I thought that, well, that you had told him . . ."

"About you?"

"About *us*."

Ana feels her heart sink. Because Letícia thinks she's here to be introduced to Ana's dad as her girlfriend, but she has no idea that reality couldn't be further away from that. Is now the time to say it all? Tell her, "I'm moving, but that doesn't mean the two of us have to break up" and wait for Letícia's reaction? Ana feels her palms begin to sweat. Best to wait a little longer. After the mini pizzas might be better. Telling her before might ruin the food. Imagine how horrible it would be to eat a mini pizza that tastes like goodbye.

"That wasn't why!" Ana says, as if Letícia had just suggested the most absurd thing in the world.

"Not *yet*," Letícia adds, full of hope.

"I just called you over because I missed you so much and couldn't wait until school starts again to see you," Ana says, changing the subject, feeling the weight of the lie make her heart sink a little deeper. "What did you tell your mom, by the way?"

"I said you had organized a surprise party for Camila, and I had to come."

"Who's Camila?"

"A girl I made up. It's not as if my mom knows who I hang out with. She's always too worried trying to figure out where my brother is and going through his stuff to try and find drugs or anything that would warrant a scandal," Letícia replies casually.

Ana takes a deep breath of relief for being an only child because, from all the times she's heard Letícia talk about her own brother, she believes the experience must be traumatizing.

"Let's go to the kitchen! I'll make us dinner," Ana says, feeling like a real adult, very much in control of the situation.

But when she takes a step forward to open her bedroom door, Letícia cuts Ana off and puts her pointer finger in front of her girlfriend's mouth, asking for silence.

"Just a little kiss," Letícia asks in a whisper.

"My dad is right there," Ana whispers back, pointing to the door.

"Just a small one, please?" Letícia begs with a little pout, which I don't know if Ana would be able to resist.

I wouldn't. And I'm *a house*.

"Okay, fine," Ana gives in, and they kiss.

It's a quick kiss that ends in a louder smack than they anticipated, which makes the two of them laugh hard as they walk to the kitchen and find Celso still at war with the wine bottle.

"Let me open it," Letícia says, gently taking the bottle from Celso's hand and pulling out the cork with her teeth.

Ana and Celso watch the scene with a mix of shock and admiration.

"It must be in my blood, I don't know," Letícia jokes, wondering when might be a good time to refrain from commenting on her family's complicated history.

Celso only fills one glass with wine before withdrawing to the living room, and the girls pretend like they've never had a drop of alcohol. Today it'll be guava juice for the two of them.

Preparing the mini pizzas with Letícia by her side is not as cinematic as Ana imagined, but it turns out to be romantic in its own way. Letícia's touch lingers a little longer than necessary when she reaches for the tomato sauce or the cheese grater. Letícia talks about her childhood memories, when her grandmother allowed her to help in the kitchen, cutting the vegetables with a yellow-handled knife that only she used. Ana listens to it all with a smile on her face, because these big family stories are so different from anything she's ever lived. It's like hearing someone tell her about an incredible trip to a place she's never been to. But in a good way, which is kind of rare. Most people who tell stories of their own trips don't know when to stop (usually it's a few minutes before the photo sequence of more than fifty gray buildings and museum facades).

While the mini pizzas cook in the old and rusty oven, and the melted cheese smell takes over the entire house, Ana wonders how long her girlfriend's smile is going to last. Letícia will certainly be devastated by the news.

What if she isn't, though? The thought occurs to Ana. The possibility of this move coming as a relief to her girlfriend's life. And now she has one more bad prospect to analyze over dinner. The count is now up to nineteen.

Nineteen bad prospects.

There isn't a proper dinner table here, because the one they have looks more like a computer cemetery at the moment, so Ana organizes everything on the coffee table in the living room. As if this were the most important dinner of her life, she places napkins at each setting, juice glasses for her and her girlfriend, and the hot mini pizzas on a glass tray.

The three of them sit on the floor around the table and Letícia takes over the conversation. Partially because she really likes to talk, but also because Ana doesn't know how to talk to her girlfriend in front of her dad, and Celso doesn't know how to behave in front of two teenagers, even if one of them is his own daughter. And, of course, there's the whole fight that the two of them had earlier, so the mood is still a little weird.

But Letícia doesn't notice anything.

"I have a cousin," she begins, between one bite and the next, "who always travels to Rio. He works as a Tupperware reseller or something. But he said they put *ketchup* on their pizza. Can you imagine how gross that is? And not just a little, either. My cousin says it's on the whole pizza, like Spackle on a wall. His words, of course. But I don't doubt him. Rio de Janeiro is a lawless land."

The mention of her future city makes Ana swallow hard and feel the food scratching her throat. Celso picks up the glass of wine and takes a completely disproportionate sip given how much his mouth can store. Ana's face burns and she compulsively rubs a napkin on her lips, trying to clean a smudge that's not there.

Letícia still doesn't notice anything.

"Let me clean up today, honey," Celso says when they're done eating. "The little pizzas were delicious."

Ana almost smiles when he says *little pizzas*. Almost.

"I'll help!" Letícia offers.

"No way, you're a guest. The two of you are off the hook to go do your slumber party stuff," Celso says, even though he doesn't have the slightest clue what slumber party stuff might be.

The two girls don't wait for him to say it again and they disappear. One at a time, they shower, wrap their hair in towels, and put on their pajamas. Ana's are twice her size, navy blue and full of stars. Letícia's consist of white shorts and a pink tank top with an owl on it.

76

"Sorry for the owl. It's the worst. The eyes are scary. My aunt gave them to me. She has a friend who sells pajamas, so she bought them to help her friend because the store was broken into, or a tree fell on the roof or something. I don't remember. All I know is everyone got pajamas for Christmas from my aunt. Even the children. It's inhuman."

Ana laughs, thinking about how any story from her girlfriend is always delivered in a funny way. She wonders what Letícia sees in her, because Ana is the girl who most lacks funny stories in this city. The story of her pajamas is *I saw them in a store window, then I went in and bought them*.

"It's cute. The owl." That's all Ana manages to say on the subject as she tries to deal with her nervousness and the bitter taste it leaves in her mouth. "What do we do at a slumber party? This is my first one."

"I don't have a lot of experience in that department, either. But I guess people, I don't know . . . do their nails?"

Ana grimaces reproachfully and, in an unsubconscious motion, hides her hands under a pillow so Letícia won't notice the size of her cuticles. Letícia doesn't notice. She barely knows what cuticles are.

"We could listen to some music," Ana suggests, tilting her chin toward the CD rack and believing that, just like music has the power to calm her confused thoughts before bed, it might also help her deal with this situation.

"Why didn't you tell me you bought *Millennium*?" Letícia nearly shouts, then picks up the Backstreet Boys album and waves it in the air.

Letícia's personality is a universe of different things. She likes sports, heavy metal, cute animals, horror movies, superhero comics, red lipstick, car parts, and boy bands. Ana has no idea how she will be able to leave this entire universe behind.

"My dad got it for me for Christmas. But I barely even listened to it," Ana says about the CD, trying her best to sound cool.

"A *much* better present than owl pajamas! You are so lucky to have a cool dad!" Letícia comments.

"You think?" Ana asks, her tight smile a mix of embarrassment and anger.

"Let's listen to it!" Letícia says excitedly while taking the album out of its plastic cover and looking around the bedroom for the stereo.

"There is no stereo in my room, I only listen to music on my Discman," Ana explains.

"No need to humiliate me with your gadgets from the future, okay?" Letícia jokes. "We can split the earphones, then. It'll just make it harder to dance together."

"Maybe we only listen to the sad ones," Ana suggests.

"Ah, of course. Just what I expected out of a slumber party."

They take the towels off their heads and, their hair still wet, snuggle in Ana's bed, sharing the headphones. Ana presses play on the device and skips straight to the second track, the only one she really likes.

"Do you know what they're singing about?" Letícia asks. "My English is terrible, so every time I listen to music from the US, I just make up what it means."

"My English isn't great, either," Ana answers. "But I think it's a song about unrequited love. Because he's like, 'You are my fire,' but then asks if he's *her* fire, too. I think he just wants to be loved back, I don't know."

"Being loved back is the best," Letícia says, pulling Ana's head closer to her chest and giving her forehead a quick kiss.

Ana almost bursts into flames. She and Letícia have already experienced some intense levels of intimacy, but never like tonight. She's afraid her dad will open the door unannounced at any point, of course, but not enough to move away. She's afraid of what he might think or hear from the other side of the door, but she doesn't mind that too much, either. All she wants is to enjoy this moment, and, if it creates any problems, future Ana will deal with them.

"This one is cute," Letícia comments, pointing at the only man wearing sunglasses on the CD cover.

"He's the least cute of them all. He's weird," Ana counters.

"I like weird. No wonder I'm dating you." Letícia laughs. "But seriously, I don't know. I think this soundtrack demands a serious conversation. Can we have a serious talk, real quick?"

Ana freezes.

"Of course," she whispers.

"I think I like boys as much as I like girls. In general, I don't know. It's nothing for you to worry about, because now I like you. It's just that when I was much younger, I thought I only liked boys, then I started looking at girls and thinking, *Okay, I'm a lesbian*, but at the same time, it's not as if I'd stopped liking boys. Does that make sense? I think I'm bisexual."

"Why are you talking about this right now?" Ana asks, still tense.

"I don't know, I've been thinking about it a lot. I think it's part of who I am, you know? And I want you to know all of me."

"I think I only like girls. And this guy's *haircut*," Ana says, pointing at the blond Backstreet Boy whose hair is parted in the middle.

"Thank you for choosing me to be the girl you like. Even though I don't have that hair," Letícia jokes, her voice full of tenderness.

As the music plays, she slowly leans in to kiss Ana.

During the kiss, the earphones fall out and get tangled in the sheets. The Discman plays to itself, without anyone to listen, and Ana feels guilt twist her stomach, because Letícia's kiss is so good and warm and tender. She doesn't deserve those kisses.

"Le," Ana says, as soon as she manages to pull herself away from Letícia's mouth. "Can we talk about serious stuff for just a minute?"

"We can take turns," Letícia says, stealing a quick kiss from Ana and burrowing her face in her girlfriend's neck. "One minute of kissing and one minute of serious stuff."

Ana feels goose bumps all over her body when Letícia kisses her neck, and she makes herself sit up on the bed to rearrange her thoughts.

"Seriously, though," Ana says. "There's something I need to tell you."

Letícia seems to notice by Ana's tone that the kissing minute is over, and she also sits up, crossing her legs. Facing each other, holding hands, they straighten up at the same time, as if preparing for an important moment, or to play patty-cake.

"Today I found out . . ." Ana begins.

That I will have to leave you?

That I don't know what's gonna happen to us?

That the end is near?

That I love you more than I thought I did because you were the first thing that sprung to mind when my dad said we are going to move and it's hard to imagine a life in which I can't call you and know that you will show up in a half hour on your bike and that helmet that seems too small for your head but still makes you look extremely adorable?

Ana had spent the afternoon rehearsing the best words, but now she can't spill it out.

"That I am moving to another city. My dad got a job in Rio, and we're leaving in two weeks," she finally says, as staunchly as she can.

Letícia falls silent but doesn't let go of Ana's hands.

Ana thinks that's a good sign.

More silence.

Lots of silence.

The silence is definitely not a good sign.

"Say something," Ana begs.

"Hold on, I'm processing," Letícia answers, her face serious.

Ana can't remember the last time Letícia ended a sentence without a smile. Terrible sign.

"So tonight is a goodbye party?" Letícia asks.

"No, we still have two weeks. I know it's not a lot of time, but still, I don't want to say goodbye. Not now. Not if you don't want to."

"We are saying *goodbye* so we don't have to say *break up*, right?" Letícia says.

"I don't know. We can figure it out together. We can figure this out *together*," Ana pleads, holding Letícia's hands more firmly with the last word.

Letícia lets go of Ana's hands, gets up, and walks around the room observing the whole area, as if she were trying to commit to memory where everything is. She picks up a hair band on Ana's dresser and uses it to tie her hair up in a bun. She does it all very calmly. Ana remains seated in the same position, as if she's hoping that the ritual of putting her hair up would provide Letícia with all the answers that the two of them need.

"I need some time to think." That's all Letícia says.

"I love you," Ana says, but the words seem empty.

A consolation prize. *I'm leaving, but here's my* I love you *for you to keep as a memento.*

"When you went all serious and said you'd learned something," Letícia says, turning off the light and coming back to bed, "I thought you were going to tell me you were a vampire. For real."

Ana can't hold back her laughter. Letícia laughs, too, satisfied that her strategy of using humor to provide some relief in tense situations worked one more time.

"If I were a vampire, I'd run away with you, go somewhere far from here. Because I'd probably be rich. And we would have our whole lives ahead of us."

"Stop talking as if you were going to die in two weeks, Ana," Letícia says.

In a way, a part of me is going to, Ana thinks.

Letícia pulls the sheet over the two of them, wondering if Celso didn't think it was weird that the two of them were going to sleep on the same bed, as there isn't an extra mattress in the room.

The truth is he didn't even notice it.

"Let's sleep, Ana. We'll think about this tomorrow."

"Can I hug you?" Ana asks.

"Always," Letícia answers.

And the two of them lie there, hugging, under the dim light of the moon that strives to cut through the clouds and reach the dark bedroom. Ana hopes for another kiss on her forehead, but it doesn't come. They close their eyes, but neither falls asleep.

The forgotten Discman had fallen between a pillow and the night-stand, the CD still spinning. Right now, the Backstreet Boys are singing track seven, "Don't Wanna Lose You Now." It would have been the perfect soundtrack to bring some optimism to this disastrous night.

Too bad neither of them is listening.

GREG

Greg is pretty sure his own aunt would kick him out of the house if she found out what he did last night.

In the brief conversation they had over dinner, he discovered she hates many other things besides Matt Damon movies. She hates Sunday TV shows with a studio audience, restaurants that don't offer free tap water to customers, people who are not brave enough to drink tap water, Hollywood sweethearts who are considered sweethearts just because they're white, songs that start on the refrain, crocheted toilet seat covers, avocado smoothies, and pirated movies.

She doesn't say any of this in a linear way that makes sense. Catarina is just bothered by her nephew's silence, so she says, "You know one thing I really hate?" and launches into something very specific, without waiting for an answer. She believes that finding a common thing to hate has the power to unite two people forever. Catarina isn't completely wrong.

But while having breakfast with his aunt the following morning, Greg feels the bulk of the flash drive in his pocket and is terrified of what might happen if she learned the truth.

I won't leave you on a cliffhanger. Greg downloaded a movie last night. The Scooby-Doo movie that Tiago wanted to watch. It took nearly four hours because the internet here is slow and unstable, and it was after midnight when Greg draped himself in the guest room sheets to watch the full movie before falling asleep.

He doesn't want to just hand a flash drive with the movie to Tiago. He wants to *have a conversation about the movie*. Talk about the photography, the script, the plot, the mysteries or whatever it is that Scooby-Doo fans like to talk about. Greg is willing to find out. He wants to get to know Tiago deeply, so that in the future they can laugh together about the time when Greg pretended to enjoy a movie with a talking dog to get closer to a cute guy.

"Are you spending the day out today as well?" Greg asks, serving himself a slice of a cornmeal cake that doesn't seem that fresh but still smells good.

"Yes. I have to seize the opportunity, having you here to watch the store. Find some gigs," Catarina says, without taking her eyes off the magazine she's holding, featuring rich people's expensive homes.

"And what is it that you . . . do . . . exactly?" Greg asks.

He's afraid of the answer. His aunt seems mysterious and not very willing to open up about her personal life (except, of course, the list of things she hates).

"I do all sorts of things, Gregório," she replies. "Yesterday I painted a wall and changed a showerhead. There are days when I give dogs baths, others when I pick up groceries for an old lady who lives down the street. I can also sew, so sometimes I fix loose buttons or mend pants that ripped right between the legs. I solve everyone's problems. I'm a friend of the neighborhood."

"Just like Spider-Man," Greg points out.

"I wouldn't know, I hate superhero movies," Catarina counters.

Greg doesn't say anything else because he's scared. Catarina doesn't say anything else because she's late.

———————

Tiago is late as well. Tuesday slows to a crawl, and Greg stares at the time in the corner of the computer screen as he waits for lunch. It's almost one in the afternoon and he is starving. Greg might have said that the feeling in his stomach is because he can't wait to see the cute emo guy again, but deep down he knows a good amount of the feeling is just hunger.

He thinks of sending one more email to Sofia Karen (it would be the third this morning; one was a long and unnecessarily detailed message about Keanu the dog's behavior, which he wrapped up with the idea of adopting a dog as soon as he came back to São Paulo), but when he's about to click the new message button, Keanu barks. Tiago arrives. With food, thank god.

"Sorry I'm late," Tiago says, probably noticing Greg's desperate look, as if he could literally have eaten the *House Bunny* DVD that's sitting on the counter from when a customer returned it this morning. Greg didn't put it away because he wasn't sure if it should go on the comedy shelf, the new releases shelf, or the instant classics shelf.

There isn't an instant classics shelf at Catavento Video, but Greg was thinking of instating one. He also wrote to Sofia Karen about this. No reply so far.

"No worries, I barely noticed the time," Greg lies, unable to take his eyes off the container Tiago is holding.

In a silent agreement, Tiago nods to indicate that Greg is free to go to the bathroom, wash his hands, and get the cutlery. Greg likes silent agreements.

He devours the plate of rice, shredded chicken, and vegetables, and only after the tenth forkful does he stop to watch Tiago playing with Keanu, throwing a chewed-up plastic ball to him. He looks just like he did yesterday: the same black pants, the same beat-up Converse sneakers, and a band T-shirt. Not the same one, which is a good sign. Greg doesn't know today's band, and the name is too long for him to be able to read without looking like he's staring at the guy, who's running between the store's shelves with Keanu. Watching Tiago entertain the dog is something he could get used to.

"I was late because I left this delivery for the end. That way I am free for the rest of the afternoon," Tiago says, making it clear he would like to spend the afternoon here.

"Why do you deliver food?" Greg asks tactlessly. And failing to notice the desire in Tiago's eyes every time they stare at each other.

I mean, it's actually very obvious.

Even I noticed it.

And I am a house.

And a video store.

"My mom owns the restaurant down the street. When school lets out,

I help with deliveries close by. I'm the cheap labor of our household," Tiago jokes. "Your aunt didn't explain?"

"She didn't explain anything," Greg answers. "Sometimes I think she doesn't like me that much."

"Impossible," Tiago says, throwing Keanu the ball one more time. "Catarina gets along with everybody. There's no one in this city who doesn't like her."

Greg tries to hide a grimace, because that's not the Catarina he found when he got here. Besides, he thinks it's really bold to assume that an *entire city* might like this one person.

"I have something for you," he says, changing the subject and leaving any thoughts about his aunt for later.

"Hmm," Tiago says, not knowing what to expect.

Greg puts his hand in his pocket and takes out the flash drive.

"Don't tell my aunt," he says, putting it on the counter.

"Britto Beauty," Tiago reads.

Greg's face flushes.

"It's my dad's clinic," he answers, pointing at the logo on the flash drive. "He gave this away to clients at the end of last year. Which is kind of silly because all his clients are filthy rich. Filthy rich people don't need flash drives."

"And you're giving me a flash drive because . . ." Tiago is very confused, the poor thing.

"No! The flash drive you can bring back later. Actually, no need for that. We have a bunch of those back home. What matters is what's on the flash drive."

Tiago holds back a laugh while adjusting his bangs in the most ador-able way possible, because there might be a million different things on a flash drive. Depending on storage, I guess. I don't understand that much about flash drives.

"It's a movie," Greg finally says. "The one you wanted. The Scooby-Doo one. I downloaded it for you. My aunt can't find out. She seems totally anti-technology."

"Maybe she just doesn't like pirate movies because that literally kills her business?" Tiago suggests.

"Hmm."

"Yeah."

"But do you still want it?" Greg insists, pushing the little object toward Tiago. He feels so stupid now.

"Of course. I won't tell anyone. It will be our secret," Tiago replies with a wink. Greg feels his insides somersaulting. "But I don't know how I'm going to watch it. We don't have a computer at home."

Greg tries to hide his shock at meeting someone who doesn't own a computer.

"We can watch it here," he suggests. "If you'd like."

"Well, I've got nothing else to do," Tiago says. "So, yes, sounds good."

Greg doesn't know how to react to this answer. Because deep down he feels hurt for being Tiago's I've-got-nothing-else-to-do. Just like he was hurt that Catarina said she hated superhero movies earlier. Any little trifle will hurt Greg.

"Can I just use the restroom first?" Tiago asks.

Greg nods, even though he doesn't know what the store policy is for customers who ask to use the bathroom in the house. He seizes the few minutes of privacy to send one more email to Sofia Karen, in the hopes that she will reply immediately.

Tuesday, January 19, 2010. 2:02 p.m.
From: geodude1993@email.com
To: skaren@brittobeauty.com.br
Subject: URGENT

I'm gonna watch a movie with the cute emo boy.

SCOOBY-DOO!

Do you think it's romantic to have a first kiss watching this movie? Do you think it's worth a try?

REPLY IN ONE MINUTE TOPS!!!

Sofia Karen doesn't reply.

Tiago comes back from the bathroom.

Keanu barks excitedly when he sees Tiago.

Mentally, Greg barks excitedly, too.

"Come to this side," he says, motioning for Tiago to join him behind the counter.

The space is tight and there's no room for the two of them to sit. After at least two minutes moving around, elbowing each other, and switching places, the two lean on the counter, a fraction of an inch away, and attentively watch the small computer screen where the movie about a mystery-solving dog is playing.

Tiago genuinely laughs at some of the scenes. He actually guffaws sometimes. Greg tries to laugh along so he doesn't let on that he watched the movie in the middle of the night and that watching it again after so little time only makes the plot holes even more obvious. But he doesn't say that out loud for he believes that doing so would eliminate his chances of kissing Tiago.

Tiago doesn't look like someone who'd kiss a boy who doesn't like Scooby-Doo.

In Greg's mind, the end of the movie would be the ideal moment to put his arm around Tiago's bony shoulders, get closer, and slowly kiss him. The afternoon sun filters through the store's door and creates the perfect mood.

But that's not what happens.

When credits start rolling, a customer comes in with two late movies and begs not to pay a fine. Greg lets her off because he doesn't want to seem mean in front of Tiago. Right after that, another customer arrives asking if they sell acai (they do not), and another one comes in asking if they have *Never Been Kissed*, which is ironic, given Greg's current situation.

Tiago seems anxious to talk about the movie they just watched, but it's as if destiny were sending all the inhabitants of Lagoa Pequena to the store, one by one. An unusual occurrence for a Tuesday afternoon that keeps Greg busy with returns, recommendations, and idle chatter.

Greg is pissed. You can tell by how his fists are closed. Tiago is lost, feeling that he's getting in the way. You can tell by how he walks from one side to the other, grabbing some movies and pretending to be just another customer so that other people don't assume he works here and start asking him questions.

"I think I'm gonna get going," Tiago says, detangling the earbuds that were balled up in his pocket.

"Okay," Greg says. "Want to take this, anyway?" He rips the flash drive from his computer and waves it in Tiago's direction.

"It'll be of no use to me," he says. "But I still want it."

"Tape it to your journal," Greg says without thinking.

"I actually do have a journal."

"Me too," Greg lies, because he wants to seem like an interesting person who keeps a journal.

Awkward silence.

Keanu barks.

"See you tomorrow, then?" Greg asks.

"Tomorrow I have practice," Tiago says. And, when he notices Greg's confused expression, he adds, "Tennis."

"You play tennis? Whoa."

Greg has never met anyone who plays tennis.

"It's fun. And it gives you strong arms," Tiago says, flexing his biceps.

You can't see anything under the two layers of black cloth that cover Tiago's body, but Greg would have given anything to feel those arms.

"See you later," Tiago says, and disappears through the garage door.

Greg stands there, not understanding how it's possible that a boy can be emo, have bangs that fall over his face, not own a computer, keep a diary, and play tennis. It's as if all his characteristics had been randomly chosen in a game of personality bingo.

Sofia Karen finally replies to his message. Greg doesn't feel any excitement as he clicks on it.

Tuesday, January 19, 2010. 5:46 p.m.
From: skaren@brittobeauty.com.br
To: geodude1993@email.com
Subject: Re: URGENT

What if you tried to get to know this guy instead of being all desperate over a kiss?

Just the advice of someone much older and totally experienced.

But if you've already had your kiss when you get to this message: HOORAY! Tell me all about it later.

xoxo
SK

Greg decides to ignore the message. Even if he's dying to ask where she came up with this idea of SK out of nowhere.

JANUARY 20, 2010

It's pathetic how the knowledge that Tiago is not going to stop by today turns Greg into a zombie, walking aimlessly around the video store and looking at the clock all the time, waiting for his aunt to come back.

Not that it's going to make any difference. Catarina's company in the house is almost as silent as being alone. But not today. Because today Greg has a *plan*. He will follow his friend's advice and get to know Tiago better. And what better way to do so than to ask Catarina questions about him?

(There are literally thousands of better ways to do it, but Greg is inexperienced with these things.)

Night has fallen by the time Catarina comes home from another day out working on who-knows-what, but today she doesn't seem as exhausted as in previous nights. Her brow is not furrowed and she's not complaining to the walls for no apparent reason. It's Greg's lucky night! (And mine.)

"Aunt Catarina," he calls to her when the two of them are resting in the living room.

Catarina is splayed on the old comfortable couch, scribbling notes in a little memo book. Greg is seated on a yellow armchair playing Pokémon.

"Yeah," Catarina answers without taking her eyes off the notes.

"You know Tiago?" Greg starts, not taking his eyes off Pokémon.

"Which Tiago? *Tiago* Tiago?" she asks, as if the two of them knew at least five Tiagos in common.

"The one who brings me lunch."

"Clélia's son. Yeah. What about him?" she asks, losing interest in her notes and staring at her nephew, curious to see where this conversation is going.

Greg doesn't know where this conversation is going. Because he didn't prepare for this interrogation. He thought that when he asked, "You know Tiago?" his aunt would start spilling out random information about the boy, therefore satisfying all of Greg's curiosity and providing him with infinite conversation topics for the next time they see each other, when Tiago isn't playing tennis or playing in a band or solving crimes with a dog or whatever else he does in his free time.

"What about him?" Catarina insists, because deep down, she feels a certain pleasure in watching her nephew's discomfort.

"He's nice, isn't he?" Greg says, because he doesn't know what else to say.

"You're being good to him, aren't you?" his aunt asks. There is a near-menacing tone in her voice.

"I am, I am," Greg clarifies. "We get along well."

Catarina smirks. "Very well. I saw this kid grow up. He's been through a lot, the poor thing. Lost his dad so early . . ." she begins.

Greg closes the Nintendo DS and focuses his full attention on Catarina because now it seems that she's going to start talking.

"Last year he broke up with his boyfriend, you see. He came to ask *me* for advice. Me, of all people."

"What did you say?" Greg asks, trying not to pay too much attention to the fact that in his mind the word *boyfriend* echoes like a siren.

BOYFRIEND. BOYFRIEND. BOYFRIEND.

"I don't really know how it works in gay relationships, so I told him to watch *Constantine*. Watching Keanu Reeves killing demons always inspires me to kill my own."

GAY. GAY. GAY.

Greg's head seems about to explode. In his home, the word *gay* is never uttered. Deep down, Greg believes that his parents won't have any issue accepting his sexuality. They're sensible people. But for some reason they keep their distance. His dad talks about his "homosexual" clients, his mom talks about the "homosexual parade" she saw in the newspaper. Greg never saw a problem with it, with feeling like a scientific study inside his own home. But hearing his aunt say *gay* as someone would say any everyday word, like *cheese*, *door*, or *lemonade*, makes him feel a comfort he's never felt before.

For a microsecond, Greg feels at home.

But he's not quite sure what to do with this feeling.

"I've never watched *Constantine*" is all he can say.

"Get it from the store. Let's watch it now," Catarina says.

It's not an invitation. It's an order.

Greg obeys, and when he's out of sight, Catarina smiles.

Maybe it's because she's about to watch one of her favorite movies once again. Or maybe she realized that her nephew is not an awful person.

Impossible to tell.

———

Greg watches the movie searching for any gay subtext that might have made his aunt choose *Constantine* as a form of advice. Except for the scenes where Keanu Reeves casually shows his abs, he can't find anything.

It's a good movie about a confused man traveling to hell and killing demons. And a great lesson about the dangers of smoking.

But no gay subtext. Just a movie based on a comic book (Greg avoids mentioning it to his aunt, who has already made it clear several times that she *hates* comics), full of action and intense scenes, watched with family after an emotionally complicated conversation.

Maybe that's the gay subtext.

JANUARY 21, 2010

Tiago doesn't show up with the food delivery.

In his place comes another guy, with a helmet and a noisy motorcycle. He drops off the food and leaves, not explaining Tiago's disappearance.

Greg is worried, but he doesn't know what to do. He could look up online what Tiago's mom's restaurant is called, find the phone number, and call to ask if everything is fine, but Sofia Karen tells him this is going to seem too desperate coming from a guy he only just met.

He's relieved he didn't share the idea of using Keanu as a sniffer dog to find Tiago. That could have sounded even more desperate. And Keanu doesn't look like he's a good sniffer dog. He's good at sleeping, barking, and running after the disgusting chewed plastic ball. Greg makes a note on a piece of paper to remember to buy Keanu a new ball when he gets a chance.

Tiago is well. He's just taking a break. Or playing tennis again. Maybe he advanced to the next stage in some tennis championship! In France! Tiago might be in France at this exact moment, and Greg is here, in the twelfth-smallest city in the state of São Paulo, worrying over nothing.

Greg hopes he'll bring a souvenir from France but knows that's unlikely. Who brings back souvenirs for some guy they've only just met?

There's a stark contrast between the cast on Tiago's arm and the black clothes he's wearing.

"Jesus Christ, what happened?" Greg asks as soon as he sees the boy coming in through the store door, the food container dangling from his broken arm.

"I broke my arm," Tiago states the obvious.

"In France?" Greg asks absurdly.

Tiago completely ignores the question because it makes absolutely no sense. Instead, he explains what happened like any normal person.

"I broke it playing tennis."

Well, like any normal and *very direct* person.

"But aren't you *good* at tennis?" Greg questions.

"I never said that!"

Greg smiles. He always assumes everyone is good at everything. Except for himself. Greg doesn't think he's good at anything. He knows he's not an idiot, but never in his life has he felt particularly smart.

"Did it hurt?" Greg asks. He also wants to ask what's for lunch today, because, as usual, he's starving, but he thinks it would be impolite to ask for food before asking if it hurt.

He wouldn't want to be impolite to the cute emo guy with the recently broken arm whom he'd *very much* like to kiss.

"I didn't feel it at the time. Then all of a sudden it really hurt. I think I passed out. I woke up in the nurse's office without a trace of pain. In the end, I thought it was cool. The cast contributes to my bad boy look."

"What's for lunch today?" Greg finally asks.

"Rice, beef Milanese, and salad. The salad is probably a little limp because of the heat and also the amount of time it takes me from one delivery to the next," Tiago says, pointing at the cast and placing Greg's lunch on the counter.

"All this sacrifice just to nourish me. Thank you," Greg says, much more dramatically than the situation requires. He was probably inspired by the smell of food.

Greg eats while Tiago watches him, and he doesn't find it the least bit weird.

"Okay if I hang out here again today?" Tiago asks.

"Of course!" Greg answers, his mouth full of limp salad.

"We could watch another movie or something," Tiago says, trying to scratch the back of his head with the arm in the cast. I think he does it on purpose. It's as if he *knows* he looks a lot cuter when he scratches the back of his head.

Greg stares at the shelves, quickly running his eye over each of them while looking for a film with the right level of romance so it can end with the kiss that didn't happen last time because no one feels like kissing after watching *Scooby-Doo 2*.

But, as if she were a spiritual guide or a dead mentor who appears as a ghost to whisper words of wisdom to a protagonist in doubt, Greg thinks of Sofia Karen's message and suggests something better.

"What if we just kept talking? I want to . . . *get to know you better*," he says, in a slightly spooky tone. "If you want to, of course. If not, we could watch *Jurassic Park Three* or *Herbie Fully Loaded*," he adds, suggesting two films that would score a D on the Movies That Make You Want to Kiss Someone scale.

"I'm down for talking. To be honest, I'd say yes to anything so I don't have to watch a movie about a car with emotions," Tiago answers.

I, a house with emotions, am a little offended by that comment.

"Okay, you start, then," Greg says, biting at the last piece of breaded steak and talking with his mouth full without realizing it. "Ask a question or something."

"Do you sometimes think about how the world is a huge place and we are very small, and no matter how long we live, it seems that a normal life will never be enough for us to try everything that can be experienced?"

Greg nearly chokes.

"Jesus Christ, what kind of a question is that? I thought you were going to ask my favorite color or animal, my dream job, you know, that kind of stuff."

Tiago smiles, moves behind the counter, and leans on the wooden top, in the same position the two of them were in a couple of days ago. They're not glued to each other because Greg moved a little to the side. He doesn't want to bump into Tiago's cast, since he doesn't know whether the arm still hurts.

"Answer those, then."

"Orange, leopard, video game developer. And you?" Greg asks, because he thinks this is how talking-to-get-to-know-each-other works.

"Yellow, otter, architect," Tiago says, without stopping to think for one second.

Greg laughs.

"You're funny."

"Why?"

"I don't know, you say unexpected things."

"What did you expect? Black, a bat, guitar player?" Tiago says, seeming a little annoyed.

"No!" Greg nearly shouts it, but, deep down, he did expect black, a bat, and guitar player.

"Because that's what everyone at school would have expected from me. But I don't even care. I like to seem more mysterious than I really am. And now, saying it out loud, I realize how ridiculous it sounds." He laughs.

Greg holds back his laughter.

"But don't worry," Tiago says. "I'm not like a character in a teenage book with a dark past who is going to take you to see an abandoned toy factory and set things on fire for fun during a monologue about how love is like a flame or something. I promise."

"Thank you for not taking me to an abandoned toy factory. I've never been in one, but I think that is the kind of thing that would scare me," Greg says, getting closer to Tiago again.

His shoulder almost touches Tiago's. Almost.

"What are you most afraid of?" Tiago asks.

Greg laughs. "Back to difficult questions, then?"

Tiago shrugs. Maybe he's the kind of person who only cares about a conversation if it involves difficult questions.

"Okay," Greg gives in. "But my answer is super boring. Probably what everyone else says. I'm afraid of being alone. Not, like, afraid *to be* alone in a place or whatever. But of reaching a point in my life where I don't have anyone else. Of it just being me and myself. I'm afraid that, if that happens one day, I won't be enough to deal with myself."

Who would have thought that Greg was also good at difficult answers?

"I get it," Tiago says. "That scares me, too. I usually pretend I hate everyone because I don't want people to think I need them. But I kind of do. My therapist says that it's my defense mechanism. All of this." He gestures to his black clothes and the bang covering his face.

"Whoa, you have a therapist! Fancy," Greg comments, because he doesn't know what else to say.

"To be honest, I wish I didn't need one," Tiago laughs.

"I have a personal assistant," Greg says, once again not knowing how to keep the conversation going. "She's my dad's personal assistant, but we talk all day, I tell her everything."

"Isn't that what a *friend* would do?" Tiago mocks.

"I don't have a lot of friendship experience," Greg answers.

"I know the feeling. That's me, too," Tiago says, running his fingers against his bangs one more time.

"Yeah, right!" Greg teases. "You brought me food on my first day! On the *first day*! That's like the secret formula to making friends quickly."

Tiago laughs. "Now I know. I'll try to hand a food container to the next one who calls me a fag and see if that works just as well."

Maybe Greg is ready to talk about *being gay* with his aunt. But he's definitely not ready for the *fag* part.

The store is silent. Keanu barks because this dog sometimes acts like an uncomfortable silence alarm.

"What is it?" Tiago asks, slightly worried. "I hope that's not a problem for you. You know . . . the fact that I'm a fag."

"You're not a *fag!*" Greg interrupts him, as if he wanted to protect Tiago from the word no matter what. The word that leaves a bitter taste in his mouth.

"Greg, it's okay. I am, in fact. I lost my fear of the word a long time ago. I think if I call myself a fag before anyone else can, there's very little other people can use to offend me. It's just another defense mechanism."

"Did you learn that from your therapist, too?" Greg asks.

"No, this one I learned by myself." Tiago cracks a sad smile that Greg decides is the handsomest sad smile of all time.

"I am, too. Maybe not so bold about it as you. But I also like to . . . you know . . . kiss boys."

He doesn't mention the fact that he's never kissed a boy before. Tiago doesn't need to know that yet. There are things people like without having to try it first. Just like any new album by Panic! At the Disco for Tiago, or any new Keanu Reeves movie for Aunt Catarina, or any snack for Keanu Reeves (the dog). For Greg, that thing is kissing boys (or any new Pokémon game).

"Funny, isn't it? That you like kissing boys, and I do, too. And the two of us here. All by ourselves in a video store. Without a chance of anyone showing up because it's 2010 and no one rents movies when they can, I don't know, put a full *Scooby-Doo* collection on a flash drive," Tiago sends him signals.

"Depends how much space there is on the flash drive . . ." Greg dodges the signals.

But Tiago is determined. Surreptitiously, he lifts his casted arm and puts it over Greg's shoulder. His forehead is sweating, and his skin itches under the cast, but he tries his hardest to maintain his Casanova look, slightly furrowing his brow as if, through the bangs, he might be able to see straight into Greg's heart. He must rehearse this look in front of the mirror because I can't deal with it.

Greg feels the weight of Tiago's arm on his shoulders and, at this point, he knows what's about to happen. He's ready. At least he believes so. His mind repeats *I'm ready, I'm ready, I'm ready* on an infinite loop, trying to suffocate the self-sabotaging voice that says *My mouth tastes like beef Milanese and limp salad, and I don't know how much of this taste will pass on to the other person's mouth as we kiss.*

Tiago comes closer.

Greg feels he is about to die at any moment.

Tiago smiles.

Greg suddenly feels alive. Will it be this way every time? Feeling like the living dead before every single kiss of his life? Greg hopes not, because the last six seconds were already exhausting enough.

Keanu barks. But this time it's not to break an awkward silence. The silence here is the sound of the improbable birth of a small-town teenage romance that believes it can overcome every obstacle in the world.

Followed by the sound of Catarina coming through the store's door.

"My god, Tiago! What happened to your arm?" she asks.

Tiago grunts in frustration.

Greg laughs in anger (and, maybe, relief).

Keanu barks again.

BETO

Adult life in the big city must have changed Lara's sleeping habits, because when Beto wakes up at 9:33 a.m., his sister is not in the bedroom. He can hear noise from the kitchen: his family making breakfast, and his mom chattering away. Having another pair of ears in the house again is not without its advantages.

The phone on the nightstand is his reminder that there's a text from Nicolas waiting for an answer, and Beto needs to gather all his strength to grab the device and start typing.

Beto and Nico are friends. If it were up to Beto, they'd be much more than friends. But he still doesn't know what to do with all the feelings he holds inside because, just like everything in his life, his relationship with Nicolas is too complicated.

It all started about three years ago on TapTop, a video app about all the things that exist in the world. Beto found Nico's profile, full of videos about *Figures on the Edge*, an Australian reality show about figure skating to pop music choreographies and drama among the participants. Beto is *obsessed* with reality shows, figure skating, pop music, and drama.

Like a true fan, he followed and commented on Nico's videos, and the two of them became close because, well, apparently no one else watched *Figures on the Edge*. The show was canceled due to the low ratings (and some gossip about one of the judges having an affair with one of the contestants and favoring him in the competition).

On the day the show was canceled, the two started really talking, because they found in each other a friend disappointed for the same reason and with the same extremely specific type of obsession. After that, the two of them never stopped talking.

Forget bumping into someone in the school hallway, neighbors with common interests, or coffee shop employees who start conversations with customers. *No one* meets that way in real life. People like Beto (shy, online, and born after 2003) meet other people while crying on the internet over their canceled shows.

There's a certain *some*thing between them, I can't deny it. It's in the way Beto smiles when he sees a new message from Nico, or on the late nights when they FaceTime while watching the same movie, counting to three so they can hit play at the same exact time.

But Beto never had the courage to declare his feelings for Nico. First, they live more than six hundred miles apart. Second, as Nico already mentioned more than once, he doesn't feel ready to be in a relationship. Third, Beto considers himself the least interesting person who's ever lived and finds it hard to believe that, in these circumstances, someone might actually *like* him.

Roberto and Nicolas are an extremely complicated match.

And that's why, a few months ago, the smile that used to appear on Beto's face every time Nico texted was replaced by a furrowed brow and the thought, *Oh no, I'll have to pretend I'm doing okay* again.

The morning sun starts filtering through the window, hitting Roberto fully in the face, and he decides to answer last night's text because, despite not knowing quite how to deal with Nicolas's possibly platonic feelings, he doesn't like to keep him waiting.

Beto

> Morning! Thanks for the compliment. Still not sure what to photograph today.

> Any suggestions?

Not even thirty seconds go by before Nicolas starts typing. Beto stares at the three little dots blinking on his screen, right next to Nico's profile picture (a shirtless Kylo Ren that he puts up just to tease Beto, who hates Kylo Ren's shirtless scene in *The Last Jedi*).

Nico

> Morning! You haven't done a self-portrait in a while. Miss your little face haha

Beto rolls his eyes because that's what Nico always does. He keeps sending these *signals* and then changing the subject. But, just like every single time before this, Beto falls for it.

He takes advantage of the sunlight, tries to adjust his hair so it looks messy, leans back against the pillow, lifts his head to hide the double chin, and takes a selfie while attempting to seem as casual as possible. Then he takes another thirty, all of them exactly the same, and sends one of them to Nicolas.

Here! So you don't miss me as much

Nico

Who gave you permission to
be this HANDSOME?

Beto smiles, but deep down, he thinks about how Nicolas would never find him handsome if he were here right now, up close, seeing Beto in 3D and whole, with all the parts he always hides out of the frame.

Nico

I also just woke up, look

The text is followed by a photo of Nico, also lying in bed. His white skin with acne scars on the forehead, his dark hair (he decided to shave his head at the beginning of lockdown), a ring on his septum, and his tongue sticking out. Beto finds it absurd how *cool* Nico is. How he seems not to care about anything. How he probably didn't take thirty versions of that photo to choose the least terrible one. Beto is certain that, even if Nico had, all thirty would have looked the same amount of perfect. Noticing every detail of the image makes Beto feel anxious, so he changes the subject.

Beto

My sister is back home. She's
staying until this whole thing is over

Nico

Ahhh that's so nice!

> Hold on

> That's good, right?

> You like your sister, don't you?

It shocks Beto how long it takes to come up with an answer. He likes Lara. Right? They never got into fights when they were younger, always shared everything they had, and Lara has never been jealous, and she never teased him. She gives him *presents*. And *advice*. And she's good at it. She's good at everything, really. Smart, capable, communicative, confident, and has an excellent sense of humor. She's everything Beto wishes he were but isn't. She was able to get out of Lagoa Pequena in just the way Beto dreamed his whole life but has not managed. And came back *of her own accord*. Temporarily, of course. But still. She was in the city where Beto always wanted to live and *still* chose to return. It's possible to love someone without agreeing with all their decisions, isn't it? It's possible to find inspiration in your sister even though the certainty that you'll never be like her annoys you a bit once in a while . . . right?

Beto thinks about all this but doesn't know how to put his thoughts into words to answer Nico's text. He takes the easy route:

Beto

> Of course! I love my sister.

When Beto finally musters the strength to leave his bedroom and face yet another Wednesday without the prospect of doing anything productive, his mom is already working, locked in her own bedroom. He can hear the muffled sound of today's first session, but Beto doesn't make any effort to try and understand what she's saying because he knows that would be disrespectful to her patients.

"Look who's up!" Lara yells from the living room as soon as she sees her brother approaching.

She's still wearing her pajamas, her hair is messy, and her eyes are puffy. But the computer on her lap indicates she's at work.

"Are you working?" Beto asks, just to confirm.

"Mhm," she mumbles, chewing on the cap of a pen and attentively staring at the computer screen.

Beto comes closer, not to snoop, but because this is the first time he sees his sister in a professional context, as an adult, making money. He wants to *learn* (and snoop a little bit, too, of course).

"Lara, you are literally watching a compilation of little choreographies on TapTop."

"This *is* work. I write about behavior and fashion. I need to know how people are behaving and dressing," she answers defensively.

"And what have you learned so far by watching this video?" Beto teases.

"Pajamas are super *in*, and also this song right here." Lara turns up the volume on her computer. "With an absurd amount of cursing, and yet I cannot stop singing it."

Beto's shoulders dance to the beat, which repeats every ten seconds as videos of people creating different choreographies for the same part play on the screen one after the other.

"And how do you turn *this*"—Beto points at the screen—"into work?"

Lara laughs, puts the notebook aside, and wraps her hair up in a bun using the pen that, a few seconds ago, had been in her mouth. It seems a little gross, but who am I to judge? I don't know the first thing about human hygiene.

"Well, I didn't realize I was under interrogation this morning," she says, crossing her legs.

"I'm serious, come on," Beto answers.

"It's too complicated to explain. Because what I write for Telescope isn't always planned. I just observe things and try to come up with ideas for articles that will make people happy. I know that I'm not, like, *informing*—not really. Or searching for a cure for COVID. Or writing news articles that *really* matter. But sometimes I might be the respite for someone who's tired of actual news, you know? Someone who just needs to forget real quick, for five minutes, that the world is awful."

Beto smiles. He likes his sister's answer.

"Is that why you decided to study journalism, then?" he asks.

"That's the pretty answer. To help people deal with their daily routine. The practical answer is: I had no idea what to do and journalism seemed like the easiest option. I don't know, I never thought I was really good at anything."

Beto rolls his eyes because he always thought she was really good at *everything*.

"I'm serious," Lara continues. "Look at Mom, for instance. Do you think going to school for psychology is just sitting in a circle and talking about feelings?"

"I'm sure that circles and feelings is some kind of official class for at least one semester." Beto laughs.

"But *still!*" Lara says after a muffled laugh. "You have to know the brain and study behavior, and she has that huge book with all the acronyms for the disorders. I couldn't imagine myself studying anything that hard."

"Right," Beto murmurs, unsure how to continue the conversation. After so much time away from her, it's as if he's forgotten how to behave in Lara's presence.

"But why do you want to know?"

"Nothing. Just thinking . . ." Beto says. *About the future, and how I should start thinking about photography as a hobby and focus on something that makes real money while I deal with the fact that I have no idea what pays well, and at this stage of my life I should have already decided, but now I feel like there's no point in deciding on things because the outside world has been overtaken by a virus and all I have left is to wait, but there are days when I think I'm not even sure if there's anything I'm waiting for. I have no expectations and every day seems like a bad copy of the day before. Besides, I've been in love for months with an online friend who's much more good-looking than I am.* "About . . . life, I guess."

Beto has always wanted to be better at the art of expressing himself. He's always wished his thoughts didn't sound like tongue twisters. He waits for his sister to ask what he's thinking about. For her to start guessing at various reasons while he answers only yes and no. Preferably just nodding, never saying any words out loud.

But Lara doesn't ask any more questions because her computer starts playing the unmistakable jingle of an incoming video call.

"Team meeting," she announces, connecting her headphones to the notebook and changing her hair to a ponytail to make herself look more presentable.

And Beto returns to his bedroom because he has nothing better to do.

During the day, Beto plays with the lens he got from Lara. It still seems surreal, because he'd have to shoot at least seven birthday parties to save enough money for one of these. He'd spent months checking the price online, wondering if it would be worth investing in a piece of equipment like this, and always concluded that the best thing to do was to leave it for some other day. And, as if she had been a hidden camera spying on him this whole time, Lara nailed this present. Almost as if . . . she knew him well?

To Beto, that possibility seemed absurd. He's the kind of person few people *really* know. And who thinks that those who actually get to know him probably regret it.

The sun is setting, painting the sky orange and purple, and Beto puts his self-deprecating thoughts aside to focus on what he sees outside.

He takes the new lens, snaps it on the camera, and looks at the sky through the eyepiece, adjusting the focus and exposure patiently (but not too patiently, because he knows the sunset won't last long), and when everything seems to be the way he wants it, his fingers start pressing the shutter button uncontrollably, taking one shot after the other.

The clicking of the camera starts as a constant, fixed rhythm but, little by little, it turns into an irritable and nearly violent *clikclicklclickclick*.

It's as if Beto believes that, if he takes pictures more quickly, all this will pass.

After the frenetic clicking convulsion, Beto takes a deep breath and looks at the photos on the camera screen. They're not bad. In fact, they look pretty great. The screen shows the window illuminating the bedroom, the orange glow coming through and creating beautiful angular shadows, the outline of the wall darker from the shade, and the clouds outside painted in a perfect gradient. Beto knows how hard it is to capture sunlight so, in the end, he is proud of what he just photographed.

In a few minutes, he uploads the images to the computer, picks his favorite, makes some color adjustments, and decides to post the photo on Twitter. He spends some more time choosing the perfect caption and then finally gives up. He writes *sunset* next to an orange heart emoji and clicks Tweet.

He closes the app in a hurry because he knows how anxious he can get over the number of likes. But I know that later, before going to bed, he will be back to check. Beto always comes back.

The family is gathered in the living room after dinner. The noise of the news doesn't even make much of a difference now. After a full month hearing the death tolls as if they were the weather forecast, the three of them have already started feeling a little numb to it, which is both sad and worrying at the same time.

"How was work today, honey?" Helena asks Lara while trying to clean the lens of her glasses on the hem of her printed dress.

"Fine. Giovana, a friend who writes for the food and healthy living section, bought fifteen pounds of sweet potatoes instead of just *fifteen sweet potatoes*, so she started a series of articles with sweet potato recipes for the entire week."

Beto laughs, still surprised at the kind of stuff that his sister's company publishes.

"And Keyla, a girl I hate, got an hour's worth of compliments from our boss because her series of articles has been on our website's top ten for weeks now. Insufferable."

"What does she write about?" their mom asks, trying to engage in conversation so she doesn't have to look at the TV.

"She created this series called *Lockdown: A New Thing Every Day,*" Lara explains mockingly. "Probably stole the idea from a foreign website. That's her specialty."

"Whoa, yesterday she tried embroidery for the first time!" Beto scoffs, opening the website on his phone and showing them the photos.

"You see?" Lara says, furious. "Look at this! Who can embroider like this *on the first try*? I bet she's been practicing for months and pretended it was her first time just to put on this performance online. Or even worse, she bought the embroidery and is pretending she did it herself."

Helena is still at war with her greasy lens. Beto focuses on the articles written by his sister's archnemesis and analyzes other things she's attempted for the first time in the last few days: guided meditation, body painting, *wall* painting, homemade Easter eggs, tango. She seems to have an amazing life, but Beto feels exhausted just from looking at the articles and imagining how much trouble it must be to learn all this stuff.

"I think you're being too cruel to your colleague," their mom comments, giving up on her mission and putting her glasses back on, the lens all smudged.

"She's not my *colleague*. She's a snob to everyone, and she's a *natural blonde*. No important social contribution in the history of mankind has ever been made by a blonde."

Beto and Helena nod, unable to disagree.

"And *yet*," Helena continues. "This might be a good thing for you two to try. Together, you know? Doing a new thing every day or something. Empty your minds of all your worries for a while."

Lara immediately rolls her eyes, and Beto feels his face burning. He hates it when his mom does that. When she subtly makes suggestions as if he were her patient and not her son. When she shows she's been observing his behavior and *knows* that he's been sad.

Beto doesn't hate that his mother cares, of course not. But the *way* she shows she cares makes him feel nervous. He can't explain why. At this point, hopefully it has become quite clear that Beto isn't great with words.

"Sorry, Mom, can't be done. There are no new things to do without leaving the house. I've already done literally *all* the things." That's the only comeback Beto manages.

"And I have no time to think of different things to do, Mom. I work all day. And I study at night," Lara adds, trying as hard as she can to get this absurd idea out of Helena's head.

"By the way, shouldn't you be studying right now?" her mom asks.

"And I *am*," Lara answers, pointing at the phone screen where a professor on mute talks to a group of students whose cameras are turned off.

Beto tries to hold back a jealous snort when he notices, once again, how *easy* Lara's life is.

"For god's sake, the two of you! I'm not asking you to find the cure for coronavirus in our kitchen. Just for you to do things together. I think it would be good for you. I can participate. We can cook, play a board game, paint a wall, build a hummingbird feeder out of plastic bottles . . ." Helena says, raising one finger for each suggestion.

Personally, I love the hummingbird feeder idea. I like seeing humans try their hand at upcycling. It always ends up looking as horrible on the internet as it does in real life.

"Fine by me, then," Lara concedes, and puts on her headphones to pretend that she's paying attention to the class.

Helena looks at Beto, waiting for her son's approval.

"Do I even have a choice?" he says, sulkily.

"It will be good for us, you'll see," Helena says, attempting to smile.

Beto can see how hard his mom is trying. He knows things aren't easy for her either, and deep down, what he *really* wants is to be capable of creating a vaccine for the virus in his kitchen. The TV, now barely audible, shows a graph with the increase in cases in the past twenty-four hours. The chyron reads in an oversized font:

THIS IS JUST THE BEGINNING.

Beto feels his skin prickle.

"I'm going to bed, that was enough existing for today," he murmurs.

Helena laughs. "Tomorrow we'll exist a little more, then. Love you, son."

"Love you, Mom."

———————

Beto doesn't fall asleep right away. When he walks into the bedroom, he enjoys Lara's absence (who's still in the living room, her face glued to her phone and a spiral notebook in her hand) to take a deep breath, without the weight of comparison, the need to seem useful, or the whole I-need-to-pretend-I'm-fine thing that has been taking over his thoughts ever since his sister arrived. This is the perfect moment to run to what is still his favorite place despite everything: his chat with Nico.

Beto

Heya. How was your day?

Nico

Whoa!!!

I was JUST about to call. To congratulate you on today's photo

With the obligatory family reunion in the living room, Beto had already forgotten the orange sunset photo he posted on Twitter earlier in the afternoon. He opens the app in record-breaking speed and smiles. One hundred and twenty-three likes. Thirty-two replies. Most of them are *What a beautiful sky!!!* or a sequence of smiling emojis with hearts for eyes, posted by people he doesn't know, hiding behind avatars of famous people, anime characters, or a potato wearing lipstick and fake nails (which he believes is a recent meme he hasn't seen yet). It's the most engagement Beto has ever had online, and as much as part of his subconscious insists that numbers don't matter, tonight they do.

Beto

Oh my gosh??? I had no idea people were going to like my bedroom window so much!

Nico

It's a great window. Mine sucks

Nico sends a photo of an open metal window facing another building. The image is dark and kind of blurry, but Beto can see the neighbor across from Nicolas, a white and slightly bald man, smoking on the balcony.

Beto

Hi Nicolas's neighbor!

Nico

HAHAHA. I feel bad for the man, he must have seen me walking around naked so many times already

Beto types *lucky him* but deletes the message before sending because he doesn't want to make the conversation weird. And to imply that he wouldn't mind seeing Nicolas walking around naked many times is exactly the kind of thing that would make the conversation weird. Better change the subject.

> Now my mom came up with this thing where my sister and I need to do something new every day during lockdown. So we can get to know each other better or whatever. It hasn't even started and I already want to give up.

Nico

> Don't be silly! That sounds like fun.

> Much better than my dad, who's playing "how many times can I start talking politics out of the blue and essentially ruin every single family interaction?"

> Or my brother, who's playing "how long can I make my mom believe that the weed smell coming from my bedroom came from the upstairs neighbor's window?"

> Or my mom, who's playing "has anyone seen the Xanax I left on top of the cabinet?"

> Haha

Beto knows Nico's family is complicated. That he writes *haha* at the end to try and downplay his own frustration. He knows Nico also feels like leaving home. The two of them have talked about it thousands of times (and many of those times ended with Beto daydreaming about the possibility of living with Nico in a São Paulo

120

apartment with a huge living room, many plants, artwork on the walls, and an office that he would transform into his own photography studio with a dark room). He feels selfish and silly for complaining about his family when it is perfectly acceptable, especially when compared to Nico's. This is Beto's worst problem. He compares himself to others too much.

Beto

Haha

He sends the answer even as his face has no trace of a smile, in the hopes that Nico understands Beto's *haha* is in solidarity with his desperate *haha*. I just wish these two would talk like normal people. Everything would be so much easier.

Beto

You're right.

Might be fun!

Nico

Do you know what tomorrow's never-attempted thing will be?

Beto

It would be just like my sister to suggest something like meditation

Or starting a vegetable garden in our backyard, I don't know

Nico

I vote vegetable garden! So you can plant tomatoes, make some ketchup, and send it my way!

Beto smiles a silly smile. Nico, for some reason, *really* likes ketchup, and knowing these small details makes Beto feel a little closer to him.

Beto

By the time I finish, from me planting the tomato, mincing it into ketchup, and sending it to you, the pandemic will already be over, so I might as well just get on a plane and bring it to you irl!

Nico

There are days when I think this whole thing will go by very quickly. There are others when it seems it will last forever.

Beto rolls his eyes when he realizes his silly I'll-bring-you-ketchup attempt at flirting didn't work and instead he led the conversation to a heavy place. He's tired of heavy places.

Beto

What kind of day was today?

Nico

Believe it or not, it was a good one. Not as good as having you here with a bottle of ketchup, but still good

Silly flirting achievement unlocked! Beto smiles.

Lara knocks lightly on the door and enters the bedroom. It wasn't the knock of someone asking if they can come in, but that of someone announcing their arrival. Her hair is again wrapped around the same pen from earlier this morning, and she's still wearing the same pajamas. Beto is *almost* sure that Lara hasn't showered today, but the grumpy look on his sister's face prevents him from commenting on it.

"I'm sorry I sounded like a silly girl earlier, with you and Mom," she says.

Beto types on his phone without taking his eyes off his sister, because he doesn't want to seem disrespectful when all signs point to them about to have *a moment.*

Beto

> I think my sister is trying to have A MOMENT with me. Back soon

Calmly, he locks the screen and continues looking at his sister, not quite sure what to say.

"Don't worry about it, Lara. I seem like a silly kid in front of Mom all the time." That's the first thing he can think of.

"Oh, but it's different, you know?" Lara answers immediately.

"Because I'm not *an adult* like you are," Beto mocks, already regretting having paid Lara any mind. His conversation with Nicolas was much better (though just as aimless).

"I swear that was not what I meant." Lara moves closer and perches on Beto's bed. "I'm not as much of an adult as you seem to think. And being home during such a weird time . . . I don't know, you know?"

"No. I don't know."

She takes the pen from her hair, shakes her head, and takes a deep breath.

"It's as if the years I spent away didn't count. As if I were still the same Lara I was when I left this place. This city . . . this house . . . I love it all here, but somehow I feel . . . smaller?" The last word sounds almost like a question.

"How can you still love a place that makes you feel that way?" Beto asks, trying to draw from his sister the confession that she, too, hates Lagoa Pequena, so the two of them might at least have that in common.

"Today when I woke up, Mom had set the breakfast table. With that horrendous cappuccino powder that tastes like plastic, but that I love. And Minas cheese. Everything I love eating in the morning was on that table," she says, clearly ignoring Beto's question. "I felt, I don't know, *special*. In São Paulo, no one makes breakfast for me. I remembered all the perks of living here. But at night, seeing the way Mom wanted us to become closer and do things together, just like when I was a teenager and wanted to go to the mall with my friends, but she'd only let me if I brought you along . . . I felt like such a . . . child."

Beto laughs. He feels that way every day.

"I feel that way every day," he says, just to reassure his sister that he wasn't laughing at her.

"Don't be silly, Roberto," Lara says, trying not to laugh because Roberto is what she calls him when she's being serious. "You've always been the little adult at home. Responsible. Going to work on weekends. You literally *save money.* I wish I were like you."

His sister's admission hits him like a punch in the gut. A *good* punch. It's as if he's starting to see himself the way Lara sees him and realizing that what she sees isn't so bad.

"All right, I have a proposal," he says, after a long sigh. "Let's do the thing Mom suggested. The whole doing-something-new-every-day thing. Together."

Lara furrows her brow, still troubled.

"But not because *she said so,*" Beto continues. "Because *we want to.* To prove to you that I am not the responsible little adult you think I am."

"And I will prove to you that I do not have the dream life that you think I do," Lara says.

"So we can get to know each other, then." Beto smiles.

Lara smiles back.

It seems like an absurd idea to him, to try and get to know someone with whom he's shared his entire life. But it's been a month of lockdown and there is no chance, not even close, that this thing is going to end tomorrow. It's not as if he has much to lose.

APRIL 23, 2020

Beto stares at the singed black disks on the baking tray. He and Lara had tried baking cookies for the first time, following an internet recipe that seemed simple enough and didn't require a huge list of ingredients.

Neither one knows if it was because they'd left the cookies in the oven for too long, or if the temperature was too high, or if it was the brown sugar they'd used instead of normal sugar because they figured it couldn't make *that* much of a difference, right? But the result was a disaster.

Beto takes a picture of the burnt cookies, anyway. Recording failures is a part of the journey.

Tomorrow they can try something new.

ANA

The following morning, after telling Letícia the truth about the move, Ana barely has time for a proper conversation with her girlfriend.

The two wake up to the phone ringing, and Letícia's mom needs her to come back home as quickly as possible. Letícia doubts anything serious has happened; she believes it's just another of her mother's attempts to show that she has complete control over her family, but Letícia obeys, anyway.

Ana and Letícia's goodbye takes place on the porch. It's cold and listless. No "I love you" because they're still too afraid to say it in public.

"We still have two weeks," Ana makes a point of reminding her girlfriend as she climbs onto her bike. "I know it might seem short—"

"It *is* short," Letícia interjects. "But we'll figure it out."

Letícia leaves and Ana locks herself in her bedroom. She spends hours lying in bed, motionless, crying in a way that comes little by little but for a long time; her eyes are constantly wet, but they never erupt in tears. It's the quiet sob of someone who's afraid of the future.

One step at a time, one step at a time, she repeats to herself. In a situation like this, holding on to a mantra that she's heard in two thousand movies seems like a reasonable idea. But deep down, the advice feels useless because Ana has no idea what her next step will be.

JANUARY 7, 2OOO

Over the next few days, Ana and Letícia speak on the phone almost daily, but with their families always around, the subject never evolves into anything more intimate. Letícia is always too busy to meet Ana, which Ana suspects is a lie. Letícia just isn't ready to have a conversation. Maybe she's hurt, and Ana blames herself for not making it clearer that the decision to move wasn't hers and that, if it weren't for her dad, she would never leave.

Celso, as distant and lost as he might seem, notices how Ana has changed. He'd expected that his daughter would show some resistance to the move, but the way she reacted was different. She's sad, and one doesn't need to be the most attentive dad on earth to see that. Not when his daughter walks around the house in her pajamas all day, not washing her hair, her eyes puffy. Not when she barely eats and spends most of her time alone in her bedroom. Not when she answers "sad" every time Celso asks her how she's doing.

I guess it's pretty obvious.

Ana burrows into her vampire books and distracts herself by taking her mind to an alternate reality where there are only mythical, eternal, young, and handsome beings, and humankind is just a passing detail. It's no good for her, because pretending that humankind doesn't exist is a terrible way to deal with the 100-percent-human decisions she needs to make.

When the move is just a week away, Celso starts packing up some of the less important things. Many objects end up going to the donation pile, and none of the furniture is coming with them.

Ana could be happy with a new bed, not a secondhand one, its feet not worn by the bites of a dog she's never met. But if it were possible, she'd sleep on the street so she wouldn't have to leave. Obviously, she wouldn't last even two days, but Ana believes she would because she's seventeen, in love, and her convictions become a bit dramatic when she's sad.

"Want to help me pack?" Celso asks on Friday afternoon, after a light knock on Ana's bedroom door.

Impatient, she gets up, opens the door, and stares at her dad. Celso doesn't know when the last time Ana washed her face was, but at this point he's afraid to ask.

Ana mumbles.

"You can start by putting away the less important things," he guides her. "And we'll organize the rest throughout the week."

Ana opens her arms and lowers her head in a gesture of surrender. "Put me in a box, then. I'm of no importance to you, anyway."

Oh my god, the drama.

"Honey, come here. We need to talk."

Tenderly, Celso grabs her by the hand and walks with her to the couch.

"YES! TALK!" I would scream if I could. But I can't. Against the rules. The best I can do of my own free will is to rattle the windows on rainy days.

"There's nothing to talk about, Dad. Everything's been decided. You made all the decisions yourself," Ana moans, throwing herself on the couch, arms crossed.

"It's hard for me, too. I didn't decide on my own because I wanted to."

Celso doesn't say it out loud, but the thought that Ana's mom is not here to help with these decisions hangs in the air. Ana is overcome with the guilt of being the one who led to her mother's death. It's hard for that kind of guilt to go away.

Ana says what she's thought her whole life: "Sometimes you wish she were the one who'd survived, don't you? Instead of me."

"Honey, no! No, never, ever," Celso replies immediately, speaking over Ana. "That thought has never crossed my mind, and I can promise you it never will."

Celso is lying. The thought has crossed his mind. But he's not proud of it.

"It's weird because I can't even miss her, you know? It's impossible to miss someone I've never met."

Celso swallows hard. Only now, after seventeen years, does he realize that he's been missing Ana's mom all alone. Talking about her has always been a complicated endeavor. He would try, in the beginning, when his daughter was just a little girl running around the house and scribbling on the walls with crayons. He would occasionally blurt out, "You have your mom's laugh," or "Your mom would be furious with all this mess." But Ana, never quite understanding whom he was talking about, only smiled and kept on playing. The subject became rarer as time went by, and Celso wouldn't bring it up because he thought his daughter didn't want to hear it, and Ana didn't ask because she thought her father didn't want to talk about it.

But today the two of them feel different, tired of sweeping the subject under their emotional rugs. Celso gets up quickly and goes to the kitchen. Ana waits, her eyes still wet, her head full of questions. He comes back with a glass of water and hands it to her.

She drinks but laughs in the middle of the first sip.

"I thought you were going to come back with a special necklace, an amulet or something, and say, 'Your mom wanted me to give you this when you turned eighteen, but I think now is the right moment,'" she confesses, still laughing.

"That only happens in movies, honey," Celso says, moving closer to Ana for a hug. "She probably would have had a special present for when you turned eighteen, but we didn't have time to think of anything. When your mom got pregnant, all we could think of was how we were going to manage to buy diapers. But if a necklace with a nice pendant will make you happy, we can go out now and get one."

Ana sighs. "It's not about the necklace, Dad. It's just that . . . I don't know. I keep trying to guess what she'd expect from me. If she'd like the person I am. If she would love me no matter what."

Celso goes silent, pondering what to say next. Ana goes silent, regretting what she just said. And in the air hovers a scream—a "DAD, I'M GAY!" that anybody would have been able to hear.

No, wait, hold on. That was *not* a silent scream hovering in the air. Ana literally said this out loud and I got lost in all the intense emotions going on. Celso too, apparently.

"Dad? I'm gay," Ana repeats, looking in the eyes of a confused and open-mouthed Celso.

"Does that mean that . . ." he starts slowly.

"I like girls," Ana explains. "*Gay* is kind of an umbrella term."

The look on her dad's face softens, because up until this very moment, he believed only men could be gay.

"Say something," Ana pleads, tired of making explosive revelations to other people just to get nothing but silence in return.

"I was surprised. Not upset. In any way. Just surprised," he answers.

"Whoa, I always thought it was so obvious. I don't know, look at me . . ." Ana says, pointing at her own body.

"I see a girl who's beautiful . . . and . . . gay," Celso says, trying his hardest to be a good dad. The last word comes out of his mouth as if it were a new dialect.

He looks at his daughter, waiting for confirmation that he used the word correctly.

Ana smiles.

"I always thought the way you are . . . The way you speak and behave was like that because . . . I don't know, I'm searching for the right words."

Because I didn't have a mom to teach me how to be more "feminine"? Ana thinks, not needing to hear the words to know what her dad means, and making air quotes in her own head.

"I think about that sometimes, too," Ana says.

The two of them take a deep breath, still staring at each other, too afraid to continue the conversation, but in too deep to leave it.

"Thank you for telling me," Celso says. "For trusting me."

"Thank you for . . . I don't know. Accepting me? And for not kicking me out of the house."

"My god, Ana! What kind of dad would do that?" Celso asks, genuinely shocked.

"Literally any other dad in this shitty little city," Ana points out the obvious.

"So that's good, right? We're going to a big city now. Rio is huge. There must be a lot of girls there. Gay girls!"

Ana laughs, still not used to her dad saying "gay girls" out loud.

"Well . . ." Ana begins, letting go of her dad's hand and twisting a strand of hair around her fingers. "There's something else. I have a . . . a girlfriend."

"Really?!" Celso says, unable to figure out how to receive the onslaught of information about his daughter who, until today, he believed had trouble being social only because of all the vampire novels she had in her bedroom.

"Is that a good *really* or a bad *really*?" Ana asks, desperate for an answer.

"A normal *really*? It's just . . . different. To know you're gay in practice, too."

Ana laughs because she'd never thought of herself as "gay in practice." She likes the title.

"And do I know this girlfriend?" Celso asks, still bewildered.

"For god's sake, Dad! It's Letícia. She spent the night here. In my bedroom. There's only one bed in there. I cried for days after she left!"

"Gosh, I thought the two of you were just good friends."

Ana's heart is heavy because, well, in a way, he's not wrong. Her eyes sadden, and she starts biting her thumbnail. What's left of her nail, in fact. And focused on this terrible habit, Ana is caught by surprise with a simple gesture. Celso comes closer to his daughter and pulls her in for a hug.

The relationship between the two of them has always been peaceful. Celso is a loving dad. But, for some reason, hugs are rare in this household.

Ana is tired of always being on the defensive, and for the first time in forever, she feels like she can rest. Ana lets herself be hugged, and the tighter Celso's arms get, the farther she shrinks, lost in her dad's chest, unafraid to be vulnerable.

"You know . . ." Celso says, stroking Ana's hair. "I once had a gay friend."

Ana squirms because nothing good ever follows that sentence, but she remains still because she wants to see where this is going.

"His name was Orlando," Celso continues. "We went to college together. He was your mom's friend, really, but she always let me borrow her friends because I didn't have many. It was the seventies, a different reality. He had to hide all the time, always afraid, but he was always in love."

"Do you still talk to him?" Ana interrupts, excited by the possibility of meeting a gay adult who can tell her that, with time, everything is going to be fine.

"We never saw each other again, and I lost his number. It's hard to keep in touch with people from that time. If only there was some virtual place where everyone could give updates about their lives just so we could know they're fine without necessarily having to get in touch with them . . ."

"Dad, you have the weirdest ideas!" Ana laughs, barely able to believe it. "Tell me more about Orlando."

"So, he had this friend . . . boyfriend, actually. They met when they were teenagers. They had been in love with each other their whole lives. He lived far away, I don't remember where. But they would meet once a year. It was the biggest event. They exchanged letters for eleven months and spent a full month together, and then had to say goodbye again."

"I hope you're not suggesting I *exchange letters* with Letícia for eleven months," Ana teases.

"No, nothing like that! It's just that . . . there was this one time. We were drinking by the lake. Him, your mom, and me. It was really for the two of them, I was just there because I was your mom's boyfriend. Kind of like a bizarre narrator-observer . . ."

I know the feeling, Celso.

"He was super excited about his boyfriend's visit," Celso continues. "Planning everything and sharing the details with your mom. She asked how they were going to cope after the month was over. It's funny because that entire year is a blur in my life, but I remember as if it were yesterday the way he looked at your mom, laughed, and said, 'How am I supposed to know? All we have is now.' And I know it's kind of a cheesy thing to say . . ."

"Yeah, super cheesy," Ana agrees.

"But to this day, sometimes I still think about it. And I think maybe it can help you."

Ana thinks about now. About everything she could do right now to make the most of her time with Letícia. But it seems so pointless to try hard to be happy today, knowing that in a week she'll be in another city, six hundred miles from here, where people put ketchup on their pizza.

This type of advice is very pretty in theory, but Ana is now gay in practice. The now doesn't seem as promising when tomorrow is already full of decisions that have been made and that she can't change. But Ana doesn't say it out loud because she acknowledges her dad is just trying to help and she doesn't want to spoil the mood. Besides, getting this hug from him and sitting here and talking feels a lot better than she imagined.

"Why are you telling me this now?" she asks.

"I don't know. Context, maybe? In which other situation could I have said, 'Well, honey, there was this gay man I knew . . .' just like that, out of nowhere?"

"No, silly." Ana laughs. "I don't mean Orlando. I mean my mom. The way you had friends together and used to drink by the lake. You never talk about her."

"I never know how much you want to know about her. Because, at least to me, these memories are really good ones, and then suddenly it becomes painful. It's a very thin line, and I don't know what that's like for you."

Ana doesn't know either, but right now she wants to know everything. She wants her mother to stop being a stranger she knows only through old photos saved in her dad's wardrobe, inside a rusty cookie tin with a drawing of the Eiffel Tower and the words COMME C'EST DÉLICIEUX! Ana wants to know what she liked to have for breakfast, how she organized her dresser, why she decided to call her daughter Ana, just Ana, no other name after, if she knew how to cook, if she was good at math, and whether she also liked vampire novels.

But all these questions together might be too much for Celso, and she doesn't want to make her dad cross the thin line between a good memory and a painful one.

"I want to know everything. Little by little. You'll have time to tell me," she says with a smile.

"Of course I will! I'm living until I'm three hundred with my consciousness transferred to a robot body, or did you forget?"

"Apparently you'll never let me forget."

"I'll stop talking about futuristic robot dads if we can start packing up," Celso proposes.

Ana jumps, pulls up her sleeves, and ties her hair back with an excitement she hasn't displayed in days.

As she gets ready to turn her room upside down, deciding what to bring to her new house, she almost doesn't think about Letícia.

Almost.

———

Packing up a whole life is fun only for the first thirty minutes. Ana had no idea how much trash she'd accumulated in her bedroom, and the more drawers she opens, the more scared she feels. The back of her closet is basically a time capsule, and Ana carefully analyzes each memory she finds there. Her school notebooks organized by year, the sticker pages intact because she didn't want to waste them, a yellow envelope with all the ticket stubs for the movies she saw in 1997, and an incomplete Pokémon sticker album because she gave up halfway through when she realized that she'd have to trade her duplicates in order to get new stickers, and that in order to do that she'd need to talk to other kids.

She throws it all away (the Pokémon sticker album is rescued from the trash by Celso, who believes that in the future it might be worth a lot of money), and the more she goes through her things, the more she feels like leaving it all behind and starting fresh in Rio de Janeiro.

That wouldn't be a bad idea.

Maybe if she got a haircut like Leonardo DiCaprio in *Romeo + Juliet* before the move, she could arrive in Rio as this new cool girl who won't need to answer the "Oh, you got a haircut?" question, because no one will ask it. That would be her official haircut.

Maybe her dad is right after all, about there being more gay people in the big city and, in a way, that makes her excited. Of course, she doesn't think about getting another girlfriend. Ana doesn't even know how she's leaving things with Letícia, and besides, she loves that girl enough to guarantee at least one year of sadness before she's capable of kissing someone else. But, as she rips her eighth-grade graduation photos in which she wore a horrible orange dress and a hairdo with two twisted little hair strands in front of her ear, Ana can't help but think of how incredible it would be to move to a different place and have friends. Friends like herself.

This kind of thinking makes guilt tighten her chest. Accepting you're moving is one thing, but fantasizing about good things the move can bring is completely different. She feels as if she's betraying Letícia, betraying Lagoa Pequena, betraying her own house.

Just to be clear, I don't feel betrayed. I'm doing great.

"A fancy dinner!" Celso says, coming into Ana's bedroom and interrupting her thoughts of guilt, hope, and longing.

"Dad, it's still four in the afternoon," she answers.

"No! I was thinking of a way for you to have a beautiful goodbye with your . . . girlfriend," he says. "A fancy dinner. This new restaurant just opened downtown, it's called All About Trout."

"From the name it sounds *really fancy*," Ana comments, rolling her eyes.

"Trout is an expensive fish, honey. I heard they have candles on the tables and live violin music. I think she'd like it. I mean, that is, if she likes trout, you know? Is she vegetarian? Some vegetarian people eat fish, don't they?"

Ana opens a big smile because she never imagined her dad would react this way when she told him about Letícia. Celso has always shown signs of being an understanding dad, but suggesting live music and worrying whether her girlfriend is a vegetarian? This surpasses any expectations.

"That sounds like a good idea, Dad. Thanks for the effort," Ana says, unable to hide a hint of worry in her eyes. "But if I were to take Letícia to dinner one day, I'd like to, I don't know, hold her hand. Over the table. Without fear. I don't know how that would be possible at All About Trout."

Celso swallows hard, maybe realizing just now that his daughter's problems are much bigger than just planning a goodbye dinner.

The phone rings, and Celso lets out a relieved breath because he doesn't know how to respond.

"Hello," Ana answers after running to the phone, and by the way her face lights up, Celso already knows who it is.

"Hi," Letícia says on the other end. "Can you talk? My mom went to the store, so I took the opportunity to call."

"I can. I need to tell you something. My dad knows . . . about us," she says, smiling at Celso, who raises his thumbs in support, then leaves to give Ana some privacy.

"Oh my god! How did he find out?" Letícia asks anxiously.

"I told him, actually. And it was fine. His reaction was very . . . positive? I don't know. I didn't really know what to expect. I told him on a whim. But he doesn't hate me. And he doesn't hate you either, obviously. Because it's impossible to hate you."

Letícia goes silent.

"Say something," Ana says, tired of waiting for people to say something.

"I don't want you to think I'm jealous or anything like that. I am so happy for you! I think that, I don't know, I think you don't know how lucky you are."

"You are my luck," Ana says impulsively.

"*Bleerghhh*," Letícia pretends she's throwing up.

This is something they do when one of them crosses the line into sappy. It's cute. Ana laughs.

"But I mean it," Ana says in protest. "Meeting you kind of changed the way I see myself."

"I miss you so much."

"Me too."

"I'm tired of pretending that things aren't going to change. But I also can't sit here thinking of how I'll regret not spending every moment by your side while I still can."

"All we have is now," Ana echoes the lesson she learned from her dad this morning, proud that she managed to make it all fit together.

"Well, *now* now is kind of hard. My mom will be back soon, and she'll need my help to put the groceries away, and we'll probably use the last bit of afternoon sun to give Billy a bath," Letícia counters very practically, completely breaking Ana's cycle of self-awareness.

Billy is Letícia's dog, by the way.

"When can you make it? Tomorrow?" Ana asks, since *now* now is out of the question.

"Tomorrow I'm babysitting my cousins because my aunt is getting waxed in a different city."

If Ana didn't already know Letícia for so long and didn't know what her family is like, she'd think those were all poor excuses not to see her.

"Sunday?" Ana proposes.

"Church," Letícia answers in the sad voice that always accompanies the subject.

"Monday?" Ana is not about to give up.

"Monday! I can do Monday! I'll make something up. I'll ask my brother to cover for me or something. He owes me one."

"I'll wait for you here. Until then, I'll figure out what we can do. But it's going to be special."

"Oooohhh," Letícia says. "Special how? Should I wear a dress?"

"No! Don't dress up too much because I don't know how to do that, so if you come in looking good and I'm just myself, we'll be too mismatched."

"As if the eight inches between us weren't enough," Letícia teases.

"You're ridiculous."

"I love you," Letícia says in a soft voice, afraid of what might happen if someone hears her.

"I love you, too," Ana says, in a normal tone of voice, because now she doesn't need to hide anymore.

She could even shout.

"I LOVE YOU VERY MUCH AND I'M COUNTING THE SECONDS UNTIL MONDAY!" she shouts, just because she can.

"No need to rub it in that you can shout it now," Letícia says, maybe resenting it a little.

"Until you can, too, I'll shout it for the two of us, okay?" Ana promises.

"Okay."

Ana hangs up in euphoria, jumping up and down and making a high-pitched sound that Celso had never witnessed. He can't help but notice his daughter's emotional range today and how the puffy-faced Ana he encountered in the morning seems like a distant memory.

"Monday it is, then, huh?" Celso says, leaning against the kitchen door frame, but sliding a little bit and nearly falling to the ground, because he's clumsy.

"Yes. It'll be something simple, actually."

"So no All About Trout?"

"No. Just a date at home. Maybe by candlelight. But we'll just hang out here. This is a safe place," Ana states.

In all my existence, I was never called a safe place before. It's so emotional I'd cry if I were able to. Maybe the next person to move in will find a leak in the bathroom.

"And how can I help?" Celso offers.

"I'll need money to buy food," Ana starts the list.

"Right."

"And would you happen to know how to play the violin?" she asks.

"No, but I think I can rehearse a song or two on the guitar . . ."

"Dad, *for god's sake*, I'm joking! Nobody wants their own dad playing live music for their goodbye dinner with their girlfriend."

Celso laughs, realizing that despite the intense emotional closeness they had today, Ana is still a normal teenager who has a hard time making friends due to the number of vampire novels she has in her bedroom.

"I just need you to leave," Ana continues. "For, like . . . two hours? Can you leave the house to us for two hours on Monday? I swear I'm not going to set anything on fire."

Celso seems to consider it.

"Or get pregnant," Ana continues, with a tight smile.

Celso opens his mouth, perplexed.

"Too soon for that joke?" Ana asks.

"*Way* too soon," he says, tapping her shoulder and getting ready to go back to the boxes.

"Thanks, Dad," she says. "For everything."

Still with his back to his daughter, Celso smiles. He didn't want to listen to their phone conversation, but the part where she screamed "I LOVE YOU!" was kind of hard to miss. And now Celso feels like this *can* be a place to talk about love.

"I love you, honey," he says, turning back to Ana and lightly pressing the tip of her nose, so the declaration feels more casual.

But deep down, he's shaking, because he's never been so serious about anything. And that is very clear to Ana, who answers naturally, almost as if the words were said on a daily basis.

"I love you, too."

"By the way," Celso says, trying to seem as casual as possible. "When was the last time you took a shower?"

"Dad!"

"I mean it. For your sake. No one wants a smelly girlfriend," he says, trying not to stare at his daughter's oily hair and puffy eyes.

"Fiiiine."

"Shower. Now!" He points toward the bathroom.

And Ana obeys because, well, what choice does she have?

GREG

"Want to stay for an afternoon coffee, Tiago? I brought some orange cake," Catarina asks with the ease of someone who did not just interrupt two boys about to kiss behind the counter of her failing business venture.

She knows what was going on. I *know* that she knows. And, once again, Catarina is delighted to witness her nephew's shame. For a woman who's lived for years with only the most adorable three-legged mutt of all time for company, watching the daily embarrassment of a teenage family member became a favorite pastime. I can't blame her. Things have been a lot more fun since Greg got here.

"I better get going," Tiago says, his pale face flushing more and more each second. "Thank you so much, but my mom must be waiting for me."

Catarina furrows her brow and brings her hands to her hips. She won't have her fun taken away from her this quickly.

"Absolutely not. I *insist*," she emphasizes, putting on the counter the container with a cake, the kind with a hole in the middle and all. "Gregório, would you make us some coffee?"

Greg doesn't know what to do. He has never made coffee in his entire life.

"I've never made coffee in my entire life," he says.

"Nonsense. You just throw some powder and water in the coffee maker and press a button. You mess around with *computers*, it's not that hard," she counters, as if computers were NASA's latest generation of rockets.

Greg doesn't argue. With a tight smile, he lowers his head and goes into the kitchen.

Minutes later, he returns with a smoky pot of coffee in one hand and three ceramic cups balanced on the other.

"Hmm, it smells good," Tiago says, feeling the moral obligation to support the guy he nearly kissed.

Tiago is lying. There is no smell. From the look of the dark, watery liquid sloshing in the glass pot, you can tell that this is possibly the worst coffee ever prepared in the history of coffee.

With all the care in the world, trying to control his nervously shaking hands, Greg fills the cups and gets a slice of cake.

The three of them drink almost at the same time. Hard to determine whose grimace was the worst.

"At least the cake is good," Greg comments, trying to ease the mood.

"What did you two do all day?" Catarina asks.

"We talked," Tiago answers.

"We watched a movie," Greg answers *at the same time* because, for some reason, he's afraid to tell his aunt the truth.

"We talked while watching a movie," Tiago tries to help.

"What a nightmare," Catarina comments, because she hates it

when people talk during movies. "And what else happened while I was away?"

She's wiggling her eyebrows up and down in an intimidating way. She *definitely* knows what she's doing. She likes it. Keanu runs from one side of the room to the other, limping on his three legs and barking excitedly. Unlike Catarina, he's not excited because the boys are embarrassed, he just senses his owner's happiness and, consequently, feels happy, too. Because that's what good dogs are like. They feel happy for people.

"Nothing much," Greg says.

"Absolutely nothing," Tiago adds.

"Nothing at all," Greg reinforces.

Catarina scratches her head, a little confused. "And the customers? Lots of foot traffic?"

Greg goes silent. It was a quiet day at the shop, nearly dead. He can count on one hand how many people stopped by today. He could add another hand to account for the people who stopped by just to ask for directions or if they sold cigarettes.

Catarina doesn't need an answer. She knows what her nephew's silence means, but she still rubs salt in the wound.

"Really? That's odd ..." She knows there's nothing odd about it. "Friday is usually a busy day, lots of clients." She knows it's been a while since a Friday has seen lots of clients. "Very interesting." She doesn't think it's interesting at all.

Greg scratches his chin. He wished there was a gentle way to tell his aunt that, well, keeping a video rental store open in 2010 is insane. Tiago straightens his bangs. He just wants to leave.

"Can you close it up, then, Greg? I'm going in to take a shower," she finally says, turning her back without saying goodbye to Tiago.

Keanu follows her because Catarina is his favorite human.

"I think she needs me," Greg says to Tiago, with the disappointed tone of someone who says, "Guess we'll have to save that kiss for later."

"It's okay, Greg. I get it. Family is important," Tiago answers with a smile.

As he closes the garage doors and wipes the store's shelves with a damp cloth, Greg thinks about the last sentence he heard. For the first time, he sees his distant aunt as family, and not only the owner of the house where he will be living for who-knows-how-long.

———

When Greg comes back inside, Catarina is already showered, a blue towel wrapped around her head, and she's wearing an old T-shirt and sweat shorts. She doesn't look at all like the stately and lively woman he met when he first got here.

"Hey," he says, settling next to her on the couch, but careful not to come too close. "Wanna talk?"

He doesn't know how to approach the your-business-model-is-outdated-and-you-have-an-important-decision-to-make-if-you-want-to-keep-making-money conversation, because nobody wants to hear that kind of advice from a seventeen-year-old.

"Why? Do *you*?" Catarina answers his question with another question. A classic strategy to avoid unwanted conversations.

"No, it's just that . . ." Greg searches for the right words.

"You're in love with Tiago and don't know what to do? I already told you, I'm no good with advice about love. I'm a failure in that, *too*."

The way she says *too* makes Greg pause. Is his aunt saying she's a failure at love *just like he is*, or is she a failure at love *as well as other areas*? Both options are depressing.

But he doesn't linger on it too long because first he needs to refute what his aunt just said.

"Wow, what are you talking about?" he answers with yet another question.

Greg is a quick learner.

"The two boys at my store counter nearly perched on each other, so in love they barely noticed I was standing at the door for almost a full minute," Catarina jokes.

Despite his aunt's laughter, Greg panics for a second. The alert system in his mind blurts out:

"Please don't tell my mom."

"Tell her what? About Tiago?"

"Anything, really. Don't tell her I'm . . ."

"Gay?" Catarina tries not to laugh. "But, my dear, she already knows."

"YOU ALREADY TOLD HER?" Greg yells, squeezing the arm of the couch so hard that his knuckles turn white.

"No! She told *me*. I thought you knew that I knew."

"But how does she know?"

"No cluc! I thought you knew that *she* knew. It's been almost a year. She called asking for advice. People must think that just because I live by myself in a secluded house, I'm freaking Master Yoda."

Greg smiles, feeling a bit relieved, but still worried.

"But she never talked to me about it," he says, looking down.

"Classic Carmem. She doesn't talk about anything. She seems to be allergic to important conversations."

Greg almost says, "Just like you," but he doesn't have the guts.

"Do you know the reason you're taking this 'vacation' here in Lagoa Pequena?" Catarina continues, making air quotes.

"My parents are getting a divorce and they need 'some quiet time to sort it all out,'" Greg answers, mimicking his aunt's air quotes.

"And they've talked to you about that?"

"No. I just overheard the two of them arguing about it in the dining room one day, while I was in the media room."

Catarina tries not to roll her eyes at the fact that her older sister has a dining room *and* a media room.

"You see? She hates important conversations. She's afraid of confrontation. It's been like this our whole lives. When she first started dating your dad, it took her *months* to talk about him at home. Because your dad is, you know . . ."

"Strict?"

"Rich and white," Catarina says. "It was almost as if your mom was ashamed of us. And all of a sudden she started going to fancy parties and golf tournaments and whatever else rich people do."

Greg nods because, well, his dad is the vice president of the Aesthetician Professionals' Golf Club. Or APGC, as the embroidery on his white vice president polo shirt says.

"After our father—your grandfather—passed away," Catarina continues, "I felt there was nothing tying me to São Paulo anymore. So I came here, got away from everything to try and find a little peace."

"And did you?"

As if on cue, Keanu Reeves shows up and jumps on Catarina's lap, snarling softly and asking to be petted.

"I think so. A little bit, at least," his aunt replies, caressing the mutt's head. "But things are changing. It's a little scary."

"What do you mean?" Greg comes closer and strokes the dog, now lying belly up on Catarina's lap.

Being petted by two humans at the same time, Keanu feels the luckiest he's ever been in his whole life.

"For starters, one of these days I woke up and there was a brat living here, and I don't know what to do with him. I'm afraid that if I feed him, he won't want to leave, but I'm not about to let the poor thing starve to death," she mocks.

Greg laughs. "*Seriously*, though, Aunt Catarina. Let's have a *serious* talk!"

Up to this point, this is the most honest conversation he's ever had with an adult in his entire life and, well, he loves it. Greg doesn't ever want to stop having honest conversations with adults.

"You know, Gregório. I know you're not stupid."

"Thank you," he says softly, so as not to interrupt his aunt's train of thought.

"It's been a while since the store was doing well. I take all sorts of gigs to keep the business afloat. And don't even look at me with that face of someone about to suggest I should close the store or turn my garage into an artisanal candle shop because those are always in, and no one will come up with a computer program that can replace artisanal candles."

"Wow, that's so specific."

"It's been suggested many times. The candle thing. The point is that all things lead to giving up being my best option. And I don't give up," she says firmly.

"That sounds like a sentence the hero in an action movie says before he sacrifices himself to save the world."

"And in the end, he saves the world, doesn't he?" Catarina says, raising an eyebrow.

"And you think keeping the store open will save the world?" Greg provokes.

Catarina thinks about it for some time. Usually she hates being provoked, but today she doesn't mind it. It might be the effect of her recent shower, which leaves a soapy smell lingering in the air, or the endorphin released by petting Keanu Reeves, which is still happening, or the simple fact that she *enjoys* her nephew's company.

"I love movies. I like how they're a collective means of entertainment to be enjoyed in silence. I like that many people can watch the same movie and understand it differently, each one with their own thoughts. I like how a list of five favorite movies says more about a person than anything else. I like recommending my favorites and, on the following day, welcoming a thankful client who loved that story as much as I did. I think movies bring people together, but not too much. Just enough. I don't like being too close to a lot of people. Movies allow for that in the right measure. That is why I opened a video rental store. And also, because when I first started, it made a lot of money."

Greg's face lights up. First, because he really likes hearing his aunt talk about something with such excitement, and second, because he's just had an idea. A *good* one. But, if Catarina is like his mom, she can only be convinced through good argumentation. And in order to do that, he will need some help. And a PowerPoint presentation.

JANUARY 24, 2010

Greg wakes up early on Sunday and, with his laptop under his arm, feels more prepared than ever to present his plan to Aunt Catarina. He talked to Tiago and to Sofia Karen and included their suggestions. He worked through the night, reading and rereading his presentation, looking for any weak spots, and coming up with answers for any possible question his aunt might ask. He's ready. More than ready, I'd say.

Quietly, Greg opens his bedroom door and lurks when he hears voices in the living room. Either Keanu learned to talk overnight or there's a man in the living room, his voice timid and deep, chatting with his aunt.

"I don't know, Catarina. His call just caught me by surprise, you know? We haven't seen each other in more than ten years," the voice says. "And I don't want him to think I've been here waiting for him this whole time, and now he can just appear out of nowhere to try and start it all over again."

"But that's what you want, isn't it?" Catarina asks.

The man laughs.

"I don't know. I don't know if I'm still in love with him, or just with the version of him I created in my head."

Greg swallows hard, still hiding behind the door frame. *What kind of a house is this? An Institute for the Care of Confused Gays?*

And, well, I have to admit that being an institute for the care of confused gays doesn't sound half-bad.

"And what do you have to lose? You're almost seventy already!" Catarina says.

"Catarina, I'm *fifty-one!*" the man yells. "Fifty-one."

"Whatever. After thirty I stopped counting the ages in between. I will be thirty-five until I turn forty, then forty-five and so forth. What matters is that this might be your opportunity to live a great romance for the first time without any fear. *How* are you not excited about this? You are the most romantic person I know!"

Greg holds his breath. Whoever this is, he needs to know the outcome of the story of the most romantic man his aunt knows. But Keanu tells on him. Walking down the hall, he lets out an excited bark at Greg that might mean either *What are you doing hiding behind the door crack like a serial killer about to murder your next victim?* or *Please give me food.*

"Gregório?" Catarina calls, suspecting her nephew might be up.

Unable to hide any longer, Greg puffs up his chest, walks out of his bedroom with a few timid steps, and goes into the living room in his old T-shirt and red pajama shorts with a pattern full of little Poké Balls.

His face goes as red as his shorts when Greg sees that the character talking to his aunt is the same as the one who stopped by the shop earlier this week. The man is unnecessarily handsome, his hair arranged in perfect firm curls, his shirt tight enough to show that, despite his fifty-one years of age, he probably seriously *lifts* at the gym.

Greg tries to associate this image with the conversation he just over-heard and can't understand how it's possible that someone like him is just about to live his first great romance. *If I were this handsome*, he thinks, *I would have already lived, like, thirty great romances.*

"This is the famous nephew," Catarina says, pointing at Greg as if he were a new piece of decor that she bought on a trip abroad.

"Hi," Greg greets his aunt's friend, desperate to run back to his room and only leave when he's no longer in Pokémon pajamas.

"A pleasure to meet you . . . Gregório, right?" the man says. "I'm Orlando."

"Orlando is a good friend," Catarina chimes in. "We've known each other since . . . forever? I don't even remember anymore."

"But we only got closer when I opened the store, almost ten years ago," Orlando says.

"When the shop wasn't yet in the garage," Catarina adds.

"My shop was next to yours," Orlando continues, and at this point the conversation is about to become a sketch of alternating sentences—a prospect that completely terrifies Greg.

"What kind of store do you have?" he interrupts the unnecessarily handsome man.

"Flowers," he answers, before he and Catarina start laughing together.

Greg has no idea if the two of them are laughing at the cliché of a sol-itary gay man selling flowers, or if it's the desperate laughter of two friends whose lines of business are extremely complicated. Impossible to know for sure, because Greg has no idea how the flower market is faring. On his end, he's never bought flowers in his life. He almost gets lost in the thought that maybe, just maybe, it would be a good idea to buy flowers for Tiago. But he snaps out of his daydreams and slaps his foot on the floor to remind himself of the reason that made him leave the bedroom with his notebook under his arm on a Sunday morning.

"Aunt Catarina, I have an idea to present to you. For the shop. But we can do it later. Can you let me know when you have a moment?" He says it all at once, getting ready to turn around and go back to his room.

"Tell me now!" his aunt says, in a good mood such as Greg has never seen. "I'm sure Lando will enjoy hearing it, too."

"Well, I've already missed out on today's mass anyway, might as well stay here," Orlando says, and sits on the couch with his legs crossed the way Greg learned from his father to be the "manly" way of crossing legs: an ankle over the other knee.

Catarina laughs again, probably at the sermon comment. Greg is not sure if it was a joke or not, and the way the two of them seem to get along makes him even more insecure. He wasn't ready to present to *two* people.

Catarina sits next to her friend, and they watch Greg walk to the middle of the living room like two proud parents about to see their five-year-old present a poem he just wrote about bees, worms, and mac 'n' cheese.

Propping his open laptop on the coffee table, Greg hits play on the presentation he spent the whole night creating. The first screen shows a photo of Keanu Reeves in *The Matrix*, with sunglasses, but Greg colored one lens red and the other blue to look like those 3D glasses they used to hand out at movie theaters a while ago, when they played poor-quality 3D movies. He thought the actor's image would capture his aunt's attention immediately, and he was not wrong. Catarina is at the edge of the couch, her hands supporting her face, squeezing her eyes to see better when Greg hits the spacebar, and the following text appears on the screen: *Catavento Cinema Club*

Catarina cracks a half smile. Orlando cracks a full smile. It's all Greg needs to feel confident enough to start.

"People don't rent movies anymore," he says. "Nowadays you can find everything online. But what is it that the internet doesn't offer?"

An image of two people hugging as they pop out of computer screens appears. Lord knows what Greg typed in the search field to find such a specific image. Good thing I was already asleep.

"Human interaction. Talking about what they just watched. Debating important subjects and expanding the movie experience."

"That's what the movie theater is for," Catarina says, starting to sound incredulous.

Greg smiles. He hits the spacebar again and the screen goes dark. A text appears in white font: *That's what the movie theater is for.* With another click, the words change slightly: Is *that what the movie theater is for?*

"In the movies, there is no agreement about debate. No one there wants to hear your opinion. Starting a conversation with strangers will just make you seem desperate. But none of that happens here . . ." Dramatic pause. "At Catavento Cinema Club."

The following page is a slide full of text, carefully divided into themes. Greg talks about each of them without having to look at the screen, such is his emotional involvement with the project.

"A monthly, bimonthly, or weekly film club—it'll depend on what you're willing to do. Customers pay for each meeting, but they get a discount if they pay for biannual packages. We set up a projector at the back of the garage to show movies. A comfortable and cozy environment. Snacks and drinks are provided through a commercial partnership with Tiago's mom. I haven't looked into that yet, but he said she'd probably be up for it. Movies carefully chosen by you, Catarina, the most beloved person of all Sunflower Street. Possibly of all Lagoa Pequena. At the end of every meetup, we'll host debate sessions about the movie's main theme. We can offer rental discounts to members who would like to take more films home to expand on the experience."

Greg stops for a breath. His eyes are locked on a stain on the wall right ahead of him, because he's not ready to see his aunt's reaction yet. He moves on to another slide of the presentation and a few uppercase words appear in different fonts:

FRIENDSHIP

EXPERIENCES

MOVIES

SNACKS

PROFIT

Finally, the presentation changes again and the words *Catavento Cinema Club* appear in the middle of the screen, next to the image of a pinwheel (or catavento), but an anthropomorphized version, with buggy eyes and thin arms on what would be its waist.

"Horrible mascot," Catarina says. "Reasonable idea."

Before she's had time to elaborate any further negative comments, Greg raises his arm, as if asking for permission to speak, and as soon as Catarina nods, he launches into his final argument. The one he *knows* his aunt will not counter.

"You will be able to explain *The Lake House* and mediate discussions about the movie, and they will *pay you* to do that." He spits the words out and ends with a smile.

Catarina smiles, too.

Orlando turns up his nose. He probably didn't understand *The Lake House*.

"We can try," Catarina says, her hands on her chin. "But on one condition."

Greg's skin prickles.

Orlando laughs.

Keanu barks.

Catarina looks at her best friend.

"We are going to do a screening in the garage," she says, raising her arm and pointing in the wrong direction, but no one dares correct her because she seems way too determined. "And you are going to invite Roger."

Catarina smirks.

Orlando's skin prickles.

Keanu goes to the kitchen to stare at the window for six minutes as he does every day, probably because he can see spirits visible only to canines.

Greg lets out a confused laugh.

"Who's Roger?" he asks, because the existence of this person suddenly is now the difference between the success or failure of the plan he created to save the store.

"Orlando's ex. From college," Catarina answers, her eyes fixed on her friend. "He's coming back to Lagoa Pequena on vacation. He texted Lando saying he'd like to meet up 'for old times' sake,' and my friend here is terrified."

Greg rolls his eyes. He always thought unnecessarily attractive people weren't afraid of anything.

"So all we need to do is invite this guy and problem solved." Greg looks at Orlando, trying to achieve the right balance of intimidation and plea in his eyes. "Right?"

Orlando has been cornered by his raised-eyebrow best friend and his best friend's cartoon-shorts-wearing nephew. This is one of the most unusual Sunday mornings of his life.

"Can we stop exposing my life now, Catarina?"

"You've just watched a thirteen-year-old make a presentation about how I should manage *my* business. I'm the one being exposed here!" Catarina claims.

Keanu comes back to the living room, barking in agreement because he'll always do anything to defend his owner.

"I am sixteen!" Greg protests.

"You'll have to expose him, too, so everyone is at the same level," Orlando points at Greg with a mischievous smile.

"I'm literally in my underwear!" Greg says.

"He's got a little crush on Tiago, you know," Catarina answers as soon as her nephew is done protesting.

"Tiago, Clélia's son? From the restaurant?" Orlando asks, crossing and uncrossing his legs like someone who needs his body to participate in the gossiping.

Greg feels his face burn of embarrassment, but he also feels something good. The comfortable sensation of seeing two adults talk about the boy he has a crush on so naturally, as if he were a kid who just said something about his little girlfriend at school. As if liking Tiago was something *to be expected* instead of *condemned*, as if it were something *easy*. Which makes him think that maybe it really is after all.

After a lifetime of uncomfortable dinners with his parents and conversations about how celebrities he doesn't know are undergoing surgical procedures he doesn't want to know about, Greg feels welcomed right as he's being categorically embarrassed by his own aunt and a gay adult stranger who is, among all the things a gay adult stranger can be, a *florist*.

"Let's be practical," Greg says, trying to divert the attention to a subject that actually matters. "We are going to need comfortable chairs, a good deep cleaning in the garage, flyers to announce it around the neighborhood, a projector, and, I don't know, a white sheet maybe?"

"I have the white sheet," Catarina says, shaking her shoulders.

"I think I can get the chairs," Orlando adds.

"I'll take care of the rest," Greg asserts, trying to sound a lot more confident than he really feels.

"Even the projector? Isn't that an . . . expensive thing?" Catarina asks, worrying for the first time about the possibility that she will have to spend money to make her nephew's fanciful idea work.

"My best friend is also kind of my personal assistant. She can help me with this."

"Personal assistant? *Pffff.* Is that what they call nannies nowadays?" Orlando jokes, taking an excessive liberty with this kid he just met.

"My family is kind of weird," Catarina whispers to Orlando.

"Technically she's more my dad's nanny than mine."

"Told you, *super* weird," Catarina whispers again.

"Sofia Karen will help me with the expensive things, Tiago will work on the sign—I hope he's better at drawing than at playing tennis—and the two of you . . . I don't know. Just be ready on the day of the first screening," Greg commands, feeling like the adult in the room.

"And that will be on the . . ." Orlando starts.

"You tell me. On the day your love from the past returns to the city. Isn't that what we agreed?" Catarina provokes.

"He's coming on Friday," Orlando answers.

"Which is in, like . . . five days?" Greg asks, already knowing the answer.

The three of them fall silent, each for a different reason.

Catarina because she realizes that the days are passing quickly, and sooner or later her nephew is going away, leaving behind a responsibility that she doesn't know if she wants for herself.

Orlando because, in less than a week, will be seeing the man he loved the most in his entire life, and he has no idea how things might work out for the two of them. *If* they work out at all in the first place.

And Greg, poor thing, because he realizes that a countdown started blinking over his head and he needs to seize every second in Lagoa Pequena to save his aunt's store and, if it's not asking too much, to kiss a guy for the first time. He feels discouraged at the possibility of his plan not working out.

Greg needs to rush, but before that, he needs to think. He shoves the laptop under his arm and turns around to go back to his bedroom.

"I can make this work," he murmurs, and forces a smile, even though he knows the two adults can't see his face anymore. I think the forced smile is for himself.

"Hey, Greg," Catarina calls him in a sweet voice, *almost* tenderly.

"Yeah," he answers, still with his back to her.

"Don't forget to remove that horrible pinwheel mascot. Please."

Greg smiles.

Keanu barks.

"Keanu would be a much better mascot!" Orlando says.

"You two are right," Greg says.

And this time, his smile is genuine.

JANUARY 25, 2010

On Monday morning, Greg wakes up early with a million things on his mind as he tries to balance the excitement of seeing Tiago and the bitter taste caused by the premonition that his days in Lagoa Pequena might be nearing an end.

He inspects every detail of the small bedroom where he's spent the last few days and wonders what will happen to his aunt after he's gone.

She will survive, of course. And so will Greg. But he has the feeling that, for some reason, this is one of those moments that will change the way he sees the world. It's a common feeling among humans. It happens when they fall in love for the first time, or when they lose someone important. When they choose a profession, or when they learn how to say no to things that they don't want to do. It happens to houses, too. When your porch is turned into a garage, when your garage is turned into a video rental store, when a new resident arrives and an old one leaves. These moments are often quick, but they leave a new mark on the line of our existence. And the mark Greg is about to make in my history is still a mystery to me.

Catarina knocks softly on the door and scares her nephew, who didn't expect someone calling on him this early. It's not even eight in the morning, and the shop won't open until nine.

"Gregório," she says behind the door. "Are you awake? Your mom is on the phone."

That takes him by surprise. Last week, his mom called three times (and his dad, zero). In all the calls, she talked only to his aunt, asked how Greg was doing, if they needed anything, and, in the final seconds, sent his son a kiss and said she missed him.

Greg never felt like talking to his mom because he didn't see a need for it. With their constant important family travels, it's not as if they weren't already used to being away many days at a time.

"Coming," Greg says, running his fingers through his hair to untangle the curls and exhaling on his hand to see if his breath smells like he just woke up. The answer is yes, obviously. And that makes him a bit more insecure about talking to his mom, because he's afraid that, even through the call, she might notice that her son is not as impeccable as she likes.

"Hi, Mom," Greg says, after stumbling out of bed to get the cordless phone from his aunt, who has been patiently waiting for him by the door.

"Morning, son. I'm sorry to call so early. I woke you, didn't I?" Her voice is a little more tender than usual. But just a little.

"You did," Greg lies because, for some reason, he wants his mother to feel guilty.

"I'm sorry. Today is going to be a long day, I have to deal with . . . a lot of things. I thought I'd talk to you before I got too busy."

Getting a divorce from my dad and pretending that nothing is happening, Greg thinks.

"I just wanted to hear your voice," Carmem continues. "Is everything all right over there?"

"Yes. Very good. The city is great," Greg says, even though he barely knows the city.

"Is your aunt too bossy?" his mom asks, with a laugh in the end.

"No. She's actually one of the sweetest people I've ever met." Greg maintains his mini-aggression strategy because, once he's started, he can't stop himself.

His mom goes silent for a few seconds, as if she were choosing the following words carefully so as not to show she was jealous of Catarina. I'm sure she was. At the door, Keanu sniffs and growls. He's sure, too.

"You'll be back next week, right?" his mom asks.

"I am? I don't know. No one told me anything."

"I asked your dad to tell the secretary to buy the return ticket and let you know."

Just like Keanu, Greg growls. But the sound is not loud enough for his mom to be able to hear it from the other side. He hates it when she calls Sofia Karen a secretary.

"I'll check with her, then," Greg says, trying to end the call. "I'll let you know if anything comes up."

He won't.

"I miss you," Carmem says.

"Me too," Greg lies.

He ends the call and throws himself dramatically on the bed, like any sixteen-year-old gay teenager who just discovered that life can be a lot lighter away from the pressure of being the perfect son. He doesn't *hate* his family. But he doesn't *miss* them, either. Lying in bed and staring at the ceiling, Greg feels guilty for thinking something like this; after all, we have to love our families, right? But another part of his brain, the part that wished he never had to go back home, reasons that Catarina is his family, too. And maybe he could just . . . stay here? Forever?

With an awkward little jump, Keanu Reeves climbs on the bed, licks Greg's face, and snaps him out of his trance of important thoughts.

One week, he thinks. One week to make the best film club ever created in Lagoa Pequena. One week to show his aunt that everything is not lost. One week to help Orlando reunite with his great love. One week, god willing, to kiss Tiago and settle the issue of the First Kiss once and for all.

And, as with any revolutionary act, this one also starts with a risky move.

Monday, January 25, 2010. 8:23 a.m.
From: geodude1993@email.com
To: skaren@brittobeauty.com.br
Subject: I have a plan

Hey, Sofia! How are things over there? A lot has happened here (no kiss) (almost!), but I will update you later. Right now, I need your help.

Do you think you can buy a projector on my dad's credit card and have it delivered here in Lagoa Pequena?

I'll explain everything later.

From your friend who needs you more than anything in this moment,
GB

BETO

It's been more than a week since Beto and Lara committed to get to know each other. Eight straight days in which they tried hard to do something different every day. Long enough that Beto doesn't have a clue what else to do. Besides the cursed cookies that left the kitchen smelling of smoke for three days, they've already tried to put together a five-thousand-piece puzzle, tie-dye a T-shirt, turn the T-shirt into a pillowcase because it was too ugly to wear, play a board game that Beto got for his eleventh birthday but had never taken out of his closet, make flan, cook beans, listen to a new podcast, *record* a podcast together, and make friendship bracelets with colorful elastic string.

Half of the things worked out, the other half not so much. Helena forbade them to cook anything without her supervision, and today, Labor Day, the three residents are plopped in the living room, each one thinking of what the perfect holiday would look like if the world weren't going through all this.

For Beto, a solo trip to a new place, with landscapes to photograph and a soft hotel bed waiting for him at the end of the day.

For Lara, an evening out dancing with friends until her hair dripped with sweat, waking up the next morning unable to remember a single thing, and eating yesterday's pizza for breakfast.

For Helena, an afternoon at a spa, no children and no worries. Nothing but aromatic candles and a masseur attractive enough to have walked out of a romantic movie about finding love after forty.

For the first time since Lara arrived, the family of three is together, has no plans, and is free to enjoy one another's company. The TV is off because, at this point, no one feels like dealing with the news. The family made an unspoken agreement that the holiday *also* means taking a break from daily reminders that the outside world is still awful. The calm silence doesn't last long before it starts to get uncomfortable. Someone needs to say something, and the three of them speak at the same time.

"I've been feeling kind of ugly," Lara says.

"Honey, when are you going to dye my hair?" Helena questions.

"What are we having for lunch?" Beto asks.

"We could dye it today," Lara suggests.

"Let's order takeout because I don't want to cook," Helena declares.

"I feel ugly every day," Beto comments.

In a flurry of questions, answers, and people speaking over one another, the family makes a decision. Helena calls a restaurant and orders three dishes. Lara puts on her mask and reasonably clean clothes to go to the pharmacy for hair dye, and Beto just stares at his phone, waiting for an answer to the *good morning* he texted Nicolas, since there's nothing left for him to do.

No answer arrives in the time it takes Lara to leave and come back, looking like someone who just ransacked a pharmacy during a zombie apocalypse.

"Christ, honey, how many people are dyeing their hair?" Helena jokes.

"Three, of course," Lara says, not sounding *at all* like she's joking.

"NO!" Beto yells right as lunch arrives.

———

During the family meal, Lara makes a list of arguments to convince Beto that dyeing his hair is, in fact, an excellent idea:

1. The siblings need something new to do today. He's never dyed his hair, and she's never dyed someone *else's* hair.

2. If he doesn't like it, it's not as if anyone is going to see it. The way things are going, the color will have faded before anyone is seen in public again.

3. "You can always wear a hat!"

4. There's no such thing as "not looking good in a hat." It's a piece of clothing. Like, I don't know, *pants*. Everyone looks good in pants.

5   External changes can trigger internal changes. Seeing yourself in a new way might help you see your problems from a different perspective and bring a bit of emotional stability.

Beto believes his sister completely made up the last argument, but since his mother, the psychologist in the room, doesn't argue, and all Beto wants is for Lara to stop bugging him, he says yes.

He may be a stubborn and determined kid, but he's *terrible* at saying no.

Beto's phone vibrates on the table.

Nico

Morning! Just woke up. Excited for another day locked in at my place.

Beto

My sister decided she's going to dye my hair

I couldn't say no

I'm sure I'll regret this

Nico

AAAAAA LOVE IT

What color?

"What color?" Beto asks out loud, without taking his eyes off the phone.

"I bought a bunch because I want some highlights in my hair," Lara answers. "So you get to choose between green, blue, or purple."

"Whoa, I get to *choose*? That's a new one," Beto teases.

Beto

Green, blue, or purple

I get to choose

Nico

Do a survey on your profile

> Sure, my ten followers that actually interact with me are gonna LOVE it

> I vote purple

Beto squirms in his chair as he accepts that, soon enough, his hair will be a different color because he's tired of arguing with his sister, and the color will be purple because the boy he likes picked it. He feels a little frustrated when he realizes that it's been some time since his choices were actually his. But then again, this is more comfortable. Isn't it?

———

"It's the BEST!" Lara shouts, leaning on Beto's shoulders as he stares at himself in the bathroom mirror.

"I look like a Care Bear," Beto points out, his mouth hanging open.

"Why do you say that like it's a *bad* thing?"

Beto is the first in the family to complete his makeover. Partly because his hair is short and *partly* because Lara was very excited to see her brother with purple hair and started with him. Helena is in the living room reading a magazine, her hair wrapped in aluminum foil. His sister is still working on her own hair and Beto needs a moment to absorb it all. He subtly excuses himself (by pushing Lara out of the bathroom and locking the door) and spends a good amount of time staring at his reflection.

This is one of my favorite parts about being a house: I have mirrors. I would be a *house of mirrors* if I had the option. Because there are always two sides to every person: the public side that everyone sees and knows, and the private side, which is intimate and personal. Put a person alone in a room with a mirror and a hidden camera, and you're guaranteed to have a good time. And since my very *existence* is like being a hidden camera, I'm always having fun.

Beto is the kind of person who tests his angles. Normally he turns his head from one side to the other, trying to feel good about what he sees. He puts his hand on his chin. Makes an angry face sometimes. Projects his lips outward a little, imagining what they'd look like if they were fuller. Then he tightens his lips to make them look thinner. He thinks that, if he were a lot skinnier, maybe he'd look like that guy who played Spider-Man in one of the fifteen Spider-Man movies.

But today all he sees is his hair. Lara did a good job, he can't deny it. For a home makeover in which his body was wrapped in an old sheet and his sister wore plastic bags over her hands because she forgot to buy disposable gloves, it's *technically* a very good result.

But it has completely changed his face. As he inspects himself, Beto tries to decide whether the change is for the better. He turns to the side, runs his fingers through the wavy strands of hair, turns his back to the mirror, and spins around suddenly, pretending to catch his reflection by surprise. He whispers, "Hi, nice to meet you. I'm Roberto, but you can call me Beto, that's what everyone calls me," as if introducing himself for the first time. He smiles. Pretends to laugh. Slowly licks his lips to see if the hairdo has added any sensuality to his personality. He laughs out loud as he determines it hasn't. He feels ridiculous, but he's having more fun than he has had in months.

Beto pulls his phone from his pocket and takes a few selfies. He tries not to think *too* much about it. He picks a random one and sends it to Nicolas.

Beto

> Do you approve? 😉

He immediately regrets the wink. The purple hair makes him feel a *little* cooler, but not cool enough to not rethink absolutely every single interaction with Nico.

Beto gets out of the bathroom and is welcomed with smiles. His mom compliments him with a disproportionate intensity, as if he has just won the Nobel Prize in Dyed Hair. And Lara is proud of her work.

"All right, I have to hand it to you. I like it," Beto admits.

And when his phone vibrates with a new message from Nico, he barely notices Lara capturing his reaction. He doesn't notice anything else, in fact, because he's too busy smiling goofily at the screen.

Nico

> Who would've thought you could look even more handsome?

———

Beto and Lara are ready to go to bed. It's almost midnight, and despite feeling like he spent the whole day in a beauty salon, Beto is happy. Light. Carefree, even. He tries to face the fact that the world remains chaotic and today was just a good, unusual day. Beto does that to diminish his happiness a little, because he has this complicated habit of thinking that feeling good is a sign that soon everything will get worse. But even when he tries hard to think of all the bad things that might happen, he knows he will remember today for some time. He knows that, in the future, this will be one of those days that evoke a thought like *Ah, remember that day when I was all happy over such a silly thing?* And, in a reality where the world is so full of bad news, it's good to have days like today to remember.

"I think you're gonna like this," Lara says, lying on the mattress next to Beto and angling her phone so he can see the screen.

Beto inspects the image. It's a picture. A picture of *him.*

"Let me see it," he says, grabbing the device from her hands.

It's the photo she took in the living room earlier. Beto can barely recognize himself. He doesn't like seeing photos of himself, and this might be why he's always preferred to be behind the camera. He also doesn't really like his arms and how his shoulders always look slumped. He doesn't like his double chin and how it becomes all the more evident when he smiles. He doesn't like phone cameras that blur the background because he knows the blurring is created by artificial intelligence and not by a lens. The outline always looks weird, and the photographer always thinks themself a professional just because they pushed a button to create the effect.

The photo he looks at now has all of it: his arms, the slumped shoulders, the double chin, a too-broad smile, all of him, his head tilted down looking at his phone, and the damn background blur.

And yet, he likes what he sees. It might seem crazy, but Beto *loves* the photo. He really does.

"When did you take it?"

"Earlier today. I was just going to send it to Gi, my roommate, because she wanted to dye her hair last year, but she was too scared to do it at home. I just wanted to prove to her that, with a few video tutorials and patience, I can do *anything*. Except I thought the photo looked really nice. I didn't even know you were capable of smiling like this," she teases.

"Lara! I smile all the time!" Beto defends himself, even though he knows that's not true.

"You laugh at your own sarcastic comments as if you were living in a monologue inside your own head. That is not the same as smiling," she explains.

"I don't do that!" Beto continues to defend himself, even though he knows Lara is absolutely right.

Lara laughs. "Ah, Beto, I don't know, maybe just accept the compliment like anyone else."

"So give me an *actual* compliment. 'I didn't even know that behind all the sadness and darkness of your soul there was still a smile fighting its way into existence' is not the best compliment you can give someone," he says, making his voice higher-pitched for a terrible imitation of his sister.

"You're right," Lara agrees, and sits up cross-legged, closes her eyes for a few seconds, and takes a deep breath. "You look so handsome in this photo, little brother," she continues, a little forced, but with genuine love.

"Thank you, dear sister," Beto counters in the same tone.

And, somehow, the two of them are finally speaking in the same dialect. In tune.

"I sent you the photo," Lara says, lying on her side and getting ready to sleep.

Riding on the serotonin in his body and the rare moment of self-esteem, Beto publishes the photo on his profile without worry, since no one will be interested in seeing his new hair. He completely ignores how the blurred background captured by a phone camera clashes with his own carefully taken, well-edited, and *nearly* professional photos. He types, *I dyed my hair, do you like it?* then deletes it. Then types, *Today was a good day*, and deletes it. Finally, he throws in the towel and settles for a bunch of grape and purple heart emojis. He doesn't know why he even *tries* to come up with captions.

MAY 8, 2020

Beto feels invincible.

It's hard to believe that—even after nearly two months without leaving the house, with his plans completely ruined, no prospects for the near future (or the far-off future, come to think of it), and the whole world marching straight toward unprecedented chaos—he could be happy.

Beto feels handsome, his photos are getting more attention than usual, his daily routine with Lara is light and pleasant, his mom has been doing a better job balancing her work hours so she can spend more time with the family, and Nicolas is still Nicolas (available, fun, unbearably handsome, and kind).

It's almost three on a Friday afternoon, and Lara is already done with work. It's all still a mystery to Beto: his sister's work routine, and how she manages to afford a life in a major city simply by writing things online, but he's given up on trying to understand.

The two of them are drinking café com leite, each in a corner of the couch, their faces buried in their respective cell phones. Someone watching from a distance might mistake them for strangers, but in the duo's dynamic this basically qualifies as spending time together.

Beto snaps a photo of his white coffee mug with WHAT WOULD JESUS BREW? in bold red letters. This was a gift from one of his mom's patients and he loves to use it ironically. He sends the photo to Nico, who almost immediately texts back a photo of a yellow coffee mug with I LOVE TUESDAYS printed next to a drawing of a cat wearing sunglasses.

Beto

That is SO specific. Who LOVES Tuesdays?

Nico

My mom has a collection with every single weekday

I only know what day it is thanks to the mugs. The pandemic has left me with no sense of reality

Beto

Nicolas, it's Friday

Nico

Oh no.

Beto's laughter is louder than usual, which catches Lara's attention.

"Who's this boy?" she says.

"What are you talking about?"

"The boy you spend the whole day talking to with your face glued to the phone."

"Lara, you really *are* turning into Mom."

"Don't change the subject, I'm talking to you," she insists, putting her own phone inside her bra and crossing her arms.

Beto points at Lara's bra and starts laughing because, well, their mother does the exact same thing. Lara laughs, too, because not even she can deny the resemblance.

"I'm being serious, Roberto!" Lara says mid-laugh. "I know there's a boy somewhere on that phone. No one smiles this much at a screen for no reason."

"His name is Nicolas," Beto answers, rolling his eyes to pretend he's just giving in to his sister's pressure.

But, deep down—*deep* deep down—he *wants* to talk about Nico. Because Nico has never been the subject of conversation with anyone in "real life." Because he thinks that, somehow, talking about Nico out loud will bring him closer.

Unfortunately, it will not.

Not the way Beto wants it.

But, in a way, it actually will.

I don't know how these things work.

I'm a house, I only know about practical things.

"And *Nicolas* is . . ." Lara says slowly, while moving her fingers as if she were teaching words to a child who still doesn't yet know how to talk.

"Nice?" Beto answers, slightly regretting playing into Lara's game.

Within thirty seconds, he realizes he can't talk about Nicolas out loud. He has no idea what to say. He's never talked about boys with anyone.

"You've never talked about boys with anyone, have you?" Lara infers.

"Okay! He's nice. And super fun. We met online because of *Figures on the Edge*—"

"The ice-skating show that got canceled?" Lara interrupts.

"There was no need to mention the canceled part, but yes, that one," Beto answers, slightly annoyed.

"Sorry, sorry. Keep going," she says, sipping her café com leite that must be cold already, but Lara doesn't mind because she loves chaos.

"Uh, that's kind of it. I think I just like him, I don't know. I can't tell. It's complicated. I think he likes me. He always sends signals."

"Uh, I *love* signals! Does he lean forward just to come closer to you? Does his hug last longer than a normal hug should when the two of you meet up?"

Beto swallows hard. He feels like *such* an idiot.

"We've never seen each other." He spits the words out in a barely audible whisper.

"What?" Lara comes closer to his brother to hear him better.

"WE'VE NEVER SEEN EACH OTHER!" Beto yells, not aggressively, just as someone who has completely lost control.

"Shhh," Helena hisses from the bedroom-office where she's seeing a patient.

"But where does he live?" Lara whispers, her face almost glued to Beto's.

"Brasília," he answers, also in a whisper, as if he were telling his sister a secret.

"Oh damn," Lara says in a regular tone of voice, completely giving up on the whispering. "I mean, it's not *that* far, but still, it's not as if people are seeing each other in person a lot these days, right? You know, even if he lived right here on Sunflower Street, it's not as if the two of you would be *able* to see each other in person now."

Beto's heart hurts with a pang when he imagines a scenario in which Nicolas lives "right here, on Sunflower Street." He would probably break *every single* COVID protocol just to see that smile up close.

"And, look, even when all this is over, plane tickets go on sale all the time. And credit card points. You can do a *lot* with points. I bought a stand mixer using points, can you believe it? Didn't spend even *one* real. It's like fake money," Lara continues, not knowing when to stop talking.

She can talk too much when she's nervous.

And she's nervous because her brother is in love with a boy who lives far away.

And she *knows* how painful that can be.

"Fine, Lara. It's not as if we're getting married tomorrow, I don't know. He doesn't even know I like him."

"You don't send signals, too?" Lara asks, curiously.

"Sometimes. I don't know," Beto answers, scratching his elbow.

"Give it to me, let me see it," Lara says, pointing at his brother's phone.

Beto lets out a hearty laugh. He really laughs, like someone who just heard the world's best joke. He's not acting. Either that or he's a really good actor (which he is not. Case in point: the times when he turns his back to the bathroom mirror and tries to catch his own reflection by surprise).

"I'm not going to show you our conversation," he finally says. "What kind of person *asks* to see someone else's phone?"

"I don't know, all my girlfriends?" Lara comments, feeling slightly offended.

"I'm not your girlfriend. I'm your *brother*. And there are things in here"—Beto taps his finger on the phone screen—"that, once seen, cannot ever be unseen."

Lara believes her brother is referring to *naughty* conversations.

Beto is in fact referring to all his failed attempts at leading the conversation in a romantic direction, which always end up with him feeling humiliated and changing the subject with memes.

"I think you should be direct with him," Lara comments as if this were the most obvious solution.

"Huh?"

"Tell him how you feel, I don't know. As difficult as it seems, at least things are easier after a conversation. After all, you can *feel* it, can't you?"

"Feel what?"

"That he likes you back, silly."

Beto thinks about it for some time. He believes so, but he's terrified of being wrong.

Every time Beto has tried to list all his fears, he's lost count after item thirty-two. His fear of rejection is almost as intense as his fear of confirmation. If Nico says no, everything will change between them. But if he says yes, everything will *also* change. And despite having spent the past three months counting the days till he can move to another city, Beto is not a fan of change. Not the kind that involves a relationship with the only guy his age who is fun, attractive, kind, and talks to him for hours and hours without either of them feeling bored.

It all must mean something, right? Beto believes it *must* mean something.

But he's terrified of discovering what.

"Come on!" Lara says, crossing her legs and rolling up imaginary sleeves because she's wearing a short-sleeved shirt. "Every time I need to make a hard decision, I consider what is the best and worst that could happen."

Beto holds his tongue and doesn't say that this is literally what any judicious person does, and that she should stop talking as if she had invented the list of pros and cons just to sound wiser and more mature. He remains silent because he knows Lara only wants to help.

"What is the *worst* that could happen?"

"Hmm." Beto tries hard to imagine the worst possible scenario. It's easy, but it hurts. "He could think it was delusional of me to imagine there was something between the two of us. And he might be all, 'I think we should stop speaking for a while,' and disappear from my life forever until we meet again in the future on some other app that probably won't be any of the ones that we have now. I'll look at all his photos—or holograms, because maybe holograms will be more common in the future—and I'll die of jealousy when I see him with a husband who's not me, and children who are not mine."

"Wow, that's intense," Lara says with a half smile, trying to focus on the conversation, but her mind is totally distracted by the whole holo-gram affair. "And what is the *best* that can happen?"

"Maybe he also likes me?" Beto says, his voice high-pitched, almost laughing at the absurd thing he just said.

"Oh, come on, Roberto! You're more creative than this."

"Fine," Beto says, and dries the sweat from his forehead with the back of his hand because this is a hard conversation. Beto hates hard conversa-tions. "He might like me. And then we'll talk a lot about what we are going to do with all these feelings. When all this is over, we meet up for the first time, and then we see if he *really* likes me, because it's different in person, you know? And, in the best-case scenario, he also loves me in person. Like, literally loves me. He says he loves me two seconds after his eyes meet mine because he can't hold it back any longer. All this hap-pens *at the airport*. Then we stop at a doughnut shop that he always talks about in the Brasília airport. I've seen photos, the doughnuts are extremely beautiful. He says, 'Hold on, I'll get us some,' then comes back with a box. When I open it, I find a chocolate doughnut with pink icing that reads, *Beto, will you be my boyfriend?* I say yes, and we'll laugh about it for years. We live happily ever after. We get an Uber out of the airport."

"Jesus," Lara says.

"Sorry. We get an Uber out of the airport and *then* we live happily ever after. I switched the order of events."

"Did you think of all that . . . just now?"

No. Beto has been scripting this moment in his head in various ways for months now. He has created a playlist that lasts the dura-tion of the trip from Lagoa Pequena to Brasília. He even knows what he's going to *wear* when he meets Nicolas for the first time.

"Yeah, just thought of it."

"I might be wrong, but I think that even if it goes the worst possible way, he deserves to know how you feel," Lara says. "It's a good feeling. And I think that in the middle of all that we're living through, everyone needs something to feel good about."

Beto lets out a long sigh and runs his hands over his purple hair. He'd never thought about it that way. He'd never looked at these feelings as a *good* thing. To Beto, love has always been like a ticking time bomb that creates more and more tension as time passes, ready to explode at any moment. And when it does, it destroys everything.

"Besides," Lara continues. "That could be today's new thing. Declaring your feelings to someone for the first time."

Beto laughs.

"*Pfff.* Yeah, right. And what would *your* new thing be?"

"Watching my brother declare his feelings to someone for the first time, of course!"

"Not a *chance*," he replies. "If I'm doing this, I'll do it by myself."

He gets up from the couch with his head up, runs to his bedroom, and closes the door behind him.

Lara cracks a smile.

In his bedroom, Beto stares at his phone screen.

This is a good feeling. This is a good feeling. This is a good feeling.

He takes a deep breath, gathering all the courage deep within himself. He was doing so well when the day started! He felt invincible! Where did all that courage go?

His hands sweaty, Beto types a message with trembling fingers.

Beto

Hey

Nico

Hey there

Beto didn't expect such a quick reply. He doesn't know what to do. Time passes, one minute, or two. Or five.

Nico

Beto?

Beto

Nothing serious

Just wanted to know what your favorite cheese is

Nico

Provolone

Or requeijão, if you consider a spread to be a type of cheese!

It's annoying how Nicolas has an answer for everything. How he doesn't need more than ten seconds to decide what his favorite cheese is.

Beto feels his stomach doing cartwheels and tying up in a knot just from imagining the possibility of Nicolas having a quick answer for his *good feelings*.

> **Beto**
> Good choice!
> I need to go take care of something
> Talk to you later

Embarrassed to death, Beto hides his phone inside his drawer as if he were able to hide from Nicolas. His courage left him, and Beto doesn't know if it will return tomorrow.

MAY 9, 2020

It didn't.

MAY 10, 2020

Not yet.

MAY 11, 2020

> **Beto**
> Hey, Nico. Are you around?
> I wanted to chat
> Nothing serious. Maybe a little
> But nothing URGENT
> Just a little

ANA

When Monday comes, Ana's fingers no longer have nails.

The last few days were busy, and my two residents dedicated a lot of time to packing their things. With every drawer they discover just how much of themselves existed here. Celso is an expert at moving, and throughout his life he has lived in over ten different neighborhoods in Lagoa Pequena (that is, nearly all of them). But this is Ana's first move. Everything she owns is here, and it is emotionally exhausting for her to decide what goes and what gets thrown away.

Ana's bedroom doesn't seem like hers anymore. The books and CDs that took over most of the space are all put away, except for Ana's current read (*The Tale of the Body Thief* by Anne Rice) and some CDs that she still listens to before bed (including the new Blink-182 album that will finally be returned to its owner tonight). The walls that were once covered in posters and magazine cutouts are now bare, and the matte white walls with a few tape markings at the corners are a little scary. There's almost nothing left of Ana here.

In the kitchen, most of the utensils are packed in bubble wrap and newspaper. The bare minimum for two people is still out: two plates, two glasses, and two forks in the dish rack. This makes Celso think that it might be possible to restart life in another city with just two plates, two glasses, and two forks. He hates doing the dishes as much as his daughter does.

The upside of inviting Letícia for dinner in the middle of the moving process is that the living room finally *looks* like a living room. All of Celso's computer parts are packed, and the dinner table is back to performing its original function. Ana bought candles (beautiful and aromatic, not the kind you use when the power goes out) and Celso even bought flowers from the Sunday street market. I can't remember the last time someone brought real flowers to my interior!

(To be honest, yes, I do. I remember everything, actually. In 1982 I had a resident who was obsessed with flowers. Her name was Elis and she lived here for four and a half years, until she met a handsome baker and moved to Italy with him after two months of dating. I hope she's well.)

"Do you have any idea how the two of you are going to deal with . . . it all?" Celso asks that afternoon as Ana looks at herself in the bathroom mirror and, for the first time in her life, tries to shape her eyebrows.

"You mean, if we're going to try and stay together?" Ana asks, impatient toward her father and her eyebrows.

"I don't know, there are ways to make it work. I don't want to seem like I'm intruding or anything, but—"

"Already intruding . . ."

"Brasil Online!" Celso kind of yells, as if he expected these words to make sense to his daughter. "Now there are free webmail services for anyone. Have you thought about it, honey? It's free, fast, and safe."

"I have my doubts about the 'safe' portion," Ana says.

"All Letícia needs is a computer and internet access and—*poof.*" Celso makes a gesture with his hands that appears to be an attempt to mimic a magician revealing his trick. "You're immediately connected."

After ripping out another hair from her right eyebrow, Ana analyzes it calmly in the mirror to see if the shape looks like the left one. It doesn't.

"Letícia doesn't have a computer at home, Dad. There's only one at school, and it's locked away in the principal's office. People still think computers are the mark of the beast, or a way for the government to control our lives, or something. You are the exception," Ana says, sounding a little harsher than the situation demands and immediately regretting it.

"I'm just trying to help," Celso says, genuinely concerned. "I don't know, it's as if the two of you are a romantic soap opera I'm following, and I'm rooting for a happy ending."

"Dad, you don't like soap operas *or* romance," Ana reminds him, unable to hold back a laugh.

"Don't I?" Celso says, wiggling his eyebrows up and down in that way that seems bizarre when dads do it, and then he disappears into his bedroom.

"Come back here!" Ana yells.

"Free webmail for all!" Celso yells back, making absolutely no sense.

Ana gives up on plucking her eyebrows; she even regrets having started it. If Letícia really loves her, she won't mind such a ridiculous detail.

"Oh my god, what have you done to your eyebrows?" is the first thing Letícia says when Ana opens the door.

Ana feels her face burning in shame and covers her forehead with her hands.

"No, no," Letícia says desperately. "I didn't mean you look ugly. Just . . . different. It's just that, well, it's on your face. It's not as if you have fake nails or something, that would have taken longer to notice. But the eyebrows are right there, on top of your eyes. And if the eyes are windows into the soul, then what are the eyebrows? Maybe the roof of the soul? No, I think hair is the roof. Eyebrows would be like the gutters that collect rainwater. God, what am I saying?"

Ana laughs, and she can already feel how much she will miss Letícia's word-vomit in her life.

"I think those would be the lashes," she answers.

"What's that?"

"The gutters are the lashes. Because without them the tears would stream straight down your face."

"But rain doesn't come out of the windows," Letícia counters.

"You better come inside." Ana steps aside, opening the way to her girl-friend and finally putting an end to this crazy conversation that wasn't going anywhere.

"Let's start over," Letícia says, stepping in. "You look beautiful!"

"You too," Ana answers as she looks Letícia up and down.

Ana really looks beautiful, wearing a loose black dress with white polka-dots, tights, and ankle boots (despite feeling a little ridiculous about wearing boots to dinner in her own living room). Her hair gently tumbles down her shoulders, and someone looking at it might think she spent hours at a beauty salon getting it done when she simply washed it.

The wonders that water and shampoo can perform!

Letícia is wearing jean shorts that look new, very old red Converse sneakers, and a light, flowy yellow top, tied with a knot slightly above her belly button, which gives Ana a slight glimpse of her belly. Her curly hair is tied in a ponytail right at the top of her head, and the only makeup she's wearing is the lip gloss Ana loves because it tastes like watermelon, and it makes their kisses just the right amount of sticky.

Ana could kiss this girl for hours without feeling time pass. She could start right now, except that her dad is still home. It's one thing to tell her dad about her girlfriend, but to kiss her in front of him is a totally different one. That would be too weird.

"Look who's here!" Celso says when he appears in the living room, dragging Ana away from her thoughts about lip gloss and Letícia's belly button.

The two girls look at Celso in shock because (1) he's not wearing the '98 World Cup hat (which particularly shocks Letícia, who had always believed Celso was bald and wore the hat to hide it, but he actually has a lot of hair and the hat is a choice), and (2) Celso is ready to go out, wearing a button-down shirt, khaki pants, and, believe it or not, dress shoes.

"Dad?" Ana asks, as if she were trying to confirm that it is really the same old Celso.

"Looking good, eh, big guy!" Letícia comments, immediately

regretting having crossed a line that she doesn't know if Celso is ready to cross with her.

"You think only the two of you deserve a special evening?" Celso says, holding the collar of his dress shirt and turning around, which is embarrassing and very sweet at the same time. "I'm going out to say goodbye, too."

"Hmm, who is she?" Letícia wants to know.

"Probably the friends who play RPGs with him every month at the public library," Ana whispers.

Celso doesn't answer, and after a kiss on Ana's forehead and another on Letícia's, he leaves them to solve the mystery by themselves.

"Wow, that was weird," Ana says.

"The forehead kiss? I thought it was sweet. And he didn't make a face when I called him *big guy*. That's a good thing, right?" Letícia comments, throwing herself on the couch. "Calling another adult Dad always seemed like such a distant concept. I don't know, I have the craziest ideas!"

Ana smiles and the two of them go silent, letting the idea that this is a goodbye dinner settle in slowly.

"There's fish," Ana says, desperate to dissipate the sadness in the air.

"Huh?"

"Trout. My dad bought it for us at All About Trout. No one in this household knows how to make fish."

"Uh, fancy! My mom went there with my dad in one of her attempts to save their marriage through expensive food. She said it's unbearable— they were playing the violin the entire time!" Letícia says.

"No live music here today, the violinist couldn't fit us in his schedule," Ana jokes, but she doesn't leave Letícia enough time to laugh before adding, "I'll set the table, then."

"Hey!" Letícia calls out. "Take it easy, there's no rush. Come stay with me for a little bit," she says, patting the couch next to her as if commanding a dog to come up, but in a romantic way. I can never understand the difference.

Ana runs and snuggles with her girlfriend on the couch, brings her head next to Letícia's chest, and listens to her heart beating.

"The two of us all dolled up just to stay in the living room. It's like spending New Year's with the family," Letícia comments, taking it upon herself to break the silence this time.

Without even realizing, the two of them already have a system in which they take turns in breaking the silence, sharing responsibility, and dealing with it all as a team.

"I didn't put half the effort into getting dressed for New Year's. Actually, I'm pretty sure I was in my pajamas when the new millennium started. That might have been what brought me such bad luck," Ana says.

It seems like New Year's Eve was a lifetime ago. The night she believed the new millennium would be the beginning of an incredible phase of her life. The night she fell asleep thinking of Letícia and everything that the next thousand years would mean in their lives. She can taste the bitterness of longing in her mouth.

"Can we be quiet for the whole evening and not talk about the future?" Ana asks.

But, at the same time, Letícia says, "We need to talk about the future."

The two of them laugh, embarrassed.

"We can't run away from this anymore, amor. We need to make a decision together," Letícia says, while slowly stroking Ana's hair.

"I think fate has already decided for us, hasn't it?" Ana bemoans.

"Fate is an asshole," Letícia states.

More silence.

"We could take a break or something. We don't have to break up. Saying *break up* gives me goose bumps, I don't know," Ana says.

"Shut up," Letícia responds lovingly. "You were the best choice I've made in my life so far. And I don't want to not have you in my life anymore, Ana. But at the same time, I don't want to hold you back."

What if I want you to hold me back? Ana thinks, but she can't bring herself to suggest it. She decides to play dumb instead. "What do you mean, hold me back?"

"As if you didn't already know." Letícia doesn't play along. "I don't know how to say this without sounding like a horrible person but, well, you know it's going to be a lot easier for you, right? You're the one who's leaving. You'll discover new places, new people, and new ways to make your pizza taste horrible. I'll stay here, living in this minuscule city where each corner holds a memory of you."

Ana had thought about that, too, and she knows that Letícia is partially right.

"I carry a memory of you in every little corner of me," Ana says, unafraid of sounding cheesy. "Except perhaps my left pinkie."

Letícia smiles, holds Ana's left hand, and brings it to her mouth to kiss her girlfriend's pinkie.

"There you go, now you have it," she says. "Just don't let all our memories stop you from creating new ones, okay?"

Ana's expression becomes sulky immediately.

"I wish I were as mature as you are to deal with all this," she says.

"Mature?!" Letícia exclaims, still holding Ana's pinkie. "I've been crying at least twice a day since last week. I keep wondering if I could manage to hide in the moving truck. I have absolutely *no* maturity to speak of!"

"That wouldn't be a bad idea," Ana says. "It's just that, I don't know, you seem so ready, you know? Sometimes it makes me angry, even. It's almost as if you were pushing me toward other people, as if you had already accepted that it all went wrong."

Letícia processes the information and opens her mouth to answer, but then she gives up and thinks about it a little longer. It's a delicate situation in which thinking before saying something can never be too much. Everyone should be more like Letícia. The world would have much fewer problems if people always thought before they spoke, even in situations that are not delicate at all.

"Amor, think about it. *Star Wars*." Letícia tries to formulate an argument.

"I know nothing about *Star Wars*," Ana admits.

"No, forget about it. They're still going to release three new movies, it's not a good example. But let's pretend that *The Phantom Menace* didn't come out last year, okay? Pretend for a moment that it doesn't exist and that all we've got are episodes four, five, and six. An excellent trilogy."

"I don't know about it being excellent, I've never watched it. You're the one saying it," Ana says skeptically.

"But I like it. I love it. And when I finished the trilogy, I didn't stop loving it for that reason. It didn't fail just because it's over. It was a hit precisely because it lasted as long as it should have."

Ana stares at Letícia in confusion.

"But you just said they're making more movies. So theoretically it's not over yet," she points out.

"Just like us," Letícia concludes, feeling that her example wasn't that bad after all, but it would definitely have been better if Ana knew as much about *Star Wars* as she does about vampire books. "Our first arc is over. And it was excellent. I'll remember it for the rest of my life. But now you're leaving and I'm staying and, I don't know, maybe one day we can meet again and start a new arc, one where things aren't necessarily going to pick up where we left off because, who knows, in the future you and I are going to be completely different people, and I can't even guarantee that you're still going to love future Letícia, you know? We can't make any guarantees, Ana. But everything we had to this point was so good! I don't understand how you can't see the beauty in it."

Ana draws a deep breath, taking in every word and remembering her dad's gay friend who once said that all we have is now. My god, Letícia is so emotionally mature. And smart. And good with analogies. And so pretty.

"I'm sorry if I'm stubborn sometimes," Ana says. "I know what you mean, it's just that . . . I didn't want all that much, you know? I wanted this to last much longer. That they'd keep making *Star Wars* movies for, like, twenty or thirty more years!"

"I wish that, too," Letícia answers, thinking first about *Star Wars* and only after about how that applies to the analogy she just made.

"And I feel that there's so much left for us to live still. We've never gone out to dance, never kissed in the rain, never did anything crazy for love, you know?" Ana says, raising a finger for each item on her list.

That catches Letícia by surprise and leaves her absorbed in thought for some time.

"Simply loving you is crazy enough for me. A good kind of crazy, of course," Letícia says. "But still crazy. Especially when we consider everything that might happen if someone finds out. I know my mom wouldn't buy fish and leave the house to give us some alone time."

The weight of Letícia's anguish hovers in the air, and Ana, once again, says a silent thank-you for having a father like Celso. She doesn't know what to say in response. What does one say in a situation like this? She feels a need to apologize for having such an understanding father, but Letícia keeps talking.

"As for other things, we can figure it out. We have the whole evening," she says, throwing her arms up and almost hitting Ana's head with an accidental slap. "How can you kiss in the rain without leaving the house?"

Ana thinks for a second. "You'll think I'm ridiculous," she says.

"I love you precisely because you're ridiculous, Ana," Letícia answers.

———

Thirty minutes later, Letícia is hanging up her wet clothes to dry in the hopes that they'll dry before it's time for her to leave.

The two of them got into the shower.

Still dressed.

To kiss.

It was a complete disaster. Probably the worst idea Ana has ever had in her entire life. But the two of them had so much fun, laughed so hard, and made corny vows to the point that they practically became a private romantic comedy in the bathroom.

"I'll never forget my first kiss in the rain," Letícia says, wrapped in a towel and wringing the ends of her hair.

"Here, put this on," Ana says, and hands her girlfriend one of her dad's bathrobes, which is probably the only thing in the house that would fit Letícia.

"Is it your dad's?" Letícia asks as soon as her eyes fall on the bathrobe, as if she were an expert on dad bathrobes.

"In theory, yes. My dad got it for free when he subscribed to one of those celebrity gossip magazines. He subscribed because he felt bad for the salesman who knocked on our door. He doesn't know how to say no to strangers. The bathrobe was just a freebie, but he never wears it," Ana lies, because Celso has worn it two or three times.

"So that means I can put this on and not worry that you'll look at me and think about your dad, right?" Letícia checks before putting it on.

"Of course, what kind of a person do you think I am?" Ana keeps lying, now unable to hold back her laughter.

Letícia laughs, too, puts the robe on anyway, and punches Ana lightly in the shoulder.

"Dude, I hate you," she says.

"That's not what it looked like when you were in the shower with me just"—Ana looks at an imaginary watch on her wrist—"five minutes ago!"

Ana smiles mischievously, which is enough for Letícia to give up on the scene she'd been making, hug her girlfriend fiercely, and kiss her neck, cheeks, and, finally, her lips. Letícia thinks about how she'll miss Ana's kisses while Ana tries not to think about how weird it is to kiss someone dressed in her dad's bathrobe.

"Now I'm really hungry," Letícia says when her lips become numb.

"All About Trout!" Ana shouts, running to the kitchen and getting the containers from the oven.

She takes her time placing them on the table, lighting the candles she bought, and setting the cutlery symmetrically next to the plates, trying to remember the correct order for each of them according to the etiquette segment she watched on some afternoon TV show. Ana gets it all wrong, but neither of them knows what right looks like, so, in the end, it's the thought that counts.

The tray of grilled trout with caper sauce fills the living room with a good smell. There's a glass dish full of rice (the whitest and fluffiest Letícia has ever seen in her life), and Ana serves two wineglasses with what's left of the wine from Letícia's last visit.

"Should we make a toast before we start eating?" Letícia asks after taking her seat.

"I think we should. It might bring luck or something," Ana answers while sitting up and holding the glass by the stem and not the base, remembering the TV show again.

"To the future!" Letícia says, bringing her glass forward.

"Oh no. I don't want to think about the future," Ana says.

"To . . . now?" Letícia suggests, still holding up her arm.

"Now is good. Because you're here," Ana says, bringing her glass forward until it lightly clinks against Letícia's. "To now!"

"Cheers!" Letícia says, because she can't resist repeating the traditional toast when the glasses meet.

Ana and Letícia take a sip of the drink and share nearly the same level of hate for the flavor of the wine. They look at each other with a tight smile, then start laughing.

"How can people drink this?" Ana asks with a grimace, and immediately shoves a forkful of fish into her mouth to mask the flavor of the wine.

"Liking wine must be a thing that comes with age or something," Letícia says. "Like putting your hand on someone's forehead to see if they have a fever, which is a thing one only learns after becoming a mother."

Ana swallows her food and feels a weight passing down her throat with it at the word *mother.*

"I'm sorry, I didn't mean to," Letícia says, regretting the comment because she knows it's a sensitive subject.

"Actually," Ana starts, taking another sip of the wine just so she can have something to do with her hands, "I talked to my dad. About my mom."

"Wow," Letícia says, not quite sure how to react. "When did that happen?"

"Right after I told him about the two of us."

"Geez, you decided to have a lifetime of conversations in a single day," Letícia comments in shock, and Ana laughs.

"Yeah, I don't know what got into us."

Ana tells her about how her dad seems like a different person when he talks about her mom, and about how he once knew a gay man. Letícia tells her she's almost sure one of her cousins is gay, too, and she really wished she could talk to him so the two of them could be gay together over Christmas because it's too hard to be gay by herself. Ana says that she wants to find out more about her mom, that she wants to see photos, see the clothes she wore, and listen to the stories her dad has to tell. Letícia says that this all makes her very happy, and that Celso seems happy, too; after all, he was better dressed than ever tonight. The two of them come up with theories about Celso's evening and what would make him dress like that to leave the house. Together they craft a story rich in detail that ends with Celso drinking whiskey at a bar and seeing a secret girlfriend whose name is Leandra who is a spy, which is why Ana has never met her.

When the two have had more than enough to eat and Letícia has fished all the capers off Ana's plate, they remain silent for some time. The awkward silence of an evening about to end. But not yet.

"Where are the CDs?" Letícia asks.

"In there." Ana points to a box in the corner of the living room.

"But it says *porcelain*," Letícia says, looking at the word written in black permanent marker.

"I was the one who wrote it. It's so the mover will be careful and not break it," Ana answers.

"The way your mind works always surprises me," Letícia says before getting up and kissing Ana one more time. "Wow."

Letícia gingerly opens the box and goes through its contents one by one.

"What are you looking for?" Ana asks.

"The perfect soundtrack," Letícia answers. "For our dance. Gee, you have so many metal albums!"

"I had a metalhead phase when I was younger," Ana lies, because it was never just a phase.

"Is this Céline Dion?!" Letícia yells, pulling out *All the Way . . . A Decade of Song* from the box.

"It's my dad's," Ana lies again.

She likes to listen to Céline Dion while reading vampire romances because she thinks it's the right ambience. She also thinks Céline Dion is very beautiful. And this specific album has a song from the soundtrack of *Up Close & Personal* starring Michelle Pfeiffer, whom Ana also thinks is beautiful. Many of the choices Ana makes in her life are based on the "beautiful women" criterion.

"I think this one will do, then," Letícia says, while she turns on the living room stereo and puts the CD on the tray. "Which song do you want to dance to?"

"Track thirteen," Ana answers immediately, since she's fantasized about this moment dozens of times in her head.

"Your dad's CD, huh?" Letícia says jokingly. She presses play on the stereo as Ana blushes.

Frank Sinatra and Céline Dion start singing "All the Way" and Letícia holds out her hand.

"Would you dance with me?" she asks with a wink.

Ana's smile barely fits her face as she gets up and wraps her arms around Letícia's waist.

The two of them have no idea how to dance to a romantic song, but that doesn't make the scene any less cute. With her head on Letícia's shoulder, Ana lets her girlfriend lead, and the two sway around in the same spot, taking timid steps to one side and the other, to the rhythm of the song (mostly). Ana's heart beats fast when she realizes she's never felt so close to anyone as in this moment. Letícia almost cries when she realizes how lucky she is to be alive right now, in this moment, next to Ana.

"You're really good at it," Letícia says, and she carefully moves a strand of wet hair away from Ana's face.

"Good at dancing?" Ana asks in disbelief because she knows she's a terrible dancer.

"No," Letícia says, laughing because she also knows that Ana is a terrible dancer. "At choosing the perfect song for a perfect moment."

Ana thinks about it for a few seconds.

"Okay, this is going to sound kind of stupid," she says, still moving her body to the rhythm of the song. "But I sometimes think that I'd like to do this for a living, you know? I don't know if it's an official profession, and I don't know if there's money in it, and least of all what I'd have to study to do it, but I'd like to be the person who chooses the songs they play in movies. The one who watches a scene, analyzes every movement, feels what the characters are feeling, and says, 'Here, take this song. It's going to be perfect for the final cut.'"

Letícia smiles. "It's not stupid. It's just very specific. But I think you'll get there. I believe in you more than anything else."

More than I believe in myself, Ana thinks. But she doesn't say it out loud because she doesn't want to turn this moment into a self-deprecating session. "What about you? What do you want to do?"

Letícia also ponders for a few seconds, but just so she can pretend she doesn't have the answer on the tip of her tongue.

"I want to be an athlete. Play volleyball for real. In competitions, go to the Olympics, win medals," she says with a wide smile.

"That's going to be so easy! You're the best volleyball player I know," Ana exclaims excitedly.

"You don't know the first thing about volleyball, Ana," Letícia answers, laughing despite herself. "But I'll take the compliment."

Ana smiles.

Letícia laughs again.

"What is it?" Ana asks.

"I have a stupid idea, too. It's more like a dream, actually. It's ridiculous, but I think about it all the time."

"I'm sure it's not as stupid as wanting to be 'the person who chooses the songs they play in movies' when I don't even know what that profession is called," Ana says.

"Okay. I imagine myself winning my medal, leaving the stadium surrounded by journalists and, in the middle of the interview, I come out as bisexual to the world, just like that. Without fear. The newspaper articles will say, 'Gay Girl Gets Gold,'" Letícia says, lifting and opening a hand in the air as if she were able to see the headlines.

"The first openly bisexual woman to win a gold medal for Brazil," Ana finishes, allowing herself to participate in the dream, too.

"It'll be a while from now, and I hope I'm not the first. I hope there are others before me. Being the first is too big a weight," Letícia says, still thinking about every detail of how she'll build her sports career.

Ana smiles because she simply loves the way Letícia sees the future.

———

It's almost eleven at night when Letícia decides to leave. Celso isn't home yet, and the two of them could have a few more minutes alone, but she doesn't want to get into trouble at home, and her clothes look dry enough that they won't raise suspicion.

"Thank you for sharing this evening with me," Letícia says, still feeling nervous as she puts on her sneakers.

"Hmm . . . So that's it, then?" Ana asks, without specifying what she's talking about.

The evening? Their relationship? Love? The capers that came with the trout because Letícia ate them all?

"For now, yes. But we don't know what the future has in store for us," Letícia answers, feeling again the weight of being the rational half of the couple.

Ex-couple?

"Wait," Ana says, and runs back to her room to fetch something, hoping that the abrupt change of subject will allow her to hold back her tears.

She comes back to the living room with a folded piece of paper.

"My dad created an email account for you. He wrote down the address and the password here, and on the back," she says, unfolding the paper and showing her the notes. "There's a step-by-step of how to receive and send emails. It's free. All you need is an internet connection. And it's much more private than, like, letters. And it arrives instantly. You can write to me whenever you want to. My email is on there, too."

Letícia takes the piece of paper and studies it carefully, as if she were reading an ancient scroll written in a dialect she's never seen in her life.

"I don't know when or how I'm going to be able to get on the internet, but I promise I'll try," she says.

"And as soon as I get to Rio, I'll call you to give you my address. And my number. But it will have to be quick because it costs more to call a different state. But we'll figure it out. I don't want you to disappear from my life," Ana says, completely giving up on holding back her tears.

"Why is the password to my email Celsoisthebest?" Letícia asks, still studying the piece of paper.

"Because my dad created it. And he's ridiculous. He said it was so you wouldn't forget about him," Ana explains, crying and laughing at the same time.

"As if I could," Letícia says.

"Forget him?" Ana asks, slightly jealous.

Letícia rolls her eyes and answers with a kiss. A slow, long kiss, just the right amount for the two of them to recall every second of it for a long time.

"Forget any of it," Letícia whispers, before opening the door to the street and leaving.

Alone in the living room, Ana lets her tears fall free. She looks at the overturned CD box and finds the Blink-182 album she didn't have the courage to return to Letícia.

GREG

Organizing a film club in a small garage without the faintest idea of how many people are going to show up is much more complicated than Greg expected.

It's Tuesday, three days before the first showing, and Greg is alone in the store dusting the shelves and stopping occasionally to pat Keanu. He deserves it.

Keanu had been a good boy the previous day, posing for Tiago, who drew the dog on the flyers announcing the club. Greg is still surprised by yet another revelation about Tiago: He can draw. And well. Luckily the disastrous tennis match had broken Tiago's left arm, and he's right-handed. In a few minutes, he was able to create a perfect sketch of Keanu Reeves (the dog, not the actor) coming out of a popcorn bucket. In black marker and his best handwriting, Greg added:

CATAVENTO CINEMA CLUB
Lagoa Pequena's First Film Club

First showing: The Lake House (2006)

208

Director: Alejandro Agresti
Starring: KEANU REEVES and Sandra Bullock
January 29 at 3:00 p.m.
at Catavento Video

Snacks for all attendees!
Admission: 10 reais
Dogs are welcome (free admission!!!)

It was at Catarina's request that they write *KEANU REEVES* all upper-case. She wanted to add "children are allowed as long as they keep quiet during the movie," but Greg convinced her that it wouldn't be very polite.

Tiago and Catarina are distributing flyers across the city. She drives to the farthest neighborhoods in a borrowed car, and Tiago bikes to the closest ones. It still strikes Greg as strange that he lives in a city where people *lend one another cars.*

It's boring to spend the afternoon without Tiago, but Greg tries his hardest to put a smile on his face every time a rare customer shows up. He hands them a flyer, mentions the film club, and watches the customer leave, looking to see if they throw the flyer out or not. Only one does, but Greg is infuriated nonetheless. It's one thing if they don't want to participate in the club, but to throw out a drawing of the most polite dog in the entire world done by the most handsome guy in the entire world? *That* doesn't make any sense!

It's past three when Orlando arrives at the store. Unlike every other time he and Greg have seen each other, today he's not well kempt and perfumed. He's wearing an old, stained T-shirt, his hair is a mess, his skin covered in sweat, and Beto believes he might be wearing butcher boots. Apparently those are *also* florist boots.

"I brought the chairs," Orlando says, wiping the sweat off his brow with his hands in an intense way, as if he were the hero in an action movie escaping from an explosion unscathed. "Give me a hand?"

Greg springs to action and makes his way to the sidewalk, where he sees a truck with a sticker that reads FLOWER VILLAGE, Orlando's store, and in the bed are about a hundred chairs piled up. Or fifty. I don't know. I'm a house who's terrible with numbers.

The two of them bring the chairs into the store, and Greg can't help but notice how, on each trip, Orlando can carry piles much taller than his because, besides being an adult who is handsome, pleasant, an entrepreneur, and about to live a great romance, he is also strong. Greg feels confused because, even though he lives in a city as big as São Paulo, he has never compared himself to people as much as he has since coming to Lagoa Pequena. This city has made him realize that he's not strong, doesn't play tennis, doesn't have his own flower shop, can't draw . . . All he likes is Pokémon, and he knows an average amount about movies. In a way that Greg doesn't quite know how to explain, that feels like very little.

"I think we're done," Orlando says after placing the last pile of chairs at the back of the garage. He's sweatier than when he arrived.

"Would you like a glass of water?" Greg asks, because he believes that is the right thing to do when standing in front of someone that sweaty.

"Yes, please," Orlando says.

Greg runs inside and comes back a few seconds later with a glass in one of his hands and a bottle of cold water in the other because he doesn't know if Orlando is the type who drinks one glass sip by sip or two all at once. Gregório Brito is a very dependable kid.

"Ahhhh," Orlando sighs after the second glass with a satisfied smile. "Thank you, Gregório."

"You can call me Greg. Everyone calls me that."

"Your aunt calls you Gregório," Orlando points out.

"Only when she's pretending she doesn't like me." Greg laughs.

"She's always been like that," Orlando comments. "Hard to win over. But she's a great friend."

Greg nods, despite not knowing what kind of *friend* his aunt is. He thinks he'll never find out, because it must be weird to have someone who's both your aunt *and* your friend.

"Are you excited about Friday?" Greg asks, making conversation because he's tired of being alone.

"A little nervous, actually," Orlando admits, leaning against the counter.

"Because of the . . . Roger thing, right?" Greg says, spreading out the words because he knows he's crossing some kind of line.

Orlando smiles and his eyes light up. Greg wonders if one day someone's name is going to make him smile like that, if his eyes are ever going to light up *that way.*

"Yeah," Orlando says. "I feel like a silly teenager in love. It's ridiculous."

Greg makes a face because, well, he *is* a silly teenager in love. Should he be feeling ridiculous, too?

"Don't worry about it, Orlando. I'm sure everything is going to work out."

"I like your optimism. Your generation is so lucky, you know? You're not afraid of anything," Orlando notes.

Greg laughs because he is afraid of a *lot* of things.

"I'm serious," Orlando continues. "When I met Roger, sheesh, those were different times. We had to hide. I had to deal with a lot of stuff. And I know we still don't live in an ideal world, that we're very far away from that. But I feel that today I'd freak out a lot less if someone saw me hand in hand with another man than, I don't know, thirty years ago."

"Even here in Lagoa Pequena?" Greg asks, wondering what it's like to be gay here.

Not that he's planning on staying or anything like that. He's just curious.

Orlando thinks for a few seconds before answering.

"Even here. It's a small rural city, there's still a lot of stupid people around. But it's not such a bad place to live. Did you know the second openly bisexual Brazilian Olympic gold medalist is from here?"

"Wow," Greg reacts, trying not to laugh at how specific the title is. "I didn't know."

"Yeah. There's probably a lot more people scattered around Lagoa Pequena just waiting for their turn to make history. In our *community*, you know?"

Greg smiles at hearing the word *community*. For the first time, he sees his sexuality not as something he is, but as a place he belongs to.

"Of course, it's not like your city. São Paulo is huge, and gay life must be a lot easier there, with all the activists and the fight for equality . . . and the parties, god, the parties. It must be a lot easier to live there. But it's good here, too."

Greg feels like saying that he's sixteen, nearly friendless, and has a terrible relationship with his parents. He wants to say he doesn't know the first thing about activism and much less about parties. He wants to say that he's felt more welcome in a week here than a lifetime there.

"It's good here, too" is all he says.

"I gotta go," Orlando says, placing his empty glass on the counter. "I still have a lot of paperwork to get to today at work."

Greg frowns, unsure what type of paperwork a *florist* would need to get to.

"See you on Friday, then?" Greg asks.

"Of course, of course," Orlando confirms. "Can you just walk me to the car, please?"

Greg follows Orlando to the garage door shyly, and now the man's body is halfway into the truck's window, only his legs out while he searches for something inside. Greg feels guilty for noticing so intently the way the tight and dirty jeans envelop Orlando's butt. First, because he's in a vulnerable position; second, because, well, Orlando is old. But, in Greg's defense, the boy has seen few male butts in tight jeans splattered with soil in his life.

A few seconds later, Orlando turns to Greg, taking a sunflower out of the car. Greg doesn't know the first thing about flowers, but a sunflower is one of the five flowers anybody is able to name.

"I gave one of these as a present to your aunt when she first moved into this house," Orlando says, pointing at me.

"Because of the street name, right?" Greg says.

"Yes," Orlando confirms. "But also because sunflowers turn toward the sun."

"Really? Quite a self-explanatory name, then," Greg laughs.

"The sunflower notices where the sun is and turns its stem to follow it. I think it's beautiful, you know? At the time, I told your aunt she was my sun, and that wherever she went, I'd always watch."

"That could either be very romantic, or very psychopathic."

"Your aunt thought it was very psychopathic, of course. But she still liked the flower," Orlando laughs.

"Where are you going with this conversation?" Greg asks, putting his hands in his pockets because that's what he does when he's confused.

"I thought you could use one of these to give to someone as a present. Someone you'll remember even when you're far away," Orlando says, handing the flower to Greg.

"Gee, who could you be talking about?" Greg chuckles and takes the flower, admiring the beauty of the yellow petals. "Was it my aunt who told you to talk to me?"

Orlando laughs. "Yes. She said she needed the help of someone who understands you better, because all she knows to do is make people watch Keanu Reeves movies in the hopes that they will draw valuable lessons from the experience."

"She made me watch *Constantine*," Greg mentions.

"Catarina has done that to me, too. Twice. It's her way of showing she cares." Orlando smiles.

Greg decides he likes Orlando.

"Thank you for the sunflower. I'll have to think about who I'm gonna give it to. And try to come up with a speech that's better than yours," Greg says.

Orlando laughs and punches Greg lightly on the shoulder. The way one does to a friend.

"Hey, don't mock my speech! Your aunt did more than enough of that at the time," Orlando says. He checks the time on his wristwatch. "Now I *really* have to go."

"Any last words of advice?" Greg asks as Orlando gets in the car.

"Put that flower in water and leave it in a bright room," Orlando jokes.

"Ah, thank you so much for handing me yet *another* responsibility," Greg counters, shaking the sunflower.

"What are you talking about?" Orlando asks, turning the key in the ignition. "No flower looks that good if no one takes good care of it. Taking care of it is the best part."

He drives off. Greg is still standing on the sidewalk, looking at the flower. And the flower is looking at the sun. And the sun is moving slowly, making time pass because, well, that is what it does.

———

Catarina is exhausted. She hung flyers in every single neighborhood of Lagoa Pequena and talked to all its residents as if she were running for city council. Sitting on the couch with her feet up, she waits for Greg to bring her dinner. Catarina hears the beep of the microwave followed by the footsteps of her nephew, who emerges from the kitchen with a just-heated lasagna in his hands.

"Thank you, Gregório," she says, not wasting even a second before taking her first bite.

"It was nothing. I imagine your day must have been exhausting," he says, sitting in the armchair in the corner of the room and flipping through the TV channels without paying attention to anything.

"Tomorrow you're the one going out," Catarina informs him, her mouth still full. "I'll watch the store."

"Going out? Are there more flyers to hang? Something to pick up?"

Catarina smiles. "There's a whole city for you to explore," she says. "You've been locked in this house since you got here. Of course, it's a small and not-super-interesting city, but you can't leave without at least seeing the lake."

Greg tries to ignore the part about him leaving because he believes that if he pretends something inevitable is not going to happen, it might end up not happening. It's kind of a naive way to go about it, but Greg doesn't have a lot of experience dealing with the inevitable.

"Is there really a lake here?" Greg asks.

"Of course there is! What a question, Gregório. It's the same as asking if Belo Horizonte has a beautiful horizon."

Greg shrugs because he's never been to Belo Horizonte.

"And the lake is . . . small?"

"It's medium-sized. But I think Lagoa Média doesn't have quite the same ring to it. I don't know. I'm not a history teacher."

Greg laughs. "All right, then, I'll figure out how to get to the medium-sized lake in Lagoa Pequena."

"No need. You think I'd send you on this journey *by yourself*? Tiago will take you. He'll stop by tomorrow after lunch."

Greg's smile is almost too big for his face. He brings his legs up to the chair and holds his knees because he's not quite sure what to do with his arms. He's not stupid. He knows exactly what's going on. First, the whole sunflower thing with Orlando, and now this. Catarina and her friend are setting him up on a date, like the reverse of any nineties movie where the kids find a date for their single dad.

"Thank you for everything you're doing for me," Greg says, nearly—*just* nearly—crying. He can tell that the two of them are about to have a nephew-aunt bonding moment and wants to enjoy every second of it.

"Well," Catarina says with a smile. "Do me a favor, then, and put this lasagna back in the microwave for another minute. It's all cold in the middle."

Catarina is not ready for a nephew-aunt bonding moment.

Greg doesn't mind. He takes the plate from his aunt, walks back to the kitchen, and watches the microwave clock count down as if it were the most exciting moment of his entire life.

JANUARY 27, 2010

This might be the most adorable scene I've ever witnessed, and I am a house *full* of memories. It's twelve o'clock sharp on one of the most gorgeous days of the last few months, and Greg is waiting for Tiago by the garage door. He is wearing a light blue button-down shirt, and his curls are perfectly curly thanks to a pomade he found in the bathroom cabinet. His white sneakers are impeccable because he spent the entire morning cleaning them with a damp cloth. The folded hem of his jeans shows off his yellow socks, the same color as the petals of the sunflower he holds in his hands. He's about to freak out, but he takes a deep breath as he watches the end of the street, hoping Tiago will come around the corner any minute now.

Tiago is late, of course. No one can be handsome, polite, good with dogs, play tennis, draw super well, *and* be on time. It simply wouldn't be fair to other human beings.

Just like milk heated on a stove that boils and spills over only when nobody's looking, Tiago shows up only when Greg gives up staring intently at the corner. He's distracted, playing with Keanu on the sidewalk, when Tiago arrives, breathless and excited.

"Hey," Tiago says.

"Wow," Greg answers.

This isn't like a *Princess Diaries* moment where Tiago appears completely transformed with a new haircut, clothes that actually fit his body, and plucked eyebrows. Tiago looks the same as ever, wearing black from head to toe, a cast on his left arm, and bangs covering part of his face. He kind of looks like someone in a band whose members all scream at rehearsal, break instruments, and throw beer at one another as part of their creative process (I'm not sure what band rehearsals look like).

But Greg says "Wow" anyway because he's just realized that he's about to have his first real date with another boy, and he doesn't quite know what to say.

"Thanks for waiting for me," Tiago says.

"As if I had a choice," Greg teases.

"Ready to go?"

"This is for you," Greg says, and looks at the sunflower without exactly handing it to Tiago.

"It's so beautiful," Tiago says with a smile, reaching for the flower.

Greg's arm hesitates, still shaking, and as the sunflower exchanges hands, their fingers graze. Greg's heart beats so fast that it might be possible to hear the thumping from across the street. Tiago, who has a little more experience with first dates and grazing fingers, seems calmer. Still, his cheeks turn a definitive red.

"You told me yellow is your favorite color," Greg says, because he thinks this excuse is a lot less weird than Orlando's thing about how "the sunflower follows the sun wherever it goes."

"And you remembered." Tiago smiles. He tries to put the sunflower behind his ear but doesn't manage it because the stem is too thick.

"I think it's best to just carry it in your hand," Greg says, genuinely worried about the sunflower's well-being.

"I can't walk around with one arm in a cast and a flower in the other. If everything goes as planned, I'll need two free hands today," Tiago says, lifting his eyebrow.

"Hmm. All right," Greg says, completely caught by surprise.

"For god's sake, give me the flower, I'll just keep it here," Catarina says, appearing out of nowhere, as if she were hiding in the store to eavesdrop.

(She was.)

"Thanks, Aunt Catarina." Greg laughs nervously, wondering how this experience could be any more embarrassing.

"Now, get out of here. Have fun," Catarina commands, taking the flower from Tiago.

I don't know what happens next. The sidewalk is my limit, and the farther they go, the harder it is to see or hear what they're talking about. But just before they reach the end of the block, I can hear one last sentence:

"This is why I needed a free hand."

Tiago holds his hand out to Greg, who looks over his shoulder in fear of being seen, but it takes less than a second for him to get used to the other boy's touch. Their timid fingers interlace, and they disappear down Sunflower Street.

―――――――

I like being a house. I really do. But today, in this moment, I wish I were something else. I wish I were Lagoa Pequena's medium-sized lake, I wish I were Lagoa Pequena *itself*, or something else capable of seeing everything. Time, the universe, fate, a ghost, a fly. Greg and Tiago are my favorite soap opera of all time. Like an impatient mother, I wait for the two of them to return, and it's almost dark when that happens.

Tiago's smile could light up this whole town. Greg's eyes look as if they've just seen the Seven Wonders of the World all at once.

"Thank you for today," Greg says when the two of them arrive at the garage door, now closed since it's late and Catarina is in her bedroom trying out new models of bow ties on Keanu Reeves (the dog) so he can be well-dressed for the film club's inaugural meeting.

Tiago laughs and points at Greg's mud-covered shoes. "I'm sorry I didn't warn you about white sneakers not being the best choice to walk along the lake."

Greg smiles. "It's all right. It was all worth it."

The two of them are silent, looking at each other for some time. It's a comfortable silence; there's no pressure. Just relief and, I don't know . . . hope?

Sunflower Street is dark and still. Some lights indicate that residents are going about their normal lives, unaware that, on the street across from Number 8 (i.e., me), a milestone in the life of two boys is currently taking place.

Greg puts his arm on Tiago's shoulder.

Tiago wraps his arm with the cast around Greg's waist.

Greg gets on the tips of his toes to reach Tiago's lips, and they kiss. A kiss that starts shy, becomes a little more aggressive, and then gets quiet again before ending. It all happens in less than twenty seconds.

"Not bad for a second kiss," Greg whispers.

Second kiss! I missed the first!

Tiago laughs. "*Twelfth*, you mean, right? Not that I'm counting."

I missed the first *eleven*!

Keanu barks and runs to the window, a pink bow tie around his neck, as if he were a canine kissing alarm.

"I've gotta go," Greg says, feeling his cheeks burn like a panini press.

Tiago steals another quick kiss, which ends in a smack and a bark from Keanu. "Thirteen is my lucky number," he whispers before walking away.

And as Greg slowly opens the gate, crosses the garage, and throws himself on the couch, I don't even mind that I missed his first kiss. I am happy that the moment was theirs and theirs alone.

———————

Catarina notices there's something different about Greg the moment he sets foot in the living room. She's no fool. But she doesn't comment on it because she feels that she's already embarrassed her nephew enough in the last few days. She likes him. She really does. Her obsession with trying on bow ties on the dog only started because she needed to distract herself from the fact that, in a few days, Greg won't be around any longer. But she'll never say it out loud.

———————

Greg can't get any sleep, obviously. No sixteen-year-old would be able to after their first thirteen kisses in one single evening. He opens his laptop and writes Sofia Karen an update. Greg misses her so much. But, before he can write the email, he sees an unread message from Sofia that she sent while he was out with Tiago.

Wednesday, January 27, 2010. 4:22 p.m.
From: skaren@brittobeauty.com.br
To: geodude1993@email.com
Subject: Re: I have a plan

Hey, Greg!

The projector you requested is on its way. I bought it at that store around the corner from your place and got next-day delivery so it will get to you faster. If all goes according to plan, they will deliver it tomorrow.

I obviously didn't buy anything without telling your father because that might get me fired, but I explained to him that you needed it (what do you need it for, anyway?), and he didn't mind. He only asked me to send a note with it that says "Dad loves you."

I'm probably at risk of crossing a professional line here, but I wanted you to know how lucky you are to have a dad who tries to make up for his emotional absence by sending you presents. My dad, for instance, only gave me the absence . . . and a predisposition to diabetes.

Anyway, changing the subject, I've attached your return ticket to São Paulo. Your mom asked me to buy it for Wednesday, February 3. I think you wanted to stay there a little longer, didn't you? But I only follow orders. Deep down, I miss you. I miss seeing you run around the apartment and interrupting me all the time when I need to get work done. It will be good to have you back, even not knowing what things are going to be like after . . . all the things that are happening over here. You'll know when your parents talk to you.

Please send me some good news to lift the weird vibes from this email.

xoxo,
SK

As if he were on an emotional roller coaster, Greg experiences a free-fall from the highest point. From thirteen kisses from Tiago to a ticket back to São Paulo in less than thirty seconds. He takes a deep breath and rereads the message. He knows it's not Sofia Karen's fault that she's the messenger bearing bad news but, still, it's hard not to blame his friend for pouring cold water on him.

Now much less excited than he thought he would be when telling someone about his first kiss, he clicks the reply button and starts typing. His fingers make their way around the keyboard lazily, as if each letter demands an absurd amount of effort.

Wednesday, January 27, 2010. 9:34 p.m.
From: geodude1993@email.com
To: skaren@brittobeauty.com.br
Subject: Re: Re: I have a plan

Hey, Sofia. Hope everything is well over there. Thanks for getting me the projector. It will be a huge help in saving my aunt's video rental store (I hope). We are organizing a film club on Friday. I'm attaching the flyer to this message. The dog in the drawing is Keanu Reeves. Tiago made it. He's really good at drawing!

And, by the way, he's really good at kissing, too!

Yes! You read that right. I will finally stop bugging you with the whole first-kiss thing because I FINALLY HAD MINE. As you know, my expectations were really high. And they were all surpassed.

Kissing Tiago after sunset on the muddy banks of a medium-sized lake was probably the most cinematic thing that has ever happened in my life. It was as if, I don't know, the entire world stopped for a second and nothing else mattered. As if everything went quiet so as not to disturb the most beautiful moment, happening right there. I don't know if every first kiss is the same, but that's how I felt. I miss you, too. But sometimes, just sometimes, I wonder how different my life would be if I could, I don't know . . . stay here?

See you soon, and thanks for everything,
GB

(Where did you get the SK thing from? I'm signing this as GB just to copy you, but my brain can only read it as Great Britain.)

He hits send. Tomorrow will be a new day for Greg Brito. The first day in which he will wake up as a boy who has already had thirteen kisses. He falls asleep while watching an anime episode on his laptop and doesn't immediately see Sofia Karen's reply. But I do, because I'm nosy and, as a house about to lose such an important resident, reading other people's conversations is the only thing capable of bringing me joy at this moment.

Wednesday, January 27, 2010. 11:02 p.m.
From: skaren@brittobeauty.com.br
To: geodude1993@email.com
Subject: Re: Re: Re: I have a plan

Not all first kisses are like that. Just the special ones.

I'm happy for you ☺

JANUARY 28, 2010

The day before the launch of the film club, Greg wakes up to the noise of a deliveryman clapping outside. He thinks it's funny, the whole clapping thing when there is a huge and very visible doorbell on the garage door, but he doesn't spend a lot of time thinking about it because he knows very well what's waiting for him outside.

Feeling like a responsible adult who's totally used to getting deliveries, he signs the receipt that the (slightly grumpy) man hands to him, then runs to the living room, excited as if it were Christmas morning. Greg opens the big box full of Styrofoam peanuts while Keanu barks and runs around him because, just like any other dog, he *loves* all kinds of peanuts, including the Styrofoam kind.

The noise catches Catarina's attention, who emerges from her bedroom wrapped in a white bathrobe and looking like she could use another three hours of sleep. Or thirty.

"What is this mess?" she asks, trying to sound mad but letting out a carefree laugh when she sees her dog rolling on the ground with the Styrofoam.

"The projector is here," Greg says, his eyes glued to the instruction manual. "But we're gonna need a screwdriver . . ."

"I have one."

"And someone who knows how to use a drill."

"I do."

Greg smiles, happy to be in a household where people know how to do things.

"So, now I think we have everything we need to make the best film club this country has ever seen!" he says with exaggerated excitement.

"For the love of god, I need coffee," Catarina says, because not even two hundred Keanu Reeveses playing with Styrofoam could have made her as excited as her nephew at this ungodly hour.

Tiago arrives to help later in the afternoon and, with Greg's and Catarina's help, repositions all the shelves in the store and organizes the chairs in rows spaced out enough so that everyone can be comfortable, but close enough to accommodate at least thirty people. They can't tell if the first event is going to be a success, but Tiago is an optimist and wants to be prepared for the best. Catarina is a pessimist and thinks that if five people come, it will be a lot. Greg is between the two and prefers not to think about it because he already chewed off all his nails and needs to get his anxiety under control before he starts eating his actual fingers.

Greg tries to act professionally. He's in charge of a pretty big project, after all. But it's hard to look at Tiago focused on work without remembering last night. It's impossible for Greg not to want to drop everything and jump straight to kiss number fourteen. It's preposterous to go from one side of the garage to the other without giggling internally every time they bump into each other "by accident."

But Catarina is here, and as much as she seems to be the coolest aunt in the history of aunts, Greg and Tiago still pretend like nothing happened.

Pretend *poorly*, I should add. It's written all over their faces how they'd like to run away and make out somewhere far away from the gaze of aunts (and dogs) (and houses).

The projector has finally been assembled. Catarina deals with the screws and Greg with the cables, connecting everything to his laptop, since the store's computer is as old as time. He *almost* starts thinking about what it's going to be like when he leaves. He almost thinks about how he could leave an instruction manual so Catarina can continue doing the showings without his help. But he chooses not to think about it.

"Aunt Catarina, I'm gonna need the white sheet so we can test the projector," Greg says as soon as he connects the last cable.

"And I need an extension cord to connect the speakers to the sockets in the back," Tiago adds, pointing at the devices he brought, borrowed from a friend who has a rock band, which, surprisingly, Tiago is not a member of.

Catarina looks at the two of them, one at a time.

"You," she says, pointing at Tiago. "Get the extension cord from the drawer behind the counter and let me help with the wires."

Tiago's lack of experience with electronics makes Catarina fear that he will set the store on fire.

"And you!" She is pointing at Greg now. "In my bedroom, in the closet, at the top, near some shoeboxes. There are a few sheets in there. Get the whitest one you can find, but check first because one of them has a pee stain from Keanu I could never wash off."

Greg makes a disgusted face.

"The sheet is *clean* and *smells nice*," Catarina protests. "It just has a stain on it."

Keanu barks in his own defense.

———

In his twelve days as a temporary resident, Greg has never gone into Catarina's bedroom. Mostly because he's never had to, but also because the room has a forbidden aura about it, like the West Wing in Beast's castle, that he never wanted to cross.

He almost knocks on the door as a sign of respect before going in, but when he enters, there doesn't seem to be anything out of the ordinary. A well-made queen bed, a nightstand with an old lamp on top, bills to pay, and a picture frame with a photo of Catarina and Keanu by the lake, next to some clothes piled up on a chair.

On the wall opposite the bed, the built-in closet takes up all the space from the floor to the ceiling, and Greg realizes he'll need the chair to reach the tallest shelf, where she keeps the sheets.

He climbs on the chair carefully, raises his arms, and feels around for the sheets on the top shelf. He pulls down the pile of sheets, but the whitest one is still toward the back. Greg silently curses his parents for the short genes they bestowed on him at birth, then he stretches his arm as far as he can to reach the piece of fabric in the back. And that's when his hand feels something . . . different. An envelope taped to the bottom of the shelf.

He shouldn't. Of course not. But he pulls it toward him, anyway. The makeshift envelope, made from an old notebook page, has become yellow with time and, judging by the thickness of it, Greg believes there's only one piece of paper inside. A photo? A letter? Written on the front of the envelope, in round and careful handwriting, Greg reads, "To the future resident of this house." It could have been a scary letter, but next to the dedication someone drew a little heart. Probably done precisely to reassure whoever found it there.

Well, *I* know who wrote this letter. I've been keeping it for ten years. But a letter hidden under sheets inside a closet can go unnoticed by an entire household. I think that, for a human, it's like a birthmark on the back of their head. They know it exists, they even know it's there, but they don't think about it.

I haven't thought about this letter in years, until Greg found it.

I don't know if it's a lack of curiosity, fear, or an impulse, but one of those things makes Greg simply fold the envelope and put it in his pocket. And only then does he return to the store holding the white sheet, but not without first making sure that there's no pee stain on it.

BETO

Beto can't explain where the courage he needed came from, but by the time he realizes what he's done, his fingers have already typed the message and hit send. This afternoon, while the rest of his family works, he lies in bed staring at his phone and contemplating the disaster that's about to happen. His texts go unanswered for a few long minutes, and he scrutinizes every word, feeling pathetic.

He thinks about deleting the last three lines, but Nicolas is now online. Too late. He's read them. The three dots on the screen blink like a countdown to complete humiliation.

Nico

Heyyy I'm around!

Is something wrong?

Beto's hands are sweaty, and he feels his face start to melt. His heart is beating at a pace he didn't believe possible. Beto doesn't know that much about heartbeats.

No way back. It's now or never. Beto takes a deep breath and starts typing.

Beto

I've been meaning to talk to you for a while. I dragged my heels and didn't quite know how to broach the subject because, I don't know, I guess I don't know how you're gonna react

Nico

You're making me worried

SHOULD I be worried?

Beto

Well it's a matter of perspective haha

Nico

Go ahead

I'm ready

I like you

Like

I LIKE you like you

I like talking to you and learning about your life and I like waking up knowing there will be a text from you waiting for me. I like the way you see the things I do and how you encourage me to be a better person. And I got to a point where I don't know what to do about this . . . feeling.

So I thought talking to you about it would be a good idea

Because, who knows, maybe you like me too, right?

We could like each other together

(From far away, but together)

It's done. Beto sends it all, locks his phone screen, and closes his eyes. He doesn't want to see Nico's response, but at the same time, he *needs* to see it. One minute goes by before Beto feels his phone vibrating in his hands. It's only then that he realizes he's been holding it so tightly that his knuckles are white, and the screen is covered in sweat.

Ew, Beto thinks.

Nico

Wow

Apparently that is all that Nico could type in *an entire minute.*

Beto

Sorry

Beto types this on an impulse because he feels guilty for the enormous discomfort he has introduced between the two of them.

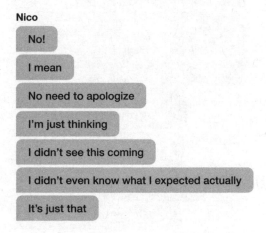

Nico

No!

I mean

No need to apologize

I'm just thinking

I didn't see this coming

I didn't even know what I expected actually

It's just that

But he doesn't say anything else. Nico doesn't complete his "It's just that." The rest of the sentence is left to Beto's imagination, and all he can imagine are horrible things.

Beto

Please say something

Beto is now plunged in despair. The screen shows that Nicolas is typing and, if he sends another *Wow*, Beto swears he is going to throw his phone at the wall and immediately thereafter throw *himself* at the wall.

Which would be a very peculiar scene to witness.

A huge block of text appears, and Beto swallows hard while trying to stitch the words together.

Nico

It's nothing NEW, you know? We've always been that way with each other, we've always been friends, but somehow there was always a THING in the air. I don't know how to explain it, but I probably don't even need to because you must have noticed it too. The way you are always the first person I run to when I have something to tell, or how I feel that my day only starts after I talk to you . . . and I'd be lying if I said I haven't thought of that before. About us. I've thought about it a lot, to be honest, but the truth is I don't really know what to do with this? Because, of course, 2020 has been a weird year, but even if it were a normal year, I'd still be here and you there. You dream about going to SP to study photography and I want to stay in Brasília to study literature, and I can't see a time in the near future where our paths are going to cross, you know? And I feel so lucky that I met you, but at the same time unlucky because I don't know where that is going to take us. You are much more of a dreamer than me. I'm a practical guy. And in a PRACTICAL way: what do we do? Do we wait? Do we keep things the same? I think that is why I never had the courage to talk about this. Keeping things the same is easier, I guess?? I don't know. I really don't know what we can do. But I don't want you to get hurt because I REALLY like you.

Beto reads the text. And rereads it. He can't understand how this bunch of sentences could mean absolutely *anything*. He can't understand how Nicolas's reply can be positive and negative at the same time. Maybe he'd been waiting for something simpler, like the answer to a little note that said only *Do you like me? ( ) YES ( ) NO*. He laughs at his own thought and thinks that might make Nicolas laugh, too.

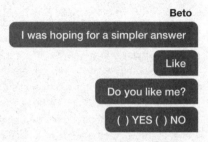

Beto

I was hoping for a simpler answer

Like

Do you like me?

( ) YES ( ) NO

Nico

(X) YES

Beto draws a relieved breath.

Nico

But it's a complicated feeling because there's nothing we can do about it now. I don't know, I might sound ridiculous saying this, but did you expect we could try virtual dating? Because I don't know if that would work for me. Not while we don't have a way to make a concrete plan to see each other. Until then, do you think we need to change? Can't we just keep things the way they are?

Beto feels he might throw up.

236

So the problem is just the pandemic? Is it just the fact that RIGHT NOW it would be impossible for us to be PHYSICALLY together? Like, what if I could hop on a plane and go there right now, what would you say?

Nico goes silent. The kind of silent that means something.

Nico

I don't know.

Beto

So the problem is something else . . .

Beto wants to cry. He *really* wants to cry. But he knows that if he sheds a tear, he won't be able to hold back the rest. And if the rest comes out, it will be noisy. And if he makes noise, he will get his mom's and sister's attention. And the last thing he wants right now is to get anyone's attention.

Beto wants the *opposite* of someone's attention.

Beto wants to disappear.

Nico

I'm not gonna give you a "it's not you, it's me" line, but maybe it is. I just think I'm not ready to deal with serious feelings today, or with anything serious, really

Beto

Sorry. didn't mean to spoil your day with SERIOUS FEELINGS

Nico

Now you're being unnecessarily rude

Beto types *UNNECESSARILY???* but deletes it. Then he types *ME, RUDE???* and deletes that, too.

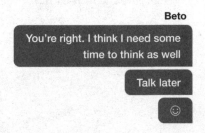

Beto

You're right. I think I need some time to think as well

Talk later

☺

And in a quick, calculated gesture, Beto locks his phone, puts it in the drawer, and spends the rest of the day staring at the ceiling, wondering how it's possible that absolutely everything could have gone so much worse than he'd ever imagined.

MAY 18, 2020

A week has gone by since Beto last talked to Nico.

He tries not to resent Lara, who thought declaring his love for Nico was a good idea. She had no way of knowing this would happen. But that doesn't mean he's *cool* with her, either. The siblings barely speak. And Helena, despite her observation skills, moves around the house completely clueless to everything that's happening in her son's head. It's not that she's a bad mother. She's just exhausted.

It's Monday evening and Lara is locked in their bedroom doing a school presentation. Judging by how stressed she's been the last few days, nearly climbing my walls, this assignment must be important.

Beto and his mom are in the living room, watching a cooking show, both feeling very sympathetic to the contestant who dropped his spinach soufflé on the floor just seven minutes before the end of the competition.

"He's going to be eliminated, poor thing," Helena says.

"Too bad. He's so . . . talented," Beto answers, because he doesn't have the courage to say "incredibly handsome."

"And incredibly handsome!" Helena compliments.

"Oh, look, Samara is going to present her dish," Beto says, pointing at the TV. "I'm sure she's gonna cry again, saying that the recipe was her grandmother's. She does it *every episode*! It kills me."

"Honey," Helena starts, carefully choosing her words.

"Ah, there it is, the crying, she's gonna cry," Beto says, completely missing Helena's worried look.

"Are you happy?"

Beto goes still and silent after his mom's unexpected question, like a dancing Santa toy that someone just unplugged. *What kind of a question is that? And on a Monday evening?*

On the TV screen, as expected, Samara cries while explaining that this is her grandmother's recipe.

"What do you mean, Mom? Of course I am," he lies.

"I was looking at the photos you posted on Twitter this week," she says, turning her phone screen toward her son and showing the series of black-and-white pictures that Beto took in the last few days: a broken glass, a tree with dead branches from the neighbor's backyard, a cloud heavy with rain, a mesh of shadows on his bedroom floor.

"You mean to tell me you *follow* me on Twitter?" Beto asks, freaking out.

"I don't. I just check it. Once in a while. I don't want to invade your space."

"Well, you're invading it now," Beto points out.

"It's just that I . . . worry," Helena says, pushing back her glasses that insist on sliding down her nose.

"It's just a series of black-and-white shots, Mom. It doesn't mean anything," Beto justifies.

"And what about this?" She points to other tweets by Roberto on the phone screen.

Another sad day, don't feel like doing anything

I wish I could just DISAPPEAR!

Sad & tired

Things I miss during lockdown: going to the movies, having some perspective, and smiling. What about you all?

The list could have kept going for a few more minutes, but Beto covers his mom's screen with both hands, because he gets the point.

"I'm just sad, Mom. *Momentarily* sad. It's normal, isn't it? Look at the world! Everyone is sad!" He points at the TV, where Samara is still crying. Or maybe she just resumed her crying.

"I know, honey. I get it. Demanding happiness from people right now

240

would be simply unfair. And it doesn't even help to think that, well, some people are in situations much worse than our own ..." Helena says, touching her son's knee in an attempt to get closer to him.

Beto frowns, tired of speaking in code.

"It's just a boy, Mom. A boy I like. I used to like, whatever," he admits. "Then Lara . . . No, not Lara. It was me. Lara had nothing to do with it. *I* decided it would be a good idea to tell him how I felt. And turns out it wasn't such a good idea, because he didn't feel the same. I don't know *what* he feels. What he says makes no sense. But it didn't happen the way I expected it, and now everything is weird. I just wanted *one* little thing to go according to plan, but since this hell of a year started, nothing works out. So then I don't know what to do, because what use is it to make plans? Just so I can fall flat on my face again? But, then again, if I can't make any plans, what use is it *existing*? Nothing makes sense."

He lets out a long sigh while Helena studies his words.

"Well," she finally says. "It sounds like it's not just a boy. It's a lot more."

"Yes. It's a lot more. It's everything," Beto says, staring fixedly at his mom's hand stroking his knee.

"We could try to find help, you know that, right?" Helena whispers. "But *right now*, all I need you to know is that . . ."

Beto rolls his eyes because he already knows what his mom is going to say. He *knows* she's going to say, "It's okay to be sad." Maybe it's that Helena is too optimistic, or maybe it's a mom thing to say everything is fine when it is not, and everything will turn out all right when it won't.

Beto doesn't even know if she really believes it or if this is kind of her autopilot to deal with everything. But now, right now, he wishes she would deal with things a little differently. He wishes she would feel his pain and understand that not everything is okay and that there isn't even a remote chance that it ever will be. And he doesn't know what to do when the protocol he's heard his entire life doesn't seem to be working.

"It's okay to be sad," she finishes.

"No," Beto answers, his voice firm and harsh.

Helena waits patiently because she knows there's more coming.

"It is not okay, Mom," Beto says after a few seconds of silence. "But I don't know what to do to change it, so then . . . I . . . I . . . don't know? I just wanted . . ."

Beto is lost for words. His face burns, and he feels like crying.

"What did you want?" Helena asks.

"To scream?" Beto whispers, feeling like an idiot.

Helena promptly gets up and leaves the living room. Beto feels ridiculous for all the drama, and even more ridiculous because the moment his mom's hand leaves his knee, he feels alone.

In less than five seconds, she comes back holding a pillow.

"Scream," she says with a smile, and throws the pillow on his lap.

"What do you mean, Mom?"

"We don't want to scare the neighbors. And your sister is giving a presentation right now," she whispers. "It's easier to muffle the scream if you put your face on the pillow like this and—"

"No, Mom!" Beto interrupts. "I know how *screaming into the pillow* works. I just don't want to seem like an idiot doing it."

Helena sits on the couch again, facing her son. Her expression is that of someone who is in control of everything and knows exactly what they're doing. What her son doesn't know is that, deep down, she doesn't have a clue.

"If I scream, too, will you feel *less* like an idiot?"

Beto thinks for a second. Probably not.

"Yes," he answers.

"Give it to me, then," Helena says, and holds out her hand to grab the pillow.

He does. A little reluctantly, but he does.

"But you . . . I've never seen you scream. You are the calmest person I know."

Helena laughs. "I am your mom. I'll do anything for you," she says, then she takes off her glasses, puts her face in the pillow, and lets out a timid scream. *"AaaaaAah!"*

Beto laughs.

"Your turn," she says, passing the pillow back to Beto, who turns it around because he finds the idea of shoving his face right into the same surface as his mom did pretty weird.

"Okay," Beto says, but doesn't move.

"Just think about everything that's making you frustrated and let it out," Helena counsels.

"I think about Nicolas every day, and wish I hadn't screwed everything up, but I think I hate him more than I hate myself because his answer was ridiculous," he says firmly.

"There was no need to say it out loud, but if that makes you feel good, go for it!"

Beto takes a deep breath, brings the pillow to his face and screams.

"*AaaaaaaaaAahh!*"

Helena takes the pillow back.

"I'm scared. I'm scared because I don't know when any of this is going to end. Adapting my work has been hard and I've been very tired," she says before screaming. "*AaaaAAaaaaahhh!*"

In a coordinated back-and-forth, like a game, mother and son let it all out. Almost.

"I feel like I'm not good at anything, just somewhat interested in photography, and I have no idea how to make a living out of it," Beto vents. "*AaaaaaAAaaaaAh!*"

"Sometimes I blame myself and I think I wasn't a good mother to you and your sister. *AaaaaaaaaaaaaAAAaaAh!*"

"Sometimes I feel that I will never be as good as Lara in everything she does, and that makes me think you like her a little more than me. *AaaaaAAAaaaaAaaaAh!*"

"Son, that's absurd! I *obviously* love the two of you the sa—"

"No," Beto interrupts. "We can have heavy conversations later. Right now we're just screaming over the stupidest reasons we can think of. Deal?"

"Deal."

"I miss going to the Japanese restaurant a couple of streets down with the cute waiter. And getting it delivered is not the same because there is no cute waiter. *AaaaaaAAaaAh!*"

"I hate this red hair. Every time I look in the mirror, I feel like Ronald McDonald, but I didn't have the courage to tell Lara I hate it. *AaaaaAaAaaaaaaAh!*"

Beto cracks a mischievous grin because hearing his mom criticize Lara, even innocently, makes him feel that he's ahead in the imaginary competition he has with her.

"I had forgotten that Lara snores, and there are nights when I need to sleep with my earbuds in because it's impossible to get any rest with all that noise! *AAAaaaaaaaaaaAAaAaAah!*"

"I can't stand the beige of my bedroom wall. There are days when I look at it and think I'm a boring old woman who will never find someone else to be with. *AaaaAAAAAAaaaaaAAaah!*"

"I also feel I will never find someone to be with, and I'm not even half your age. *AAAaaaaaAAaaaaaaaaaAaAAAAAAAhahahahhah!*"

The scream turns into laughter.

The laughter turns into guffaws.

The two of them laugh as they haven't in a long time, and then, their faces red from all the screaming and laughing, they take a moment to catch their breath.

"Enough. Enough. I can't take it anymore," Beto says, still out of breath.

"I will miss you so much, son," Helena says with a melancholic smile.

"What do you mean?"

"You know. When you go do your things. Leave home. Go photograph the world. Abandon me here, all by myself," she answers, adding a bit of drama to the last part.

"Do you really think I'll make it?"

"Of course you will, Beto," Helena says, and puts her glasses back on. "Things are going to work out. Right now, it's kind of hard to know when, but everything will be okay."

Beto hears his mom's old sentence, but, this time, he doesn't feel that she's just repeating a slogan. He believes her. For the first time since the year started, Beto *actually* believes it will be okay.

"Thank you, Mom," he says, but feels that just thanking her is not enough. "And don't worry. Your hair still looks nice. You look beautiful. And you don't look like Ronald McDonald. Pfffff."

He barely manages to finish the sentence and laughs again.

Helena laughs, too. What else is there to do?

"Jesus Christ, what is going on?" Lara says, finally emerging from the bedroom.

"Nothing, honey. We were just laughing together."

"And screaming," Beto adds.

The two of them start laughing again, and he feels happy to have this moment, these past few minutes, shared exclusively with his mom.

A moment all their own that no one will be able to invade.

Lara gives up trying to understand because she's tired from her presentation.

"Oh no," she says, looking at the TV. "Did I miss the end of *Super Cheflings?*"

"No, *Super Cheflings* is on Wednesday. Today is Monday. It was just regular *Super Chefs*. With grown-ups," Beto explains, surprising himself at the precision of the information he is able to offer.

"I'm so exhausted I already completely lost any notion of *weekdays*," Lara comments, massaging her temples and squeezing in between Helena and Beto on the couch.

"How did the presentation go? Did everything go well?" Helena asks.

"The professor's son appeared in the middle of class and kicked a Peppa Pig plush on the camera, so we had to wait a few minutes until he set it all back up. It was funny. But the presentation went well. My group got the highest grade," she answers, with the same level of excitement that someone might describe what they had for lunch that day.

"Congratulations, honey!" Helena says, much more excitedly.

And Beto doesn't feel jealous nor rolls his eyes the way he always does when Lara says something that reminds him how great at everything she is. In fact, he feels proud of his sister. He thinks that, even though she's so exhausted she forgets which day it is and gets confused about when *Super Cheflings* airs, she can still work, study, and get the highest grade on an assignment. And, well, that is, indeed, reason to be proud.

"You're the best, Lara," Beto says, *genuinely* believing that she is.

"Thank you, family," Lara answers, her voice still tired, pulling the two of them into a hug.

Beto smiles when he hears the word.

Family.

———

Beto drinks an entire glass of water before going to bed. The whole screaming-with-his-mom thing made his throat sore. When he goes into the bedroom, he doesn't turn off the light because Lara is lying in bed with a book, but when he comes closer, he realizes she was using the book to support her phone and is actually just endlessly scrolling her Instagram feed.

"Please don't tell Mom we didn't do anything new today, please. I don't have it in me to think of anything," Lara says as if she were confessing a secret.

"Well, I did," Beto says, and he can't help but feel like the champion of the Who Is Doing New Things Every Day Competition.

Maybe he's always like this. Competitive. Maybe it's a star sign thing or whatever. I'm a house, I don't know anything about star signs. I've already tried to figure mine out, but I don't know if, for houses, you should count from the beginning of construction or the end. Or when the first resident moved in, since while no one was living here, I was not a house, just a place. There were too many variables, so I gave up. My sign is all signs. Or none. It doesn't matter.

But Roberto is a Scorpio.

"Oh, you did? What?" Lara asks, not as curiously as her tone of voice suggests.

"I talked to Mom. In a more . . . serious way? Intense. I don't know, I felt like we were talking about *important* things."

He doesn't include the part about screaming into pillows. First, because it was a private moment between the two of them, and second, because he believes Lara would find it ridiculous.

"So you talked like two *adults*, then."

"Yeah, I guess that's what it was."

The word hovers in the air. Beto was never afraid of becoming an *adult*. In fact, he's always wished it above everything else. To work, save money, leave Lagoa Pequena, live by himself, see the world, own coffee makers that make different types of coffee, to like coffee. That's what being an adult is, isn't it?

Because if it is, Beto is 100 percent ready.

Unless adults aren't allowed to be insecure about their body.

And their professions.

Or their purple hair.

Or the constant thought that, when it's all over, they will die alone.

Or the wish to go back in time and never have declared his feelings for Nicolas in the most passive-aggressive way possible.

If all that is allowed, then from the height of his seventeen years of age, Beto is ready to be an adult.

"Mom hates the red hair, doesn't she?" Lara asks out of the blue.

"Wow, that question came out of the blue."

"Stop trying to dodge it," Lara insists. "Did she say anything about it?"

"No," Beto keeps the secret safe. "Why do you think that?"

"She left the door ajar while seeing a patient one day. She was wearing a hat, Beto. A *beach* hat. Indoors."

Beto laughs. "Maybe it was part of the treatment for that specific patient, who knows," Beto answers, not really knowing if there really is a patient who would need to be seen by a psychologist wearing a beach hat. "All I know is that she wanted to change the color of her bedroom wall."

"Ugh! That beige really is horrible." Lara pretends to vomit. "We could paint her bedroom walls for her. As a Mother's Day present."

"Lara, Mother's Day already passed."

"Jesus, I really need some sleep."

And in less than two minutes, she's already snoring.

MAY 20, 2020

The siblings paint their mother's bedroom walls a weird green. It's kind of mossy but slightly bluish; the can calls it Cloudy Horizon. I don't know what horizon has *that* color, but if I saw it one day, I'd run the opposite direction. If I had legs.

But Helena likes it. In fact, she *loves* it. She smiles a goofy smile as she examines her new wall, trying to ignore the paint stain that fell on the rug that cost a lot more than a rug should ever cost. Overlooking the stain is more mature than trying to determine who's to blame.

Beto is to blame; he bumped into the paint can while taking photos of Lara. His sister's pose was too unusual for him not to photograph it: on tiptoes like a ballerina and her arms raised as much as possible to paint the details in the corner of the wall with a thin paintbrush. In his defense, the photo looks amazing.

"I never thought that the lockdown was going to turn me into an artist," Lara tells her brother later, as he edits the pictures he took throughout the day and she pretends to work. "Hair dyeing, wall painting. The next steps are painting pictures, painting nails—"

"You could do my nails one of these days," Beto says without thinking. "That would be a good first."

"Do you want the Instagram nail extensions, with those plastic crystals glued to the tip?" Lara teases, hoping that the answer is yes so she can find an outlet for her *obsession* with Instagram nail extensions.

"No. Just black nail polish. Kind of smudgy, for a rebel look."

"Kind of like the guy who owns the restaurant a couple streets down?" Lara asks. "He's, like, thirty and still emo."

"He's my greatest inspiration," Beto informs.

"Does he still live here?"

"Probably. Nothing changes in Lagoa Pequena."

"Yeah," Lara agrees. "Nothing ever changes."

The family spends the night gathered in the living room watching *Super Cheflings*.

It's a thrilling episode in which children between nine and thirteen years old prepare three dishes (appetizer, entrée, and dessert) in less than two hours, then serve the meal to a renowned chef who will criticize them lightly enough to avoid legal trouble but harshly enough to make some of the children cry on basic cable.

In short, just another episode of *Super Cheflings*.

Lara applies a nearly dried-up black nail polish she found at the bottom of her mom's nail polish case on Beto's left hand.

With his right hand, he looks at his Twitter timeline, emotionally avoiding anything that might remind him of Nicolas. It's an exhausting exercise, considering that everything reminds him of Nicolas.

"Give me the other hand," Lara demands, and Beto drops the phone to focus his attention on his freshly painted nails.

He thinks about how fun it would be to send a photo of his nails to

Nicolas, and how he would joke he has painted his nails for the first time, Beto can already say he's breaking *all* the gender barriers.

Beto laughs to himself.

Lara huffs when Beto's laughter causes his hand to shake and she smudges his index finger.

Silent minutes go by and, with ten painted nails, Beto walks around the living room waving his hands and blowing on his fingers.

"Roberto, you can't blow on them like that, it'll get all smudged!" Lara provokes.

"I'm admiring *your work*, leave me alone," he answers.

"Shhhh," Helena chides. "The two of you, be quiet so I can watch the show. They're about to eliminate the red-haired girl I like, poor thing."

The siblings stop talking. Helena pushes her glasses to the tip of her nose so she can see the TV better. The three of them watch in silence as the red-haired girl gets eliminated from the kids' cooking show. Helena nearly cries.

Beto's phone vibrates on the arm of the couch, but he doesn't pay it any mind. Probably a *Let's meditate?* notification from the meditation app he downloaded at the beginning of lockdown and only used twice.

The phone vibrates again, *really* asking Beto to meditate.

The third vibration sounds urgent, as if to say *ARE YOU GOING TO MEDITATE OR WHAT?* Beto reaches for the phone, determined to delete the app and never try meditation again in his life, but what he sees on the screen are three texts from Nicolas.

Nico

I know it's weird, me texting out of nowhere

I just wanted to say I am very proud of you

SIXTY THOUSAND LIKES!!!!!!!!

With his hands shaking, Beto uses one finger, now painted with dried-up black nail polish found at the bottom of his mom's nail polish case, to open his Twitter notifications tab.

For some reason he cannot understand, the old sunset photo he reposted next to a recent photo that shows the same window but a dark cloudy sky outside has captured the internet's attention. Likes, comments, and reposts with the caption *Photo by @Betojpg* fill his eyes. This time he screams without waiting for the pillow.

ANA

JANUARY 14, 2000

Watching the moving truck depart is a lot less dramatic than Ana had imagined. For starters, it's not even a *proper truck*. A pickup truck, maybe? Ana doesn't know the first thing about moving vehicles.

The company her father hired sends the truck/pickup truck very early on Friday morning, and a couple of employees come in to quickly gather boxes and the furniture that was already disassembled. Everything happens in a few minutes, and Ana feels surprised at how easy it can be to simply disappear from the face of the earth (when one is working for a millionaire technology company willing to pay for your entire move).

The personal items and a few boxes with fragile and expensive computer parts that Celso was afraid to leave in the movers' hands are coming with them on the plane.

The car ride to the São Paulo airport will take a few hours, but it's enough to make Ana nervous, since she can't remember the last time she saw her dad drive. She's also nervous because she's never been on an airplane in her life. Ana knows it's irrational to be afraid of airplanes, but a part of her believes that when she's up there, seeing the world from an entirely different perspective, she will feel like screaming.

She needs to remember to ask her dad if it's wrong to scream on an airplane. As in *legally* wrong. Because she knows that socially it's not the best.

The two of them are on the porch watching the truck drive away. Celso scratches the palm of his hands in the way he always does when he's nervous. Ana watches the truck drive down Sunflower Street and feels her heart tighten with the knowledge that, not too long from now, she will be the one driving away.

"Celso?" a voice suddenly calls, making the two of them turn their heads at the same time.

Ana doesn't recognize the owner of the voice, a tall white man with broad shoulders and a stern jaw, the sleeves of his red shirt rolled up to his elbows. He's accompanied by a Black woman with short curly hair and red lipstick whom Ana recognizes. She's the owner of the video rental store down the street.

"Hi?" Celso answers, caught by surprise.

Ana puts her arm on the porch rail and leans on it to watch the scene attentively. She loves seeing her dad interact with other adults, which is an almost rare situation, but always fun.

"Wow, it's been so long! It's me. Orlando," the man says. "You remember me, don't you?"

Ana nearly jumps at the man's name. Because this *has* to be "the gay guy" her dad used to know. No one knows two Orlandos in the same city. That means this stranger used to be her mom's friend. Ana feels her heart beating fast, but she has no idea what to do about the feeling.

"Of course, of course. I remember you. It's just that . . . This is funny . . . It's just that last week—"

"Hi, nice to meet you, my name is Ana," Ana jumps in, before her dad can say, "I was talking to my daughter about you, the only gay person I know because, you know, *she's* gay, too."

Orlando's eyes turn to Ana, and he cracks a smile. It's the look of someone who opens a present on Christmas Eve and *actually* likes what they see inside the box, no need to pretend.

"Hi, Ana," he says, still smiling. "Wow, you look so much like your mother. The nose, exactly like hers, how can it be?!"

The morning sun is flashing right in front of her face. She has to narrow her eyes to see well, but even so, she can't tell if there are tears in his eyes or if they're just naturally shiny.

Ana hopes it's the second option, because she wouldn't know how to deal with a total stranger crying in front of her because of her *nose*. She also hopes that the naturally shiny eye thing is part of gay genetics. She would *really* like to have naturally shiny eyes.

"This is my friend Catarina," Orlando introduces the woman next to him, who smiles, offers her hand, and initiates a clumsy cycle of greetings.

"The video store owner!" Ana says.

"Ah, yes, I knew your face looked familiar," Celso adds.

"Yes, that's right, I've seen the two of you there," Catarina says.

An awkward silence settles between them.

"What are you doing around these parts?" Celso asks, trying to show interest but sounding like an inexperienced interrogator.

Ana laughs.

"Catarina is thinking about moving to this street. To live closer to work and everything. We're looking around for places to rent."

Celso puts his hands on his waist and flashes a proud smile.

"We're leaving today! Number Eight will be vacant very soon," he says, pointing at me.

This gets Catarina's attention, and she carefully examines every detail of my facade.

"An excellent house!" Celso continues. "Spacious living room, this big porch right here, two bedrooms . . . Are you married? Do you have kids?"

Once again, Celso has the best of intentions, but something about the way he enunciates the questions while slowly running his hands through his full head of hair makes it seem like he's *flirting* with Catarina.

Ana laughs again and Orlando joins her. The two of them exchange a quick look, as if to confirm that they're sharing the same interpretation of this conversation (they are).

"No, no!" Catarina answers firmly. "That's my worst nightmare."

"Marriage or children?" Celso asks.

"Both," she answers with a laugh.

No one laughs with her.

She notices the discomfort in everyone's faces.

"Maybe a dog. I'd like to adopt one," she adds to soften the mood.

Ana smiles, wondering if, in her new Rio de Janeiro life, she'll be allowed to have a dog, too.

"Which neighborhood are you moving to?" Orlando asks, diverting the focus from his friend.

"Another city, actually. We're moving to Rio de Janeiro," Celso answers.

Catarina frowns.

Orlando smiles supportively.

Ana looks down.

"Wow," Orlando comments. "A *big* move, then! How lucky of me to have been able to find you before you left, and to see Ana, who's so big now. I hope you will be very happy there."

I doubt that, Ana thinks.

"Me too," Celso answers.

"Dad, I'm going inside," Ana says, and Celso nods.

"It was a pleasure to meet you," Orlando says. "Good luck in the new city."

I'll need that, she thinks as she walks slowly into the living room.

From the front window, Ana watches the adults talking outside. Orlando laughs, Catarina is still analyzing the house's details, and her dad is talking excitedly about something, moving his arms more than necessary. She's afraid he might be asking for advice on how to deal with his recently out gay daughter to the only other gay person he knows and hasn't seen in who knows how long. She's afraid of what other people might think of her. Even though she knows that, at this point, nothing else matters. The opinions that the residents of Lagoa Pequena have about her don't matter anymore, and even though that should be a good thing, it still leaves a bitter taste in her mouth.

The rooms are almost completely bare. It's only a matter of time until there's nothing left in here. Just another couple of hours before I cease being a home to becoming just real estate again. A building without someone to build their story inside me.

Ana grabs her backpack, the only luggage left behind, and turns over everything she's bringing to distract herself during the trip. The flight from São Paulo to Rio de Janeiro takes less than an hour, but Ana still brings her Discman, earbuds, extra batteries (which she's afraid will be discarded at the airport because she read somewhere that electronic devices can mess with the plane), two books longer than five hundred pages each, a neck pillow her dad also got as a freebie when he subscribed to the tabloid magazine, and a brand-new ruled notebook that she intends to use as her life journal.

I'm a house and know *nothing* about planes, but I'm pretty sure Ana won't be able to listen to music, read two books, sleep, and write in her journal in less than an hour. She'll probably spend most of her time looking out the window and imagining how, from above, people look like little ants, and how human existence is small and ephemeral when we look at things from afar.

Well, at least that's what *I'd* do if I ever traveled by plane.

She sits on the floor and inspects the living room walls from the height at which she used to see the world when she was a child.

My living room, now that it's empty, already looks bigger. But, looking from this angle, it appears gigantic. Ana thinks about how she grew up here, while the walls around her stayed the same size. She remembers when she watched *Alice in Wonderland* with her dad for the first time on the television. She thinks about the scene where Alice becomes a giant inside the White Rabbit's home, her legs sticking out of the door and her arms out the windows. At the time Ana laughed at the absurdity of the scene, but that's how she feels right now. Forced to grow quickly and unexpectedly until she no longer fits in here.

She used to love that movie, and the memory of having watched it with her dad here is the type that was locked inside her, untouched, and just needed a little push to come back to the surface.

Alice in Wonderland made her dad cry, and at the time she didn't understand why. What kind of an adult cries watching a surreal animated movie?

Only later, in her teenage years, did Ana get to understand that what had made her dad cry was longing.

———

Ana's mom's name was Alice.

Up until this exact moment, Ana had never stopped to think about the fact that she shared an initial with her mom. And, apparently, the shape of her nose.

Throughout her life, Ana always thought about her mom in a weird way. She'd thought about the consequences of her departure or the guilt she carried. She'd thought about her dad's loneliness and how everything that had happened had shaped her relationship with him. But she'd never thought about *Alice.* It was here that Alice became pregnant. I was the first (and only) home Ana has ever known. And now, lying on the floor and looking at every detail of the living room attentively, she tries to imagine her mother's footsteps in here.

Ana puts together a mental collage, using photos she's seen and the few stories her dad told her, to re-create a version of her own mother.

She imagines Alice doing the dishes in the sink and walking to the bathroom in the middle of the night while pregnant to pee for the fourth time. She imagines her parents laughing together, watching the street from the window, arriving home soaking wet after a storm, and hanging the clothes on the backyard's clothesline when the sun returned.

"Honey? Are you all right?" Celso calls, catching Ana by surprise.

Lost in her own thoughts, she hadn't noticed he'd come back.

"I'm all right. Just looking at the house one more time," Ana answers, eyeing her dad up and down and smiling at how he looks like a gentle giant.

Celso doesn't ask any more questions. He lies down next to her, not minding the back pain this is going to cause him.

"It was a good house for us, wasn't it?" he comments, looking at the walls from the same angle as his daughter. The two of them small against the huge living room.

"I liked living here," Ana says. And, taking a deep breath because she doesn't know how her dad is going to react, she asks: "Did Mom like living here?"

Celso laughs. It seems like a good sign.

"Ana, she *loved* it. She liked the name of the street and said that even the electricity bill felt like a love letter, because the envelope read 'Number Eight Sunflower Street.' She used to like waking up early and sunbathing in the bedroom window before they built that huge building next to us. She would have been devastated if she found out, because she *really* loved the way the sun hit the window in the morning. She liked the porch and had always wanted to get an inflatable pool so we could ·

cool off on hot days, but I never agreed to it because I didn't want people passing by and seeing two adults inside an inflatable pool. How silly of me, isn't it? Today I'd agree to it."

"And you're only *now* telling me this?!" Ana teases. "I've always wanted an inflatable pool on the porch!"

That's a lie. An inflatable pool on the porch hasn't even crossed her mind, but knowing that it's what her mom wanted makes her want it, too.

"We'll have to arrange for a new house, then," Celso says, hiding from his daughter the information that the building complex they are moving to in Rio has a pool and an ocean view.

I should feel jealous, since I'm losing the two to a building complex with a pool, while I will remain here, a small house with a porch and two bedrooms, squeezed between two buildings on a street that makes any mail seem like a love letter. But I'm not. I'm happy for Ana and Celso.

"Will it sound too ridiculous if we, I don't know, maybe . . . *thank* the house?" Ana suggests.

"Maybe a little," Celso laughs. "But okay, you go first."

Ana feels her face burning, a little embarrassed at her own idea. But at this point she has nothing left to lose, right?

"Thank you, house. For taking care of us this whole time. I will miss you," Ana says in a near whisper.

"Thank you, little house. It was really nice living here," Celso adds.

I would cry if I could.

"Thank *you*," I would say, if I could.

As quickly as the moment started, it comes to an end. Celso props himself on his elbows, then stands up to carry on with the day's tasks.

"The video store lady is going to talk to the real estate people. She might move here."

"She seems nice," Ana says, getting up as well because it would be ridiculous to keep talking to her dad from the floor.

"I'm gonna go get the car. We need to leave in a bit. Do you want to come with me?"

Ana thinks about it for a second.

"Can I stay a little longer? I'll wait for you here," she says.

Celso wrinkles his nose.

"I promise I won't run away and live under a fake name for the rest of my life," she says.

"Ah, there. I feel a lot better now. Be back soon," Celso gives in, before getting his keys and disappearing through the front door.

———————

Ana looks around her bedroom for the last time to make sure she's not leaving anything behind. She opens the closet, checks behind the door. She's not leaving anything.

Except, of course, the love of her life.

Ana doesn't know how long her dad will be, but she thinks it's long enough to execute a last-minute idea. She runs to her backpack, pulls out her journal and a pen, and starts scribbling in a hurry. I don't read it because, at least for now, I decide to respect her privacy.

When the page is full of words written in hurried (but still beautiful) handwriting, she rips it out of the journal. Then she tears another piece of paper from her journal to create a makeshift envelope, which she addresses "To the future resident of this house." With a piece of tape that was stuck to the closet door (and that used to hold a poster of *Titanic*, since Kate Winslet was on the list of Women Who Are So Beautiful They Deserve a Space on Ana's Wall), she sticks the envelope to the back of the top shelf.

———————

"Let's go, let's go, let's go!" Celso hurries her.

The rented car is parked by the porch, with the trunk open and full of her dad's junk. Ana tries to fit her backpack in there, and it becomes the hardest Tetris match of her life.

In the end she gives up and decides to carry the backpack on her lap.

Celso turns the key to the front door for the last time and, taking a small camera from his jacket pocket, snaps a photo of the facade.

"So we'll never forget your first house," he says.

Ana sighs, knowing it will be impossible to forget me.

Everything is in the car, but something seems amiss. Celso looks around and then at his wristwatch, as if he were waiting for the right time to be late. Ana thinks that maybe her dad wants a rushed trip full of strong emotions, but that makes no sense because Celso generally hates strong emotions.

He finally smiles in relief when he sees, at the end of Sunflower Street, Letícia's bike approaching.

She's pedaling as hard as she can and almost falls off the bike when she slams the brake by the sidewalk.

"I'm so sorry, Celso. I didn't want to be late. It was my mom that—"

Celso just closes his eyes, points to Ana, and turns his back to the two of them.

"What are you doing here?" Ana asks, unable to move.

"One last goodbye. Your dad told me what time you were leaving and . . . well . . . here I am."

Letícia is sweaty, her hair smushed by the helmet, her breath shallow from crossing Lagoa Pequena by bike. But she's here. And that's all that matters to Ana.

"Five minutes," Celso yells, still with his back to them.

Letícia comes closer and holds Ana's shaky hands, as delicate and fragile as butterfly wings.

"Hmm," Letícia mutters, with the air of someone who tried hard to be on time just to realize they didn't prepare anything to say. "I hope you have a good trip. A safe trip."

"I'm afraid of flying," Ana confesses, the first thing that comes to her mind.

"Ah, it's a little scary at first, but you'll get used to it. We always take a plane to visit my relatives in Belém. When it starts going up, you get butterflies in your stomach, you know? You'll feel your body getting light and heavy at the same time. But it's fine. Closing your eyes might help."

Ana tries to make mental notes of it all, but she's too distracted by Letícia's beauty.

"Thank you for coming. I d-don't . . ." Ana stutters. "I wasn't ready to say goodbye again. I didn't want this to be happening. I just wanted our story to . . . work out."

Without letting the other hand go, Letícia brings one finger to Ana's lips.

"Shhhh," she whispers. "Stop that. Stop saying we didn't work out. We worked out *so well.* I wouldn't trade even one minute I spent with you for anything else in the whole world."

"But . . ." Ana protests.

"We worked out *so well,*" Letícia repeats.

Ana finally smiles. Her eyes are wet and, in a way, shiny.

Letícia's finger slides from Ana's lips to her cheek to stroke Ana's face in a simple but very intimate gesture.

Ana blabbers the next foolishness that comes to mind: "Your Blink-182 CD. I never returned it. It's in my backpack, if you want to get it and—"

"Of course I don't," Letícia answers. "You can have it. To remember me by."

"But I didn't leave you anything to remember *me* by!" Ana counters, regretting not having thought of a present.

"I have this whole city to remember you by, Ana. And I will keep only the good memories, okay?"

"Okay," Ana whispers, feeling deep down (but *really* deep down) that everything is going to be all right.

"One minute!" Celso announces.

How can you fit a love the size of the world into one minute?

"I'd really like to kiss you, but it's okay if you're not ready to do that in public," Ana says, looking around and seeing some people walking down the street, going about their normal lives.

Lagoa Pequena's opinion on her sexuality might not matter to her anymore, but it does to Letícia, since she's the one staying.

"I think I'm ready," Letícia says, and then inches closer to Ana and brings her lips to her girlfriend's.

The last kiss is sweet, slow, and good. Ana feels her body grow light and heavy at the same time, and she thinks of it as a test for her first takeoff.

"Thank you for having loved me so much," Letícia says when they move away from each other.

"Thank you for having allowed me to love you," Ana answers.

The two of them look at Celso, still with his back to them, rubbing his eyes like someone who's either crying or having an allergic reaction (he's crying).

"Dad, shall we?"

"One last thing. Stay where you are," Celso says, and turns around with his camera in his hands. "Say cheese."

Ana and Letícia hug and smile for the picture.

———

I can't hear what happens after father and daughter get in the car. I choose not to pry into Letícia's thoughts, who's standing on the sidewalk watching the car drive away and, after it disappears, looks up at the sky.

I wish the two of them had had more time together, but, for now, I know it's not possible. I wish I could see the photo Celso took. I was in the background, and I know I look good in photos, but I might have blinked.

Another joke, on the house. I don't blink.

I root for a better future for Ana and Letícia. It probably won't be here. They're too big for Lagoa Pequena. But the house that harbors a love as big as theirs will be a lucky one.

Just like I was.

GREG

I don't know if it was the flyers, Catarina's popularity, a desire to watch *The Lake House*, or the complete lack of better things to do on a Friday at the end of January in Lagoa Pequena, but at three in the afternoon there are twenty-two people sitting in the store, ready for the movie. Greg runs around with a badge hanging from his neck that has STAFF written on it next to the drawing of Keanu Reeves in a bucket of popcorn. Tiago made the badges because, apparently, he takes event planning very seriously.

"All good with the projector? Is it working?" Catarina asks, cracking her knuckles to keep her anxiety under control. She has a badge, too, hanging discreetly from a scarf wrapped around her neck.

Catarina looks radiant. Her tight curls are styled in an updo and, for the first time since Greg arrived, Catarina is wearing makeup. Her perfectly applied red lipstick contrasts with her brown skin, and her eyes are accented by a golden eyeshadow and what Greg believes to be eyelash extensions (but no, it's just mascara. Greg doesn't know the first thing about lashes). She bites her lip and holds her breath as she inspects the familiar faces sitting in her garage.

268

"Everything's in order, Aunt Catarina. I've tested it. Three times," Greg appeases her.

"And the food?" she asks.

Greg looks over his shoulder at Tiago, who's manning a table by the entrance, full of drinks and snacks prepared by his mother. He gives a thumbs-up to Tiago, who replies in kind, adding a wink and a kiss. Greg wants to *die* because, in an effort to appear less intimidating for this special event, Tiago brushed his bangs away from his face, which makes for an even better view of his perfect features and dimples when he smiles.

"Gregório?" Catarina calls him again, because Greg has spent literally five minutes staring at Tiago.

"Yes!" he says when he snaps out of his trance. "Everything is all right with the food. Now all we have to do is start."

"Do I need to make an opening speech?" she asks.

"I don't think you *need* to, but if you want—"

"I do," she says without hesitation. Catarina positions herself in front of the screen (well, the white sheet) and claps to get everyone's attention.

All twenty-two people go silent immediately because Catarina is the kind of person everyone wants to listen to when they have something to say. The twenty-two people look extremely happy to be here. The twenty-two people turn into twenty-four when Orlando arrives with another man who must be about his age. Without making a fuss, the two men take a seat in the last row. Orlando smiles and nods at Catarina, who had been waiting for her best friend before speaking.

"Good afternoon!" she says, then clears her throat and smiles. "I'd like to thank everyone for coming to the first showing of Catavento Video's very own film club. You all know this is a very special place to me, and your participation might help keep this garage working. Today we will be showing an extremely romantic movie that's hard to understand unless you're paying very careful attention, so please do not talk during the film. And, yes, I'm talking to you, Marta." She points at a white woman with gray hair who's whispering in her friend's ear. "Keanu Reeves built his career on emblematic characters, saving the world, questioning the system, and blowing things up. But in *The Lake House*, we see another side of the best actor of this generation: a man who's sad, melancholic, and in love. At the end of the movie, we will discuss the plot and answer questions. Whatever question you want to ask, I'll definitely be able to answer it, because I've watched this movie an absurd number of times."

Greg holds his laughter, not knowing where his aunt got all this inspiration from.

"Before we begin, I'd like to thank my nephew, Gregório." She pauses. "Greg. For the idea. For having organized everything and encouraged me to do something different. Because everyone who knows me *knows* I hate change. But this one wasn't so hard to accept."

The room goes silent, and no one knows what to do until Tiago starts clapping. Then everyone claps, Catarina takes a seat in the front row, and Keanu Reeves (the dog) jumps on her lap. Greg turns off the lights, turns on the projector, and the film begins. He tiptoes to the entrance and gets a chair to sit next to Tiago. It's the best seat in the house, since from here he can watch everyone (including Orlando and Roger, who, as soon as the lights go off, inch a little closer and lean on each other's shoulders). But also because Greg is sitting next to the most handsome boy in town, and no sad, melancholy Keanu Reeves (the actor) will ever hold his attention more than Tiago, who is now looking at the screen and smiling. His face is lit up from the projector, and his eyes wander between the movie, his feet, Greg, and the ceiling.

The two remain silent because, to be very honest, no one is brave enough to break Catarina's rules. But exactly thirty-three minutes into the movie, Tiago holds Greg's hand, and they stay that way until the end.

———

"No, they live in different *eras*, but on the *same planet*. It's not a movie about *aliens*," Catarina explains, making exaggerated gestures with her arms.

The movie is over, and the discussion is heated. As expected, half the audience didn't quite understand the movie's timelines and, the more people argue, the more occupied Tiago becomes selling popcorn, home-made chocolate truffles, and cans of soda. People tend to get hungry when they're confused.

"Hey." Greg timidly approaches Orlando and his companion.

"Greg!" Orlando nearly screams in an attempt to make himself heard amid the gaggle. The garage feels like a very large family's Christmas party. "Roger, this is Gregório, Catarina's nephew I told you about."

"Good things, I hope," Greg jokes, immediately regretting sounding like his mom at one of the rich-people parties his dad always drags them to. "Very nice to meet you."

Greg holds out his hand and realizes Roger is holding a sunflower. Greg laughs, imagining the moment Orlando gave it to him, with that whole speech about the sun.

"Very nice to meet you, Gregório. My name is Roger," the other man says. His handshake is a lot stronger than Greg expected.

Roger seems to be a little older than Orlando, more mature, more experienced. His skin is brown, a little lighter than Greg's, and his shoulders are wide. He wears thick-rimmed glasses that make him look like a man who knows a lot about many things, and his hair is shaved so short that, depending on where you stand, he might appear bald.

"Hmm," Greg mutters. "Enjoying your time in the city?"

He has no idea how to maintain a conversation with an adult who looks like he knows a lot about many things.

"Very much enjoying it." Roger smiles. "I've missed it. I really like it here. I might be back to stay this time."

Orlando's eyes light up upon hearing this.

"To stay, really?" Greg asks Roger, but his eyes are fixed on his aunt's friend, who's smiling a goofy smile.

"I think I've done my share of traveling around the world. I've come to realize that I belong here," Roger answers, but he is *also* looking at Orlando.

This is the weirdest conversation ever.

"See you around, then," Greg says, stepping back to give the two of them more time to talk.

He can't help but wonder if one day he will experience anything like this. If one day he will be responsible for his own decisions and able to choose to stay. If adult life holds for him a beautiful love story with someone who will make his eyes shine.

———

The film club goes until late, and the sky is dark by the time the last customer leaves. The discussion turned into an open vote to decide which movie they would show next, which then turned into a party where everyone was eating, drinking, and chatting.

Greg feels relieved that he made the event work. Catarina feels proud because she's never seen her store so crowded.

Tiago volunteers to stay a little longer to help clean up, and Greg insists that his aunt should go back inside with Orlando and Roger to pop a bottle of wine and talk about whatever people over thirty-five talk about.

He isn't *excited* to take down the screen (sheet) and pile the chairs on top of one another, but he'll do anything for some alone time with Tiago.

"Congratulations! It all worked out!" Tiago says while closing the garage.

"I wouldn't have made it without your help," Greg says, his heart clenched and happy at the same time.

With the door closed, the two boys are alone in the garage, only the light filtered through the cracks of the door illuminating them. That's all they need to go at each other with a kiss that lasts exactly six minutes and eighteen seconds.

"Wow." Greg takes a deep breath when they finally move away from each other, both gasping for air.

"I'm getting my cast taken off next week," Tiago mentions, pointing at his left arm. "I can't wait to hold you properly."

Greg opens a mischievous smile that lasts two seconds before reality hits him.

"I'm leaving next week."

This information doesn't seem to shock Tiago, but it still hits him hard. He leans against the wall, slides to the floor, and gestures for Greg to sit next to him.

"I kind of assumed that would happen," Tiago says, putting his unbroken arm around Greg's shoulders and pulling him closer. "I think that's why I was so insecure about this whole thing. I didn't want to invest time in a summer romance. It seems like a thing that only happens in the movies."

"Well," Greg sighs, and cuddles against Tiago's chest. "I guess your plan didn't quite work, did it?"

"It's all your fault," Tiago whispers with a silly smile on his face. He runs his fingers through Greg's curls and stares at the wall.

"I wish I could stay, you know?" Greg says, throwing the idea out there to see if it makes more sense when he says it out loud instead of just keeping it locked in his head.

"Stay here? In Lagoa Pequena?" Tiago scoffs. "What an idea, Greg! You live in a city that has everything. There's *nothing* here."

Greg bites his tongue so he doesn't say "You're here" right away, but after two seconds of silence, he realizes that, yeah, Lagoa Pequena has Tiago. But that's not the *only* reason he wants to stay.

"But here I have family that I feel actually likes me. Just the way I am, you know? And a dog. And an infinite supply of movies in the garage. And, well . . ." He pauses before he finally says, "You're here."

Tiago wants Greg to stay, too, but he doesn't say anything. He knows it would be too much to ask, and he doesn't want to deal with the weight of it in the future. Instead, he just lowers his face and covers Greg's head with approximately a thousand little kisses.

"Ow," Greg complains.

"Did I hurt you?"

"No," he answers, then sits up straight on the floor, puts his hand in his back pocket, and pulls out a piece of paper.

It's the letter he found in his aunt's closet that has remained untouched in his pants pocket since the day before.

"What's that?" Tiago asks, craning his neck to get a better look.

"I found it in my aunt's closet. It looks like someone wanted to hide it, but not enough to make it impossible to find," he answers, turning the envelope around.

"'To the future resident of this house,'" Tiago reads. "A letter written by someone who lived here before Catarina. Interesting," Tiago ponders as he rubs his chin like a real detective or one of the characters from Scooby-Doo.

"It might be a letter from my aunt to someone who will live here in the future, I don't know," Greg says, running through the possibilities.

"No, that isn't Catarina's handwriting. I know her handwriting because she always sends us Christmas cards with a photo of Keanu wearing a Santa hat."

Greg ignores the pang of never having received a Christmas card with a picture of Keanu wearing a Santa hat, even though he is literally part of Catarina's *biological family*. Maybe family really is something you choose.

"You're not gonna open it?" Tiago provokes, breaking the silence.

"No," Greg answers immediately. "I don't know. Maybe it's confidential."

"The envelope says it's for a *future resident*. In theory, you are now a resident. For a limited time, sure, but right now, in this moment, you are. You better seize the opportunity while you still live here."

Greg could have interpreted Tiago's advice in myriad ways, but he chooses to believe that he is speaking exclusively about the crumpled letter in his hands.

"We could just open it, see what it is, then put it back," Greg suggests, throwing a *we* in there so he won't feel guilty by himself.

"*Yes!*" Tiago says in support, holding back his curiosity and managing not to rip the letter from Greg's hands to open it himself.

"Okay, let's see what we have here," Greg says, gingerly opening the envelope as if he were holding the most fragile piece of paper in the entire world.

He takes out a notebook page that has been folded four times. It's in the same handwriting as the envelope, but the letters seem tighter and smaller:

Lagoa Pequena, January 14, 2000

Hi,

If you have found this letter, you're probably living in Number 8 Sunflower Street (unless you're someone from the real estate company who found it by accident. If that's the case, please put the letter back where you found it. It's not for you).

I don't know you, and I think that, by the time you read this, I will be far away from here. But I couldn't go without first leaving a note. This was my house for my entire life. I don't know what it's like to live somewhere other than here (but I'm about to find out). For seventeen years, I fell asleep and woke up here every day (in the large room, which used to get the morning sun before they built that huge building next door), and today, only moments before I have to move to a new city where they put ketchup on pizza, I've realized how much I'm going to miss this place. I thought I'd just miss my girlfriend. Or ex. I think we broke up. I don't know yet. Everything is kind of weird right now. But the point is that I will miss the house, too. My room, the front porch, and the details on the door frame in the living room, which, if you look closely, look like a smiley face.

So, person who lives here now, take good care of this little house, okay? It was here that I literally became a person. Every memory I've had to this day was formed inside these walls. But I think I'm only taking the good ones with me.

I hope you will make some good memories here, too.

With love, A

Greg and Tiago remain silent for a moment, taking in every word from the letter and trying to unravel the details of what they just read.

"It was a girl. A *gay* girl!" Greg comments, marveling at the coincidence.

"It might be a boy. You can't tell."

"A boy with handwriting this beautiful, Tiago? Yeah, right."

"Hey!" Tiago protests. "My handwriting is pretty. I think."

(It is.)

"*Gay*," Greg whispers into Tiago's ear.

"That doesn't matter right now," Tiago says, pretending to be mad but really he just loves it when Greg whispers things into his ear. "I thought the letter was cute. What are you going to do with it?"

Greg thinks for a moment. "Put it back?"

"No." Tiago laughs. "I mean what are you going to do *about* it? This letter made its way to you for a reason, I think. It was hidden in the closet for *ten years*, Greg. It feels like destiny."

Greg looks at the piece of paper with the slightly yellowed borders. His eyes fall on the last sentence.

"Well," he says with a smile that carries a hint of sadness. "I think I'll follow this letter's advice and make some good memories here."

And with that, the two of them kiss for another six minutes.

Or more.

It's not like I was *timing it*, okay?

FEBRUARY 2, 2010

Greg leaves Lagoa Pequena tomorrow. He doesn't have much to pack; all he has is a small backpack with a few clothes and some knickknacks. But he still spends a good amount of time calmly folding every T-shirt and thinking of the memories from the last few weeks. He stares at the walls of the smaller bedroom, the shelves full of old DVDs and cardboard tubes containing posters that probably used to decorate the store.

It's a simple bedroom, with a small window and nothing much. But it's not what's in it that makes Greg's heart so tight. It's not about *things*. It's about people. And the dog, too. Greg wants to stay, but he doesn't know how to ask that. It seems too absurd. He's capable of requesting a super-expensive projector from his dad's assistant without worry, but asking for a big move like this makes him tremble with fear.

He feels like his entire family is afraid of change.

His parents, for instance, dragged on a horrible marriage for over ten years because of their fear of change. His aunt literally still runs a video rental store because she doesn't want to change.

And then there's Greg, at sixteen, full of innocent dreams, thinking he can move cities (and, in doing so, completely change his life) and receive the immediate support of his family. It would never work out.

The bedroom door is ajar, and Catarina knocks on it as Greg folds the same T-shirt for the hundredth time, his eyes fixed on the light of the moon filtering through the window.

"Hey," she says in a whisper. "I made you a goodbye dinner."

Greg shakes his head in an attempt to disperse his bad thoughts. "Wow," he mocks, clapping slowly. "You *made* dinner?"

"Oh, please, Gregório, I ordered pizza! Five-cheese, it's your favorite."

"I've never told you that! How do you know?" Greg looks truly scared as he asks himself if his aunt has supernatural mind-reading powers.

If she did, this is when she would hear Greg begging to stay and things would be a lot easier.

"Tiago told me," Catarina confesses, sticking by the decision not to tease her nephew on his last night with her.

Greg smiles, still confused because he doesn't remember telling Tiago that specific detail, but they've spent so much time talking nonstop since they first met, it's no wonder Greg doesn't remember everything he shared.

"Thank you for thinking of every detail."

"I don't even *like* five-cheese pizza. I think it's silly to waste pizza with a flavor that's just five times the same thing," Catarina mentions. "Goes to show how *great* of an aunt I am."

She brings her hands to her hips and raises her head as if waiting to be applauded for her personal sacrifice on behalf of her nephew.

But what she gets is a hug. Out of nowhere, without warning, Greg embraces his aunt for one or two seconds, and she barely knows how to react. He doesn't know, either. It's the most embarrassing hug in the history of hugs. And yet, they're both smiling when they let go.

***

Catarina loved the five-cheese pizza, but she avoids showing too much satisfaction because she's a proud person. The two of them look at the empty pizza box on the dining table, in a silent war to determine who will overcome their sluggishness to get up from the couch and put it in the trash.

A war they both want to lose.

"Wanna watch a movie?" Catarina asks, still unsure how to deal with the strange feeling that her nephew's unexpected hug left in her chest.

"Hmm, no," Greg answers, dispirited.

"Do you want some help packing?" she insists.

"It's just a backpack, there isn't that much to pack."

"Do you want me to leave you alone so you can get some sleep?" She plays her final card with a tired laugh.

Greg thinks about how to answer her. He takes a deep breath, opens his mouth, and thinks a bit more. It takes him more than a full open-mouthed minute to gather the courage to say something.

"You know, Aunt Catarina, I want to *stay.*"

"What do you mean?" Catarina plays dumb.

"*Stay* stay. To live here. For a while, I don't know. But it's the kind of thing that's complicated to ask because, well, who shows up out of nowhere like, 'Hey, can I live in your house?'"

Catarina brings her hand to her chin, pretending that she hasn't spent the last three days thinking about this.

But Greg is not done talking.

"I know you like to be alone. Just you and Keanu." Greg points at the dog lying on his little dog bed next to the couch, unaware of the serious conversation taking place in this room. He is, after all, a dog. "And I don't want to get in the way, you know? I don't want you to be my *mom*. But I like it here. And I wish I could stay a little longer."

"Gregório—" Catarina starts in a serious tone, looking right into her nephew's eyes, but he interrupts her.

"I know. I know you're going to say it's ridiculous that I want to move to another city because of a boy. But there's more to it, I swear! I feel free here. Maybe *free* isn't the right word. I feel like . . . I feel that I don't have to walk around holding my breath all the time. This place feels like home to me. And that's all thanks to you. It's not as if I like you more than I like my parents or anything like that, I like *everybody*, I promise. The thing is just that, I don't know. I think I like myself more when I'm here."

That did it. Catarina starts crying. For the first time since she moved here (March 23, 2000), she's crying over something other than the ending of *Point Break*.

"You didn't need to give me the full speech. I was ready to say yes when you first brought it up." She laughs, drying her wet eyes with the back of her hand.

The twinkle in Greg's eyes is brighter than the moon outside.

"In my defense, I always thought you hated me," Greg says, crying and laughing at the same time.

"I generally hate *children*. But when they arrive like this, all grown, ready to work at the store, and they already know how to clean the house and wash their own underwear, I really don't mind it as much."

Greg laughs even harder, and they enjoy the few minutes of extreme happiness before they have to deal with the rest.

"You want to stay, I'll *let* you stay, but things aren't so simple. We have to call your mom."

"Piece of cake. I'm sure my parents will celebrate or something," Greg says, feeling sorry for himself.

"That's not quite true, Gregório," Catarina counters, her voice heavy and serious. "Your life isn't like that movie *Matilda*, where you live with two horrible parents, and at the end you show up with adoption papers that you *found in a library book*, they sign them, and then take off."

Greg goes quiet for a moment, reflecting on how his life is *literally* like the end of that movie.

"Well, let's give her a call. Get the phone," he orders, feeling that his palms are starting to get sweaty.

But before Catarina can get up to get her cell phone from the bedroom, someone knocks on the door.

Greg runs to get it. It's Tiago. Greg nearly dies a little because, after his aunt said *yes*, he couldn't imagine that his evening could get even better.

"Heeey," Tiago says, waving his arms above his head.

"You took off the cast!" Greg says.

"And I came straight here to give you a *two-armed* hug. And to get my sunflower, which I left behind."

"Who is it?" Catarina yells from the bedroom.

"It's Tiago," Greg says.

"Hi, Aunt Catarina," Tiago yells as he walks into the living room.

And Greg nearly explodes, because never in his life has he felt so at home.

———

Tiago decides he's not leaving anytime soon and, after Greg and Catarina fill him in on the whole situation, the three of them put their heads together to come up with the most convincing argument of all time.

"We need to think of every detail. Every argument my mom might use not to let me stay."

"School will be the first one," Catarina says. "You go to school, right?"

"I do, Aunt Catarina," Greg answers, laughing a little at his aunt's inability to comprehend the daily life of a sixteen-year-old. "But there are schools here."

"There must be a good cheap one," Catarina says, trying to remember the last time she paid attention to a Lagoa Pequena school. Which isn't easy, considering she's the kind of person who crosses the street when she sees a group of teenagers.

"It can be good and expensive," Greg mentions right away, displaying his financial privilege. "I mean, it's not as if money is a factor for my dad."

He feels ridiculous.

"College entrance exams," Tiago adds, trying to change the topic because he sees how uncomfortable Greg feels. "You realize you're a junior in high school, right? Any college plans?"

Greg scratches his head, completely confused. "I don't know, but I've been in a college prep course since last year. My dad wants me to be a doctor or something that will make more money than that. I haven't found a way to tell him it's not gonna happen."

"Roger is moving here. He's a history teacher and is going to teach a prep course downtown," Tiago says.

"Which Roger? *Roger* Roger?" Catarina asks.

"Yes, Orlando's boyfriend."

"His *boyfriend*? Orlando didn't tell me anything about that!" Catarina protests, completely beside herself.

"Relax, he hasn't told anybody anything yet," Tiago says with a laugh, trying to assuage Catarina. "But I'm a restaurant owner's son. I know *everything* that's happening in this city."

Greg smiles, bemused at all the small-town stuff he didn't understand until a few weeks ago.

"Good for them. But back to the matter at hand!" Greg says, clapping his hands.

And, as if on cue, Catarina's cell phone starts blinking and vibrating. The small screen shows that *Carmem (Sister)* is calling and, before giving into his despair, Greg wonders for a moment how many Carmems his aunt must know that she needs to specify their relationship in her contacts.

There. Now Greg is desperate.

"Pick it up, Aunt Catarina!" he demands.

"You pick it up," she counters.

The phone is still vibrating.

"For the love of god, *somebody* pick it up!" Tiago begs.

Both aunt and nephew take a deep breath, almost at the same time. Catarina puts her hand on Greg's shoulders, her biggest display of tenderness yet. At least in terms of humans. She's always tender toward Keanu Reeves.

Greg grabs the device, presses the green button, and brings it to his ear.

"Hey, Mom," he says, swallowing the lump in his throat. "I need to ask you something."

BETO

MAY 23, 2020

Contrary to what many might think, thousands of likes on a Twitter photo did not bring Beto immediate fame and fortune. He's just a boy posting photos of his window, after all. It's not as if he became a meme, or were really funny. But still, the event brought some good things.

New followers are now supporting his work, and some of them are actual famous photographers whom he'd always followed. Beto pretends he's used to it and tries not to seem like a *fanatic* every time someone important starts following him.

He also got paid for an original photo for the first time in his life. *Actual* money for a photo that's unrelated to a wedding party or gender-reveal party. The image of the sunset was purchased for a virtual exhibit (though Beto doesn't quite understand how that works, he accepts that all the normal events have had a virtual version since the beginning of the pandemic), so he just signed the release form and received money without any effort. The dream life.

He receives emails from people asking if he does artistic nudes (*I'm seventeen!* is his answer to those), trying to book in-person photo shoots in São Paulo (*We're in the middle of a pandemic!*), and who simply took time out of their day to say they liked his work and found a little inspiration from his photos (*!!!!!!!!!!!*).

Beto doesn't know how to take compliments.

But everything that's happened since the photo went viral for no apparent reason is like fuel to Beto. All this validation motivates him to take photos practically every day and, as much as he hates to admit, it is so nice to receive compliments from people he doesn't know.

It's Saturday morning, and Beto is leaning against the living room window, using the lens he got from his sister to focus on a hummingbird perched on the street's power cable. The sky is clear, not a cloud in sight, and the neighborhood is quiet. Ever since the lockdown began, Beto has always felt that the absence of people in the streets made everything look like a zombie apocalypse and the end of the world. But not today. Today, for no reason at all, he feels at peace.

The secret to surviving one day after another, Beto learned, is to enjoy these moments of quiet and erase all the awful things happening in the world from your mind. Because these moments are too short. You blink and they're gone. And Beto wants to make today's quiet moment last as long as possible (the year's record so far is forty-six minutes).

"Take a photo of me!" Lara demands, coming into the living room out of nowhere, with her high-pitched voice that completely breaks the quietness.

Beto takes a deep breath and turns around to face his sister.

She's posing with her eyes closed and an exaggerated pout, and her face is covered in a green face mask. Beto laughs at the scene and snaps a shot of his sister.

"There," he says, after pressing the shutter release button at least five times. "Now leave me alone."

"We need to decide what new thing we're doing today," Lara says, sinking into the couch.

She's still taking their project seriously, despite all the signs Beto has sent that he can't stand it anymore.

"You leave me alone, how's that?" he suggests. "That would be a new thing."

Lara laughs because she knows he's joking. Beto laughs also because he's too happy to keep up his grumpy act.

"Are you and that boy talking again?"

"Nicolas."

"Yeah. Don't dodge the question."

"No. He told me that my photo started going viral on Twitter, and I answered with a bunch of shocked emojis. You know, the ones with the blue face and white eyes, kind of panicking."

"I know the one."

"And that was it."

"That's all?"

"Yeah."

"Wow." Lara sighs. "I expected more, based on how you described the emoji in such detail."

"I'm sorry, Lara. Nothing happens in my life," Beto mutters as he detaches the lens from the camera and puts it away carefully.

"With all the awful things happening to people right now, having nothing happen to you is kind of a good thing, no?" Lara reasons.

And she's kind of right.

"But I'm okay now. There are times when I think back to when I confessed my feelings for Nicolas," Beto says, holding back an embarrassed laugh. "I feel ridiculous saying it out loud. But I think I just wanted something to *happen*, you know?"

"Totally normal," Lara answers, biting her nails.

"And, like, it's not as if I don't like him anymore. I do. But, I don't know, I guess before I told him, I thought it might be nice to have a virtual boyfriend? And it's not even that I wanted a boyfriend. I don't know if I do. But that's the thing. I wanted to *feel* something. I wanted to feel like my life was moving forward. Because everything was so still, but then thousands of people online decided they like what I do, and suddenly that felt like enough, you know? I don't feel quite so still anymore. I used the pictures I took over the last few days to apply for a scholarship in a virtual portrait photography course. I thought it would be good to learn something, to keep my mind busy, and it's crazy to think how that replaced what I felt for Nico. It didn't *replace* what I felt, right? They're two separate things. But it filled out the emptiness of nothing happening because now several little things are happening, and I guess for now that's enough."

Lara blinks slowly, twice. "Wow?" she says. "I came to say good morning and chat. There was no need to *pour your heart out* to me like that."

"Sorry," Beto says, feeling ridiculous again. He urgently needs to stop feeling ridiculous about every little thing.

"No need to apologize, it's fine. Just let me know if you're going to talk more because I need to take off this mask in two minutes," she says, pointing at the green goo covering her entire face.

"You can go take off your mask in peace," Beto says, giving her a thumbs-up. "I've said everything I had to say."

Lara gets up, does a big stretch in the middle of the living room, and, before walking to the bathroom, turns around to face her brother again.

"Can I just give you one piece of advice?" she asks.

"Shoot."

"Talk to Nicolas."

"Last time you suggested that, it didn't go too well," Beto says with a laugh, trying to hide the lump that immediately forms in his throat from the thought of talking to Nico again.

"No, silly," Lara says. "*Really* talk. In an honest way. Everything that you just told me. It might work out. Just so the two of you don't have this bitter taste in your mouths forever."

Beto instinctively swallows his own saliva, hoping to taste bitterness. "I'll think about it. Thank you."

"I'm always here for you, okay? I know it might seem depressing to vent with your older sister, but I'm here."

"I know," Beto answers, completely hiding the fact that he shouted into a pillow *with his mom*, which is definitely more depressing than venting with your older sister.

Lara bows and turns to go to the bathroom, but she stops halfway.

"Oh! One more thing," she says in a whisper. "Talk to Mom later. To see if she knows anyone who can see you. You know? For therapy and stuff."

Beto smiles and nods.

Lara winks at him.

That's the way they find to support each other. To show that they care for each other.

MAY 27, 2020

Wednesday is *Super Cheflings* day. The ideal time for Beto to lock himself in the bedroom for some privacy while his mother and sister eat popcorn and stare without blinking at the TV in the living room. Beto thinks it's the finale. Either that or the premiere of *Super Kids Cheflings*, which is a spin-off of the cooking competition for kids, except featuring *even younger children*. Beto is definitely feeling a little lost in the reality TV schedule.

Sitting in bed and leaning against the wall, he holds his phone, his mind set on a conversation with Nico, even if it's the last one (but he hopes it won't be).

Beto

Hey. Can we talk?

The answer comes in almost immediately.

Nico

Sure!!! Everything ok???

Beto tries not to think too much about the number of exclamation and question marks in Nico's text. And also about the fact that there was a time when a conversation between the two was just routine, but today it's enough for Nico to suspect that Beto is not doing too well.

Can I call? Don't want to type everything hehe

Can we do a video chat? I want to see your purple hair again!!

A few months ago, Beto would have thought that was yet another sign from Nicolas. After all, who talks to anyone like this unless they are madly in love with the person? But today Beto knows that the way Nico says he wants to see his purple hair again only means that he wants to see his purple hair again.

And yet, Beto shakes his head to get his wavy (and, at this point, faded) strands of hair in order, in a way that seems casual but also looks good. Before he starts the call, I swear to god, he moistens his fingers with saliva and adjusts his eyebrows.

"Hey," Beto says, as soon as Nico's pixelated image appears on the phone screen.

"Hey! One sec, ijhnojhony hnnejction roojhible," Nico answers, which I think means "One sec, I'm going to the balcony, the connection in my room is horrible."

Or maybe "One sec, I'm in so much agony, the injection is really very durable."

I really can't tell.

Beto looks at the blur on his screen and patiently waits as he organizes his thoughts to say everything he wants to in a direct and coherent way.

"There!" Nicolas's voice echoes. "I'm on the balcony. Now I can see you better."

I got it right.

"Hey there," Beto says in a direct and coherent way.

"I will never get over that purple hair of yours. I want it for myself, too!" Nico compliments him, trying to break the weird mood that has already settled in their thirty seconds of conversation. "So, what's up? What do you want to talk about?"

Beto takes a deep breath.

About a lot, he thinks.

"I wanted to thank you for telling me when my photo blew up on Twitter," he says, because he thinks it's a mild way to start the conversation.

"Ah, that was nothing. I was bursting with pride, you know? But since you just answered with a bunch of emojis, I thought you still needed more time to, I don't know, process everything?"

"Oh. I didn't know what to answer at the time. It was pretty intense. I didn't even know the little notification icon on Twitter could go up to three digits."

Nicolas laughs, and the sound, even though it breaks down because of the internet connection, makes Beto laugh as well.

"Don't forget about me when you become famous," Nico says.

"No one becomes famous posting sunset photos online, Nicolas."

"You might be the first, who knows."

"And I'm sorry about how I reacted when I found out you wanted nothing to do with me," Beto says out of the blue, without any hint of subtlety as he leads this conversation to the complicated part.

Nicolas seems surprised. He stands still for some time. One might think the connection froze again, but he blinks twice and clears the doubt in Beto's mind. He's just surprised.

"Wow, Beto, easy," Nicolas finally says. "Everything about that sentence is *so* wrong. First, because you don't have to apologize about how you reacted to something. Second, because it's not that I don't want anything to do with you. I just don't know what I want right now. Things are . . . hard."

They've known each other long enough for Beto to realize it's not just a *Do you like me or not?* thing that's making Nico feel so distressed.

"What is happening? Do you want to talk?"

Nico takes a deep breath.

"My mom. She caught the virus," Nicolas says, and then continues to talk immediately when he sees the worried look on Beto's face. "It's okay, it's okay! Nothing to worry about, everything is fine now. It was just a complicated process. An *actual* lockdown for her. I was living at my cousins' just to be safe, the whole family had to do a million tests, and the doctor had to give her, like, three different medicines until she was finally *well*. But it's still very scary, you know?"

"And why didn't you tell me anything?" Beto asks, feeling stupid that he, once again, is putting himself at the center of the conversation.

"It was when we had our talk," Nico laughs. "I was going to tell you after you were done, but kind of couldn't. I didn't want it to seem like I was using my sick mom as an excuse to make you feel sorry for me or something. It's complicated. I had a lot on my mind. I still do.

But these weeks without talking to you every day . . . it's been hard, you know? Because you've always been—and I feel stupid saying this, despite the fact that it is true—my safe haven. Talking to you was always the easiest thing in the world. But, suddenly, it's not anymore."

"I'm sorry" is all Beto can say.

"Relax. Everything is fine now."

"Is it really? No, really, yeah?"

Ten seconds of silence.

"No, it's not," Nico blurts out.

The two of them laugh because, honestly, what else is there to do?

"You know," Nico continues, "I reread our conversation a million times. I think I was kind of an asshole. I asked my cousin if she thought it was emotionally irresponsible of me. She didn't know what emotional irresponsibility is because she's not on Twitter, so I had to *explain* it. It was the most painful conversation of my life."

"Probably not as painful as last time we talked," Beto comments, regretting how rude he was to Nico in such a difficult time.

He promises to himself (mentally, for a second) that he will never again be rude to Nico in difficult times. Or in the easy ones.

"I wish everything would just go back to normal."

Beto pauses to think before answering. He's not sure if Nico is talking about what's normal between them or about the world from a few months ago. Both scenarios seem kind of unlikely.

"I think it'll be hard to go back to normal after everything I said to you. I don't know, like you'll always be careful with your words so you're not leading on the boy who likes you," Beto says firmly, determined not to sound sorry for himself.

"Beto," Nico says, even more firmly. "I *like* you, too. I told you so. It's just that *right now* everything is weird, and I don't know what to do. There's no running away from this, I don't know what to expect from the future. And I know you've been waiting for this year for, like, your whole life. And it's horrible when things don't happen when we want them to. But I'm patient and can wait a little longer."

"I get it. I know you're right. I can *rationally* think about it and see you're right. But have you ever had the feeling that you're just waiting for something to happen, and the thing never really happens? It's as if that . . . that good thing was just around the corner, saying, 'Be there in five,' but then five minutes go by and it never arrives."

"I feel that way all the time." Nicolas laughs.

"And every little thing that comes my way seems like it's going to be the Big Thing, but it never is. I thought it would be my move to São Paulo, and then that it was going to be my relationship with you, and then a picture I took, which a thousand people saw. But it never is. I feel like a character in one of those three-hundred-page books we read and then think, *Jesus Christ, all these people are going to do is* talk? *Is* anything *going to happen?*"

"I like that kind of book," Nicolas admits.

"I *know.* You've recommended, like, three to me. These everyday stories without even a hint of adventure. Not even a villain," Beto teases.

"Sometimes we're the villain."

"Or the system."

"Ah, the system is *always* the villain. Even in stories where it's not mentioned."

"I don't want to be the villain in your story," Beto says. "I don't know what I want to be for you, but please don't let me be the villain."

Nicolas laughs, puts his arm behind his head, and smiles in a way that makes Beto want to melt into a puddle right on his bedroom floor.

"You could be the best friend who's secretly in love with me, and I'm secretly in love with you, and we're both living on an emotional roller coaster for years, full of missed opportunities, while destiny plays tricks on us, until one day we run into each other at the airport when we finally have everything we need to be together, but then unfortunately you're on your way to Italy and I'm off to Rio de Janeiro. Then years go by, and we meet again. In Italy! We kiss in the middle of a vineyard during sunset. You hold up the camera hanging from your neck and I say, 'You're taking *another* picture of the sunset?' And you say, 'No, I'm taking a picture of something far greater.' Then you point the camera at me and take a shot of my glowing face. The frame grows wider, as if we were being filmed by a drone moving away, showing all the grapes in the background. Black screen. The end credits roll. The end."

Beto wants to laugh and cry at the same time.

"I can't believe you came up with a love story that takes, like, twenty years to work out, just so in the end you get a free photo session. You could have just paid me, you know?" Beto laughs.

"Sorry if that went too far," Nico says.

"It's okay. My version of us is almost like a movie, too. But a lower-budget one. You pick me up at the airport and ask me to be your boyfriend with a box of doughnuts."

"Pfff. Boring. I can do better than that."

"All right." Beto smiles. "High expectations, then."

"You got it."

"All right."

"Everything is going to be okay, Beto."

"It will."

"One day."

"One day."

The two of them stare at each other for at least three minutes, smiling and making stupid faces, not knowing what to say next.

This time, Beto doesn't feel desperate to say something. He's not in a hurry to make a move. He hates waiting, hates not having plans, hates this *what if . . .* ghost hovering over them. But right now, in this moment, everything is fine.

And tomorrow is a new day.

MAY 28, 2020
Thursday, May 28, 2020. 9:13 a.m.
From: geodude1993@email.com
To: photobeto@email.com.br
Subject: A question

Hey, Beto!

Hope you're doing as well as possible (no one is truly okay in 2020 haha).

This might be a little weird, but I saw your photos online. The ones you took from your window. I immediately felt at peace, like I was home! So then I zoomed in on the photos, looked at the details, and sent it to my aunt just to be sure I wasn't going crazy. And, in the end, I thought it would be best to send you a note.

Of course, you don't need to answer if you don't want to. I don't want to make you uncomfortable. But do you live in Lagoa Pequena, SP, by any chance?

And if so, do you live at 8 Sunflower Street?

Because your bedroom window is very similar to the window of the bedroom where I spent the end of my teenage years. Unforgettable five years.

If so, I hope the house is treating you as tenderly as it treated me.

Thanks for your time. Sorry if this seems intrusive.

And congratulations on the photos. They look beautiful.

Warmly,
Greg

I AM KEANU REEVES.

The dog. Not the actor. Thought I'd make that clear.

Another thing I find important to clarify: I did not die. I'm still alive. A little old, but alive. This isn't the kind of story where the dog *dies*, you can keep reading without worrying.

Almost ten years later, after my humans and I moved out of Number 8 Sunflower Street, here we are again. I'm wearing a bow tie that Catarina picked especially for this occasion. It is red and has a pattern of little white bones. I personally hate bones. But I don't know how to articulate that to my owner. She has a hard time decoding my barks most of the time.

Anyway, here we are.

Catarina, Greg, and I standing in front of the house again.

But first, I should add some context. I'm a context-loving dog.

I spent my whole life sitting on Catarina's lap watching movies with ambiguous endings and, honestly, I'm tired of stories where I need to *interpret* the ending. Interpreting is exhausting for a dog (and from what I've gathered, nearly impossible for humans). I'm also a happy-ending-loving dog. So here are a few:

Orlando, Catarina's florist friend, got married in 2012. It was the biggest party I've ever seen, with the largest number of sunflowers per square feet imaginable. They made me bring the rings to the altar. I made people cry emotionally as I walked down the yellow carpet carrying a little basket in my mouth. I almost let the rings fall because it's hard to balance on three feet, walk in a straight line, have people taking photos of you, *and* keep your head up while wearing a dog suit that Catarina bought online.

But it all worked out fine.

I paraded around the party like a star, and everyone would call me over to pet me and feed me.

I was sick the following day.

We left Number 8 in 2015, right after Greg graduated from college (of all the majors in the world, he chose library science, following the family tradition of working with things no one uses anymore because everyone owns a cell phone nowadays). The house was too empty after Greg left, so we moved to an apartment closer to the town's movie theater.

Oh, yeah. Catarina *bought* the movie theater. After getting a loan that made her cry at night for some time and partnering with her rich sister, she now owns the only movie theater in Lagoa Pequena, where she still hosts film clubs showing Keanu Reeves films every Wednesday for free. And it's a special theater—the only one in the state that lets dogs in.

It's a mess. I love it. I've made a lot of friends there.

The email from Beto, the photographer standing in front of us, arrived years later. He and his sister are putting together a special personal project. I remember how Catarina laughed that day, talking about how young people these days call *everything* a personal project. She took the opportunity to mock Greg's personal project once again (an Instagram account where he shares his Pokémon embroidery).

But the point is: Beto and Lara, his sister, are gathering data on everyone who lived at Number 8 Sunflower Street for the past fifty years. Or a hundred. Or a thousand. The details sometimes escape me because I get distracted by people's shoes.

"We're going to take a photo of you posing with a serious face looking straight at the camera, like those old-timey family photos. And then we'll take some more relaxed ones, talking, laughing, that kind of thing. Sound good?" Beto says, positioning us in front of the house and holding a camera the size of a car.

"Got it," Catarina says, going dead serious, her eyes staring at the camera with the intensity of a laser beam.

I love my owner.

Click. Click. Click.

The shutter goes off a thousand times, and it's nearly impossible to hold a pose.

"Okay, now relax," the photographer instructs.

I loll my tongue because, well, that's my trick. Everyone *loves* it when I let my tongue hang like that, and I use it to get absolutely anything I want. It never fails me.

Everyone laughs. Greg picks me up, I lick his face, and I immediately regret it because Greg has a beard now. Ew.

A dark shadow approaches and it takes me a moment to tell whether it's a spirit or a person. (I see spirits. Every dog does. It's a long story and totally unrelated to what I'm trying to tell you here.)

It's a person.

No apparitions hanging out on Sunflower Street today.

"Tiago!" Catarina cries.

"Tiago?" Greg repeats.

"The emo guy who owns the restaurant a few blocks down?" Lara whispers to her brother, thinking no one is listening, but I am because I have super hearing and huge ears.

"What are you doing here?" Greg asks, and from the way he clutches me against his chest, he's either terrified or excited.

"I called him. So he can be in the photo, too," Catarina says with a mischievous smile.

"Who's the handsomest boy in this whole city?" Tiago says in a baby voice.

Believe it or not, he's talking *to me*. I'll never understand the baby voice thing. I'm practically a *senior citizen*, but I don't mind. I wiggle my feet to get away from Greg's smothering arms and jump on Tiago, lick his face (no beard!), and get my fur all over his black clothes.

"Can we take another picture, please?" Catarina asks. "One with Tiago."

"Of course, of course," Beto answers, promptly bringing the camera up to his face.

"Did he live here, too?" Lara asks, writing this all down in a notebook like a real journalist.

"No," Tiago answers.

"Kind of," Greg says at the same time.

"He did," Catarina also says at the same time.

It's hard to follow all the people talking, despite my super hearing and huge ears.

"He's an honorary resident," Catarina clarifies. "He'd spend the whole day in the video rental store I ran in the garage."

"Hmm. Interesting," Lara says, scribbling even harder in her notebook.

"Yeah," Tiago says.

Leaning against his chest, I can hear his heart going at a hundred thousand beats per minute.

"He and my nephew have an unresolved love story." Catarina spills the beans because, at her age, she has nothing left to lose. She says whatever she wants and ends every sentence with the same silly smile.

"God, everyone who lived in this house is gay," Lara whispers to her brother, once again thinking no one can hear.

"*Aunt Catarina*," Greg murmurs between his teeth, his voice sounding like he'd give anything to have a hole open under his feet and swallow him up.

Catarina just smiles for the photo, and we hear Beto's camera go *click, click, click*.

Deep down, all Catarina wants is for her nephew to be happy. I know that because she talks to me at home. She says, "Ah, little Keanu, all I want is for Greg to be happy." And I think that is one of the most noble feelings in the world.

The photo session ends, Lara interviews each of them for a few minutes, and I go back to the ground, from where I listen in on everyone's conversations and try not to get distracted by shoes.

"I didn't know the garage used to be a video rental store," Beto tells Greg while Lara interviews Catarina.

"Ah, yes, this is where Catavento Cinema Club started. And then it moved to the movie theater downtown, you know?"

"Yeah," Beto says, looking like he does *not* know. "Another thing I discovered when I was trying to track down everyone who lived here was that the guy who created TapTop used to live here before you, did you know that?"

Greg looks confused. So does Tiago.

"The video app. One of the most famous in the world? TapTop, haven't you heard of it?"

"Yeah," Greg answers.

He totally hasn't.

"I'm taking photos of him and his daughter next month. He's retired now, but his daughter's super busy. She travels the world with her wife, who's training for the next Olympics or something."

"No way!" Tiago exclaims.

"The second openly bisexual Brazilian Olympic medalist?" Greg asks. "A friend of ours told us that once. I never forgot it."

"And then you told me," Tiago says, looking straight at Greg for the first time since his arrival. "I never forgot about Letícia, either."

The look they give each other burns with the heat of a thousand pizza ovens. Beto moves away when he realizes he's interrupting the moment.

Greg and Tiago go on reminiscing over the past, and I'm almost sure I see their hands graze. They interlace their pinkies for a second, then let go.

Almost sure.

I can't be certain because, well, there I was, staring at shoes again. Tiago's have a lot of laces. It's hypnotizing.

The interviews are done, and I run around, excited to leave because Catarina promised she'd take me for a walk around the lake after we were done.

She didn't promise it *per se*, but she did put three plastic bags in her purse, and I know what that means.

"Thank you so much for your time," Beto says, saying goodbye to everyone with a handshake, and to me with a head rub. "And, Greg, thank you for the email you sent me. It's kind of what sparked this project."

"No need to thank me," Greg answers. "I remember when I first saw that picture you took of the window, I could see myself in it, you know? I remembered my teenage years in that bedroom. The first night I spent there, the day I downloaded a Scooby-Doo movie to impress Tiago, only to find out later that he didn't even like Scooby-Doo, and he just said that to make fun of me."

"I spent two years *pretending* I did because I didn't know how to tell him the truth," Tiago says, laughing.

I always feel a little offended by this story. To a dog who's curious, scared, and hungry at the same time, Scooby-Doo is kind of a hero.

"And on the day your photo popped up on my feed, wow, things were hard. I really needed that. I needed to remember what it was like to feel at home. I miss living here, but I realized that a house is not just a place. It's up to us to turn a house into a home. And there might be a cracked tile in the bathroom or a door handle that falls every time we slam the door. Sometimes we look at other people's homes and think, *Wow, if I lived there, I'd be happier.* But, in the end, the feeling of being home doesn't come from a place. It comes from within."

Catarina nearly cries.

Tiago holds Greg's hands firmly this time, and now I am *really* sure I saw them holding hands.

Beto smiles, feeling proud that he was able to inspire a good feeling in someone with a photo he took.

And Lara scribbles in her notebook, rushing to jot it all down because she probably didn't expect Greg to come up with a motivational speech out of nowhere moments before they say goodbye.

"Could you repeat the last part?" Lara asks, her eyes still glued to the paper. "I think it would be a good quote to end our article."

"The thing about the door handle falling when you slam a door?" Greg asks.

"No, before that."

"The thing about the tiles?"

"Before." Lara is losing her patience.

"It's up to us to turn a house into a home," Tiago whispers.

"Yes!" Lara shouts. "Thank you."

Under the light of the afternoon sun that's now burning his scalp and making him squint his eyes, Greg looks upon Number 8 Sunflower Street once more, smiling as if he's just learned the most important lesson of all. A lesson that has been right here, under his nose, the whole time.

It's up to us to turn a house into a home.

ACKNOWLEDGMENTS

This was the hardest book I've ever written. Despite being a "Jesus Christ, all these people are going to do is *talk*? Is *anything* going to happen?" kind of story, *This Is Our Place* came to me in 2020, a year when every day seemed to contain three hundred more years, and escaping reality to write fiction demanded a huge amount of effort. In Ana, Greg, and Beto, I found a way to see problems that were different from mine, and, just like the house who can't see beyond the view from its windows, I had to try hard to look inside and imagine every kind of story that might happen between four walls. I'd never have been able to finish this project if I didn't have such incredible people by my side, and now it's time to give them proper thanks.

Rafael, my lockdown, adventure, and life partner. Thank you for holding my hand every time I feel incapable, and for showing me every day that the future can be good if we take it one day at a time.

Mom, thank you for teaching me the true meaning of *home*, and for always leaving the door open to me. I love you to the moon and back, and then there and back again just to be sure.

Taissa Reis, my agent, friend, and confidante. Thank you for believing in my work for both of us when I couldn't do it by myself. It is thanks to your professionalism, passion, and companionship that this story will reach so many households in Brazil (and around the world!).

Veronica Armiliato, my editor, friend, and gossip partner, who was thrilled by the idea of this book from our first conversation and cheered it on until the end. There's a little bit of you here and in everything I write.

To the entire team of Editora Alt, the publisher that has been taking such good care of my books, since the first one. Thank you for always welcoming me and for never doing anything less than the best to ensure that my books will be in the best shape by the time they reach readers. A special thank-you to Agatha Machado and Paula Drummond, who arrived at the final stages but are already part of the family.

To Igor Soares, for the sweet words, and to Gih Alves, who read it before anyone else and reacted with the excitement I needed to believe that, yes, this book is special in its own way.

To all the amazing people at Scholastic for making the US edition of this book possible, and for believing in the stories I have in me. To my editor extraordinaire, Orlando Dos Reis, thank you for all your thoughtful input, your keen attention to detail, and all the fun we had in the process. Larissa Helena, you've done it again! Your translation is spot-on, and I know I can always count on you to give voice to my characters in English and get them ready to meet new readers across the world. David Levithan, thanks a million for always hyping up my books. To Stephanie Yang for doing such an amazing job designing the book and cover, and to Douglas Lopes for illustrating such a welcoming cover. And to Janell Harris, Cindy Durand, Jody Corbett, Priscilla Eakeley, Maddy Newquist, and everyone who helped bring this book to US readers.

To my friends who, at this point in my life, are family. Lucas Fogaça (Fogs!), Lucas Rocha, Vito Castrillo, Mayra Sigwalt, Thereza Andrada, Iris Figueiredo, Duds Saldanha, Barbara Morais, João Pedroso, Aureliano Medeiros, Luiza Souza, Isadora Zeferino, Gui Almeida, and Bruno Freire, I'm counting the days until I can hug you all.

To all the people who read my books and see a little bit of themselves in them. Who talk about my characters with love, who recommend these stories to others, and who have been patiently waiting to meet Number 8 Sunflower Street. You lend purpose to everything I do, and encourage me to be a better writer and, more important, a better person. I don't deserve all that love, but I'll receive it with an open heart.

And, finally, to my aunt Rosane, who left us this year and whom I miss like an empty room that I am constantly trying to fill with good memories. Thank you for caring for me as if I were your son, for rooting for me at every single moment, and for encouraging me to study and brush my teeth because "there's no use being rich if you're stupid and your mouth is ugly." Love you forever.

ABOUT THE TRANSLATOR

Larissa Helena is an editor, rights consultant, and translator. She has translated numerous titles into Portuguese and English, including *Where We Go from Here* by Lucas Rocha and *Here the Whole Time* by Vitor Martins, co-winners of the 2021 Global Literature in Libraries Initiative Translated YA Book Award. She lives in New York City with her partner and their dog, Zee, who they have decided will live forever (the dog, not the partner!).

ABOUT THE AUTHOR

Vitor Martins lives in São Paulo, Brazil, and, in addition to writing, works as an illustrator and translator. His first novel, *Here the Whole Time*, was co-winner of the 2021 Global Literature in Libraries Initiative Translated YA Book Award and a finalist for the 2021 Latino Book Award for best young adult book originally in Portuguese. He believes that representation in young adult literature is a powerful weapon, and his main goal as a writer is to tell stories of people who have never seen themselves in a book. Follow him online at vitormartins.blog and on Twitter and Instagram at @vitormrtns.